welcome!
browse, sit awhile or borrow.
but, please
RETURN TO:

The
Bureau
Of
INTERNAL
AFFAIRS

The wrong side of right

*a Gumshoe & Fox
Crime Story*

by

Myron Ferdig

Prologue

Day off and the Rams have a bye! Just my luck! Swazer cursed under his breath. He had known it for three weeks, but it was still upsetting. After all, how many Sundays during football season did a police detective have off! He would have bought a ticket, and maybe one for a close friend -- one Jeb Tolling. Much more fun with a buddy. But instead, he watched the Miami-Jets game on the tube -- alone.

A quick check of the medicine cabinet showed only a few Aleves left, fridge showed only six more vials of OLVs for Archie, his Mom's eighteen year-old Persian cat, and a couple of Modelo Ambers in the fridge door. Definitely time for a supply run.

He strapped on his service weapon complete with shoulder holster -- a task which, after five years, had become so much a habit, he felt undressed without it. Then he locked the house, hopped into his Ford F-150, and pointed it toward the local pharmacy.

A group of three, hooded, young fellows and a loud, young female with frizzy green hair was horsing around at the bus-stop as he approached. The leader of the foursome, wearing a purple hoodie, raucously shoved past him into the establishment, followed by his entourage. Bradley frowned, but waited with furrowed brows and more than a modicum of patience. "You're welcome," he whispered with a sarcastic smile and followed them in.

He stopped to chat with Lindsay at the front counter.

"How's my favorite policeman?" Lindsay asked.

Heads turned to identify the cop, among them the rude foursome. They elbowed each other, threw out a few audible "pig" expletives, and continued on ahead.

"Day off; need Aleve, cat food, and beer," Swazer laughed.

"That's a terrible diet!" she frowned and winked at him. "How's your mom?"

"Grumpy as ever. You'd think I live with the Queen of the South. I gave her a light lunch a couple hours ago; 'too hot! not enough peanut butter!' She's still recuperating from her fall, but getting better every day. Good talking to you, Lindsay."

He meandered through the beer aisle, picked up a carton of Modelo Negra, then continued on, adding a large bottle of Aleve on his way to the pharmacy counter at the rear.

Henry Tatum, pharmacist, smiled and waved a greeting as Bradley joined the queue of six others waiting in the pick-up line.

A couple of people ahead of Swazer, an older gentleman and the green-haired female, started a shoving match. Bradley then observed with a frown, that another of green-hair's buddies, the purple-hooded fellow, pushed seventy-year old Martha Dingle out of line just as she reached the counter. Swazer yelled, "Hey man! Take it easy. The lady was ahead of you!"

The youth turned and growled, "Shut the __-up, Pig!"

Henry shot a concerned look at Bradley, just as the hooded guy reached out, grabbed Henry's arm, pushed a silver hand gun in his face, and demanded drugs.

Seeing that he didn't have good leverage with the druggist, *Purple Hood* let go, and grabbed Martha's arm. Folks began to scatter.

Pulling his service weapon, Swazer shouted, "Let her go, or I'll drop you where you stand!"

Purple Hood wheeled and fired his pistol at Swazer. Bradley returned fire -- two shots. Someone at Swazer's left opened fire on him. Swazer returned fire; patrons were screaming, ducking, seeking shelter, and exiting the establishment.

Bradley shouted, "Call 911! Get some cops over here, now!" He went to check on Martha. Customers continued to flock out the door, scrambling to escape. Swazer thought he saw *Purple Hood's* silver pistol go flying across the floor -- everything happened so fast.

When the smoke cleared, Swazer had a bullet hole in his shirt at the shoulder, two young perps were dead, including *Purple Hood,* and no guns were found . . . other than, of course, Bradley's. He called Morris with the news. Then he went to comfort Martha Dingle, his mother's best friend.

The 911 call brought two squads. Remaining patrons gave their accounts of the activity; then asked to exit the store before the doors were locked. Henry Tatum brought the cat medication over and sat with the young detective on a couch and awaited the inspector.

Morris and another officer arrived within the hour, questioned those present, relieved Swazer of his service revolver, told him to take his purchases home, and await further instructions.

The Bureau Of INTERNAL AFFAIRS

The wrong side of right

a Gumshoe & Fox
Crime Story

Chapter 1

The year 2019 had come and gone: national elections were over (although the smoke had certainly not yet cleared), Americans had had their tryptophan fix -- complete with stuffing and jellied cranberries, had opened their gifts, and made their resolutions. It was Tuesday, January 21, 2020.

Liz (her given name was Betty-Anne McConnell, but we never used it) was back at her desk. (*Because of her injury I had given Liz a few more days off after the holidays. She had been shot during a gunfight in Key West, Florida while on a recent assignment -- but that's a different story.*)

"So, Fox," I said, looking at the notes I had hurriedly scribbled on the white board yesterday, "what do we know about Bradley Swazer?"

"You already have it encapsulated right there, Bossman, and we went over them twice already. We know he was off-duty; we know he shot two perps at Ocean Drugs in Redondo; we know he said the guys had guns; we know two or three customers, along with the druggist, confirm while two or three deny; we know that no guns were ever found; we know he's 6'1" and wears boxers . . . oh, I don't know, Gumshoe," she frowned. "He's your friend. I've met him only a few times."

"Funny lady, Fox. Okay, you have the deposition

printouts Morris sent over; read them to me once more -- and be serious for a minute."

Fox blew out a breath, rolled her eyes and shook her head. She began.

"Bradley Swazer -- Sunday, November 24, 1620 hours. 'Entered Ocean Drugs to pick up a prescription - Pharmacist Henry Tatum on duty. There were as many as 15 customers in the immediate area. Henry seemed nervous, motioned toward a fellow ahead of me in a purple hoodie [later identified as Marvin Rollins] who was brandishing a silver 9mm -- demanding pharmaceutical drugs.

Rollins pointed the gun & threatened to shoot Henry. Then he reached for a lady [Martha Dingle] to use as a hostage. I think I heard someone yell "look out Martha." I was busy. I pulled my weapon and fired two shots. He fired simultaneously, I felt a sudden jerk at my shoulder [discovered later a bullet had hit my holster]. I don't know how many shots were exchanged. As he fell, his weapon skidded across the floor.

One of Rollins's companions to his left [identified as Elroy Tinney] fired at me as well. I saw the flash, and returned fire. I yelled for someone to call 911 while I took statements from witnesses still on scene.

Neither gun was recovered. Marvin Rollins died at the scene. Elroy Tinney died enroute to the hospital. Some shoppers had gone, so I was not able to obtain statements from all. Two patrons [the lady shopper -- Martha, along with Annie Bunch -- see affidavits p.3a] and Henry verified seeing weapons; however, two others, [Louisa Calumba & Thomas Trout -- see affidavits p.3b] denied their existence.

Conclusion: I know Rollins and his companion had guns; hell, my shirt has a bullet hole! That guy had at least three buddies outside who came in with him -- they probably grabbed the guns and ran out. My use of deadly force was appropriate.'"

"Read that bit from Martha what's-her-name about the perp trying to grab her arm, Fox, and then the one from the pharmacist. Not everything gels."

"Uhhh, okay. Here's what Martha says:

'That hoodlum was very scary. He was high on something. He grabbed my arm and jerked me toward him, his gun in his other hand. Henry, my pharmacist, yelled, 'Look out'! About the same time the other man -- Lara Bradley's son (he's a policeman) shot him. I don't know what happened to the gun. I was just happy he was there. I have a terrible bruise on my arm.'"

"And, let's see, Henry . . . ummm, where is it now . . . okay, Henry says:

'The young thug demanded opioids -- fentanyl, oxycodone, whatever I had -- I told him all I had was Zyrtec. He showed me his gun and threatened me. I saw Bradley and gestured for him that I was in trouble. Then the perp grabbed my arm, but since I was on the other side of the counter, he let go and grabbed Ms. Dingle. Someone, a woman, I think, screamed, Look out, Martha! -- something like that -- That's when Bradley shot him -- I think four times. I don't know what happened to his gun, but he had one -- a silver one, like a Saturday Night Special. I didn't see the other youngster shoot, or his gun, but I believe Bradley. He had one.'"

"Now read what that Thomas Trout fellow says. The 'no gun' guy."

"Fine . . . but did you think he'd say something different this time, Gumshoe? He says:

'A fellow walked in and asked for a prescription. The pharmacist yells at a lady nearby, she panics, screams, someone else cries GUN! and the cop starts shooting. There wasn't another gun; I never saw one; just a panicky reaction with the shouting and the cop shooting.'"

"Now I may as well read the last one," she smirked, "you're going to demand it anyway." She gave me another look.

"This is from Louisa Calumba:

> 'I never saw a thing, just heard seven or eight loud pops. It was chaotic for a few minutes; people were running around, some ran out of the store. If there were other guns, someone may have run out with them.'"

"I'm done, Gumshoe. I've read these depositions three times. Let's go have some lunch; any bright ideas we can discuss them over a beer. Then we should go see Swazer."

"Pretty bossy for my underling, Liz," I chided. "I think we'll *first* see Mr. Swazer, after which we'll have a meal somewhere close to the cop shop."

"If we must, Bossman, but why do you always get to make the big decisions? . . . don't answer that!"

We closed up the office, hopped into my Caddy, and headed for Hermosa Beach.

* * * * *

Sergeant Swazer was expecting us; big, broad smile as he stepped out from around the intake desk to shake hands. It seems the big boys up at IA weren't through with him just yet -- consequently, he had been riding that desk for over a month while their investigation into the shooting continued.

"They should have dropped this thing long ago, Mr. Garrett. I'd have thought they simply forgot about me, except that every Monday the inspector gets a notice that the file is 'progressing'. I don't even know what that means anymore -- 'progressing'. I should be out on the streets.

"Have you seen the old man? He's being run ragged, budget maxed out, handcuffed -- can't hire any more cops, and here I sit. Like they're watching him squirm, Mr. Garrett, right along with me."

"Yeah, well, the 'old man' gave us all the eye witness depositions, and authorized a per diem," Fox said, "so we're covered with the precinct -- right, Bossman?"

"Absolutely," I nodded. "We'll have you walking a beat in no time, Bradley." I winked at Swazer while avoiding Fox's eyes.

"Oh, thanks!" he frowned at me.

"On to something else, Swazer. What was this about guns disappearing from lock-up? A couple of questions: Who brought them in? Is lock-up under a camera? Who mans the cage? And did you take them?"

Liz looked sharply at me, frown on her face. Then with a puzzled look, she turned to Swazer for his response.

"That goes back almost a month, Mr. Garrett. You should be asking Morris, not me."

"But right now, I'm asking you, Bradley."

"Well, I didn't take them . . . let me look at my notes." He gave us a lame smile. "I always jot down notes. You never know." Bradley thumbed through his desk files, pulled out a thin folder and opened it. "Aah, yes, December 5. Okay, here we are, the guns.

"Two cops, Friday and Smith from Inglewood station, handed me the paperwork; guns came in a sealed box. I glanced over the paperwork -- three weapons: one Glock-23 and two 9mm. Paperwork had serial numbers and photos attached. Looked in order.

"I questioned how and why guns from Inglewood would be transferred to Hermosa; they replied that it had been approved by people above their pay-grade, so I called down to Vern Yardley -- duty cage officer that day -- to pick it all up. Then the two cops from Inglewood volunteered to walk the guns down to Vern. They knew him, they said."

"This Smith fellow, was that Frank Smith by any chance?" I asked.

"Yeah! You know him?" I shook my head, glanced at Fox, and raised an eyebrow.

"Anyway," Bradley continued, "I was busy so I agreed. That's when the confusion started. I never saw Friday or Smith come back up. In retrospect, I figured the guns were walked right out the downstairs door by the two from Inglewood and never delivered. Yardley confirmed -- he never saw anyone. I feel pretty stupid."

"Continue," I encouraged.

"On December 7, Morris asked regular cage officer, Denny Moore, about the guns. Denny reported that no guns had been checked into the cage.

"I called Inglewood. Those guns had been processed as part of an 'anonymous gun recovery drive' in Inglewood on December 4 and sent on." Bradley looked up from his notes and frowned.

"Like I said, Mr. Garrett, I feel stupid, but I was involved only as I questioned how a gun recovered in Inglewood could show up in Hermosa Beach."

"What's protocol on gun recovery, Brad?" Fox asked.

"When guns are surrendered, serials are logged, they're photographed immediately at the recovery table, then brought into the precinct -- that's protocol."

"One more question, Sergeant. To your knowledge, did the guns go through ballistics?"

"I questioned Robles from IA about that when he came in a couple of days later for an update on my shooting; I wanted that info for my file, but he ignored my question, so, I'm not sure," Bradley replied.

"We'll be in touch, Bradley. Did you happen to jot down badge numbers of Smith or Friday?"

"No, sir. Didn't seem necessary -- they wore the uniform."

"Thanks, Swazer. You take care. We'll see you out there soon."

"Not soon enough," Bradley growled.

We started out the door. "Aren't you going to see Morris while we're here, Bossman?"

"No, Fox. We're going to lunch. If I know Morris, he'll swing by this afternoon for a chat."

"Right," Liz smiled, "and a cognac."

*****

After a quick burger we headed back toward Manhattan Beach. I turned to Liz. "So, Miss, what did we just learn?"

"That's easy, Bossman. Our burgers are just as good as Hermosa's, maybe even better. Oh! you mean our visit with young Mr. Swazer? . . . Still looks cut and dried to me. A good shoot. Cut him loose, I say."

"What about the three confiscated guns, Liz? Don't you wonder where they ended up? I think we'll make a slight detour." I pointed the Caddy toward Inglewood.

Chapter 2

"What do we hope to accomplish in Inglewood, Gumshoe?" Liz shrugged. "They don't know us from Popeye the Sailor. Why do you think they'll even give us the time of day?"

"Lots of things we don't know, but we can always try. Think positively, Liz."

GPS said to turn right at the next corner; I turned right.

*****

Desk sergeant Gibson's brows furrowed as he listened with half an ear to my query.

"You say you're missing some guns?" he yawned. "Where'd you last see them?" Then he became more serious. "Inspector Morris called -- told us you would probably show up here.

"I heard about your, that is, Hermosa's problem. We don't have any answers for you. Captain grilled the boys that took in weapons that day -- a good day, really. We took twenty-seven weapons off the streets, most of which went into our cage: two went to Gardena and six to Hermosa. The two for Gardena were delivered, so they're accounted for. Ballistics proved them to be clean."

"No! Wait! Wait!" Fox said, shaking her head. "I'm confused . . . there were six guns? Sergeant

Swazer says no guns made it to Hermosa. From what you're saying, there are six guns in the wind, not just three."

"I trust Bradley is telling us the truth, Officer Gibson," I added. "No guns reached Hermosa from Inglewood, Gardena, or Internal Affairs. Now, I'd like two things if possible: I'd like a copy of the transport paperwork, and to know who physically walked it and the guns into the Hermosa precinct. Can we get that info from you, please?"

Gibson nodded. "Sure thing. Be right back."

*****

Five minutes went by; then ten. I looked at my watch and raised an eyebrow to Fox. "This guy's having some prob . . ." Gibson returned, flanked by two officers.

The first to speak was on Gibson's left. "Understand you're a private investigator, Mr. Uh . . ."

"Alan Garrett," I finished for her, "and this is my associate Liz McConnell." I handed her a card. She looked at it and smiled.

"Gumshoe and Fox! Real cute. So, you're the Gumshoe," she nodded to me, "and that would make you," she sized Liz up, "the Fox. I'm Captain Wallins, by the way."

She reached out for a handshake. "So why are Gumshoe and Fox in our house asking about matters that should be strictly police business?"

"Inspector Morris asked us to delve into the Ocean Pharmacy shooting on Sunday, November 24 involving one of his officers," I smiled. "There was confusion surrounding some purportedly missing guns. Our investigation raised a couple more questions we'd like to clear up before we move on. You know, one thing leads to another -- in this case, more questions . . ."

"And more confusion," Fox interjected, frowning.

"Which brings us to your station," I said, ignoring Liz, "and, well, here we are."

"I'm listening. What are the questions?"

"According to the Hermosa desk sergeant, your boys, Smith and Friday . . ." I began, looking directly at Wallins, but she only raised an eyebrow. The two cops with her frowned, but said nothing.

I continued, "They delivered some weapons to Hermosa on December 5. Paperwork was in order according to the desk sergeant. He says he initialed the transfer file. Three guns in a sealed cardboard box. Supposedly, they went into lock-up.

"On December 7 the cage officer reported no guns were present; today Fox and I asked for copies of transfer paperwork, but the entire folder was missing. We decided to visit you folks to get copies of your originals, Captain."

"Interesting, Mr. Private Eye. I'll just say, I appreciate your dedication. Unfortunately, we just discovered, thanks to you by the way, that all of our paperwork is missing as well. Come into my office; I'll share what we know."

Chapter 3

Tires screeched to a stop at the sidewalk in front of our shop as Fox sprinted (with a limp) to unlock our side door. I was just pulling a couple of things from the trunk as she turned, shouted something unintelligible, and disappeared inside.

I jerked up. "Wha....?" Conked my head on the trunk lid and chose a choice expletive before I followed her inside.

Inspector Morris stood at the front door; I buzzed him in, then checked my crown. My fingers came away red and moist; Fox came out of the wash room looking guilty.

"Sorry, Bossman, I was in a hurry and . . . oh! you're bleeding! How did you cut yourself?"

"You yelled something and I . . . ." I shook my head. "Forget it. It's fine." I turned to Morris who had been watching -- showing a smile from ear to ear.

"Inspector! How can we help you?"

"You were in my house today, talking with Swazer. Make any headway?"

"You already knew there were no guns and no paperwork, didn't you, Morris? What were we supposed to learn that you overlooked?"

"When I heard it was Friday and Smith that brought the guns in, I knew something was awry, I just didn't know what. I'm assuming you didn't finish there. You continued on to Inglewood, right?"

Fox blurted out, "How did you know that, Morris?" Then she turned, "How did he know that, Gumshoe?"

"We're his legs, Fox; he knew we wouldn't take a breath until we came to a logical resting place. Saves him running around."

Fox went to the cabinet and pulled out three glasses and an open bottle of Martell cognac. I nodded my head as she placed a glass in front of each of us.

"So, did you find anything interesting, Alan?" He lifted his glass as a toast; I responded in kind.

"Matter of fact, yes," I said. "First, Inglewood has neither a Friday nor a Smith, which we had already figured; second, we know twenty-seven guns were turned in -- Captain Wallins says Inglewood kept nineteen -- they have a maximum twenty-five-gun rule in their cage; they turned the others over to IA for ballistics testing.

"IA officers, Ramos and Sidney, told Wallins they'd deliver the weapons to willing precincts. You let them know that Hermosa was willing."

"Yeah, yeah, I remember," Morris took a sip and nodded.

"We called Gardena," I continued. "Two guns made it there, delivered, not by Smith and Friday, but by Ramos and Sidney themselves."

"Slimy sons-a-bitches!" Morris growled. "New hot dogs from Internal Affairs. Ramos has been coming in every week to tell me the Swazer shooting is still under scrutiny. Come to think of it though, he didn't show his face in the last week -- simply called it in."

"Don't you vet these people that walk in off the street, Morris?" I grinned. "Did you get his badge number or at least get his calling card?"

"Badge? Card? Now that I think of it, Alan, no!"

The inspector pulled out his cell phone, punched in a number, and excused himself. "Hello! Chief? Inspector Morris out in Hermosa. Everything's going well. No, no -- just need to clear up a loose end or two, trying to put Officer Swazer back in the field. Oh? . . . Is Ramos in the building? Oh, no! Sorry to hear that, sir . . . how about Sidney? . . . I'll wait . . . Is that right? And no one said? . . . Okay, thanks! . . . Yeah, please send me that notice and his official mug shot? . . . yes, just a minute . . . Alan! What's your fax number? . . . Right. Thanks, Chief."

"Damn, Alan," Morris shook his head, pounding on the desk. "I must be getting old; how could I have allowed a phony to walk into my house without checking his creds?" The inspector closed his eyes, filled his lungs, then released the air slowly. Then he swirled the cognac around in his glass and stared at the liquid before taking another sip.

The fax spat out a black and white photo. I glanced at it before Fox grabbed it from my hands. "You must have seen these guys, Inspector. Is this Ramos or Sidney?"

"That's Ramos. He's the only one who visited the precinct. Never met Sidney. Captain Delaware says Ramos quit just three weeks ago. But get this. He says Sidney was only a clerk on staff at IAD, he lasted only five or six weeks, caught falsifying reports, and trying to blackmail several cops in the department.

"On November 23, Captain Delaware gave all precincts a head's up. Says he must have missed us. Huh! So Sidney wasn't even an IA officer!"

"You're sure this is Ramos?" Liz asked matter-of-factly as she tacked the photo to the corkboard.

"Ramos! I just told you!" Morris confirmed, cursing under his breath.

I couldn't resist a flippant run at Morris: "You taking statins for your cholesterol? I read an article recently saying older folk, especially men, should stay away from statins. Messes up brain activity. Google it, Morris, I ain't lying."

"Statins, schmatins! You playing with my head, Garrett? I simply allowed a mistake to continue. Now I intend to arrest that SOB and put Bradley back on the street where he can earn his keep."

"Wait a minute, Morris. Have you found and interviewed that green-haired lady or the families of the dead perps?"

"No, Alan. I told you I'm short-handed and need help. The IA boys sent us some paperwork, but it turned out to be worthless. Nothing substantial."

Fox broke in, "Of course not, sir; what IA boys sent the reports over? Ramos and Sidney, right?"

"Oh! right, Ramos and Sidney! Crap!"

"Not totally on you, Mr. Inspector; your chief should have arrested Sidney on the spot when he was caught changing paperwork," Fox offered.

"Statins, Inspector, I'm telling you." I raised my Martell snifter. "But, don't worry, Carl, we'll take care of you. And stop mollycoddling him, Fox -- tell it like it is! Damned old man is losing his cognitive perception, is all. He can't help it, but it doesn't excuse him."

Morris held out his snifter. I poured. He looked at Fox, saluted her with the cognac, and smiled.

"You're the other reason I visit this establishment."

*****

"I'm serious, Gumshoe; that Captain Delaware should have notified Hermosa of the breach in protocol."

"Perhaps not Delaware; perhaps someone down the line, Fox. It wouldn't take much to have a message erased or set conveniently aside."

"Are you saying withheld purposely?" Fox frowned. I shrugged.

"Worth considering. We have a whole string of loose ends: phony cops, phony names, allowing a dirty clerk in IA to slide, then a message regarding that travesty from the highest level undelivered, then delivery of empty boxes, then missing guns. Anything about that sound suspicious to you? Poor Morris. Shouldn't have jostled him quite so hard, huh?"

Fox simply rolled her eyes. "So, what now, Bossman?"

"Tomorrow we nose around Internal Affairs downtown, see what kind of chatter we pick up."

"We'll never get close to city hall, Gumshoe; you're kidding yourself if . . ."

"I know a guy."

"Right. I'll see you tomorrow, Bossman, I have an appointment with a physical therapist for my leg. It's still a bit tender."

Bidding her a good afternoon, I poured another two fingers of Martell, sat and stared at the white board. I shook my head, stood, erased, re-wrote until I was satisfied.

"Time to head for *Pop's*," I told the flip board, "but, I'll be back." Grabbed my fedora, left my Cadillac locked behind the chain-link gate, and walked up the short distance to *Pop's*, the moniker the family had christened my little bungalow many years before. It sits at the end of a cul-de-sac, just two-three blocks above the Manhattan Beach Pier.

Pop's was named for my pop, a fireman, now retired, who -- with my mom, had signed it over to me while she was still alive. It was, and still is to some extent, a meeting place for poker nights, pot lucks with his squad and families. My old man just recently decided to vacate the place for a sweeter offer, so I'm now batching, but I would never change the name. It was, and always will be, *Pop's Place.*

Chapter 4

After my morning run along the beach, I walked to my office, glanced at the wall clock -- 7:14 -- then showered. As I was toweling off I caught the distinct smell of fresh coffee. *Aah, that would be Fox,* I thought as I combed my hair. I was wrong. I opened the washroom door to Pop's friendly face.

"Morning, Alan. Who's the guy?" he asked, handing me a coffee and nodding toward the cork side of my board.

"That's Ramos, a dirty Internal Affairs cop. Don't know much about him yet, but I intend to find out. Good brew, Pop. And a good morning to you! How's Rita this morning?"

"Still asleep, I expect. We were out late last night. Went to a Clippers game -- Clippers won. That Harrell had a great game! By the time we arrived home it was after midnight."

The phone rang. "Garrett."

"Bossman, I have news."

*****

By the time Fox drove her car into our lot almost an hour had elapsed. Pop and I were discussing his upcoming marriage when Liz came through the side door with an anxious look on her face. "Turn on the news, Gumshoe." The way she said it, I felt obligated to turn on the office TV.

Fox sat, eyes fixed on the tube. A camel was walking through an office, trying to convince her it was hump day ... I checked ... he was right. I shook my head and laughed. "What news, Fox?"

She shushed me with a "Quiet, please! Wait!"

Another commercial came on. Fox took the opportunity to speak. "Remember yesterday you had a hunch and took a detour to Inglewood?"

"Yeah."

"Well, yesterday I had a hunch on the way home and went to the hospital to see Ramos, the IA dude. He was still in a coma, and there was a cop at the door. The cop told me there were police concerns for his safety."

Pop broke in, excused himself with a, "You two are busy. I'll get out of your way. Swing by tonight, Alan. Rita will be putting together a lasagna."

In answer, I said, "I'll call you, Pop." Liz waved a goodbye.

Turning to Liz, "What was the cop's concern?"

"That's what I asked as well, but the cop says . . . oh, wait! The news is back on.."

> "Headline for this morning is the report of a double homicide at City Hospital in downtown Los Angeles. Lauren is on site. What can you tell us, Lauren?"
>
> "Well, Frank, details are still coming in, but from what I know, at approximately 6:05 this morning a gunman or gunmen shot and killed two police officers and escaped. A nurse says that one of those deceased was a patient, while the other was guarding that patient's door. I'm told there will be an official briefing at ten a.m. . . . back to you."

"Gumshoe, I was there! I talked to that young guard. He's dead and so is Ramos!" Fox poked the remote button to turn off the TV. I poured a mug of coffee for her.

"Two hands," I instructed, noting she was visibly shaken. "Take a few minutes, close your eyes, take a few deep breaths. You want to go home? Take another day?"

"No! I feel safer here with you, Alan. I'm just glad I went there last night and not this morning. I could have met the assassin."

"So, I suppose there's not much point in going to city hall today," I determined. "May as well move to step two. Was there anything else the guard had to say last night we should consider?"

"Maybe. He was actually mumbling to himself as I approached -- things like, *'beyond help, supplying guns to street people, corruption, streets will run red'.* I didn't pay much attention, I just thought he was blowing off steam.

"When I came close, he said, 'Sorry Ma'am, you can't be here.' I said, 'Hoping I could get a statement from Officer Ramos.' He said, 'You'll have to leave now.' As I left, he started again with the mumbling. Something like, *'this goes deep, really deep.'* Strange, huh?"

"You sure he said supplying guns to street people?" Now I was frowning. "Like maybe the homeless?"

"I didn't know how to read it, Bossman, but now that you say it, yes. You mentioned step two -- what's that?"

"Let's head to the drug store in Redondo, and see if they kept the video tape from November 24."

"Oh, they wouldn't have it after thirty days would they, Gumshoe?"

"Humor me. Let's go find out."

*****

Fred, the manager at Ocean Drugs, told us the

tape had been scooped up by the police the same day of the shooting. "I have his card around here, somewhere," he said, pawing through his desk drawer. "Aah, here it is -- an Inspector Morris. I remember, now, another detective asked for the tape later, but I explained to him that it was already gone."

"How did he take that news?" Fox asked.

"Surprised and disappointed," Fred replied.

"Did he leave a business card?"

"No. Once he found out there was no video feed, he literally spun on his heel and walked out. Tried to take a strip off my butt as he left."

"Interesting. So you had another fresh feed rolling when the second cop waltzed in, right?"

"Oh! I do believe we must have," he nodded to a female associate. "Heather, we have that tape, right?" The lady disappeared. She reappeared a few minutes later, holding a portable monitor, and waved us over to view the video from the evening in question. I studied the clip for a few moments.

Looking at Heather, then back at Liz. "He didn't look too pleased, did he Fox? Like Heather, here, should have known he would be swinging by for that tape."

"He was a jerk!" Heather quipped. "Comes in like we, in the store, are subservient to him. Tries to brow-beat Mr. Brant. I wasn't about to show him diddly squat!"

"Believe me," Fox assured her, "we appreciate your giving us a look."

"You can have it. I have another. I kept a copy from the afternoon, too," Heather winked. "I always make a copy when there are . . ."

"Problems?"

"Yeah, problems. You want to look at it?"

"If we may," Fox said, "and thanks!"

As we walked out, Fox quipped, "Well, that was fun." She shook her head. "So where to now?"

Chapter 5

"Dammit! Jill! Get in here!" Captain Delaware literally screamed, slamming a meaty fist on his desk. "Who else did we 'conveniently' forget? Tell me, Rainee, who besides Hermosa?" The chief was furious.

"Everyone was advised, sir, all twenty-one divisions," Sergeant Rainee responded, racing in from her desk in the outer office. "Give me a minute; I'll show you the transaction record."

"Damn right, you will!" Delaware shouted after her. "Embarrassing as hell to find that some impostor worms his way into the Internal Affairs office," he mumbled to himself.

The young sergeant returned with the fax transactions for December 6. "See? It shows all twenty-one divis . . . ooops! Sorry, Chief -- Hawthorne, Hermosa, and Long Beach failed to go through. I should have scanned the transaction page."

"Just great! Fax that notice to all three with the photo right now, Rainee, then take the rest of the week off!"

"What?" Rainee straightened to her full five-nine,

a red flush rising in her cheeks and throat. She walked briskly to the door, closed it quietly, and turned on her heel, her face a picture of controlled rage and disbelief. "You need me in this office, sir. I am and have been the "go-to" person in this office for almost fourteen years -- five years before you came aboard.

"Marchinson hired Sidney, not me! And you signed off on it. I put in a requisition for new office equipment in July; you denied it for budgetary reasons.

"And I recommended Gordie Pritkins for IA eight years ago and Tom Gates two years ago -- Tommy happens to be the most thorough officer we have. A year ago, I was the officer who found discrepancies in your findings involving Aikens and Mariam Gill. I could go on and on! In fact, I have held my tongue over many *snafus* that cross your desk for signature.

"Now, if you set me on the sidelines for a few days over a temper tantrum, you will destroy our relationship and the smooth-running of this office. In fact, I think I shall seek employment elsewhere!"

Delaware turned red and stood, staring at his Sergeant. Finally, he spoke: "You're right, Jill. You do need a new fax for our office. Order one today. Thanks, Sergeant. Please leave the door open. It's a bit stuffy in here."

*****

The present . . .
(Wednesday afternoon)

"How's the leg, Fox? Okay to run a few more miles before we call it a day?"

We were on Manchester in my Caddy, sipping coffee and munching on our choice of donuts from

Randy's -- Inglewood's world-famous icon.

"I'm good to go, Bossman. Where we goin'?"

"Back to Hermosa." I dialed a number, nodded to Liz, "making sure the old man is there."

*****

"Thought I'd see you again before the day ended," Morris laughed. "What else should I know? Oh, before you begin, a call came in from IA. They'll be sending over paperwork by 4:30. Bradley will be back in the field starting tomorrow morning. Now, your turn, Mr. Private Eye."

"We just came from the Ocean Drugstore. Lady there says you have the tape from the afternoon of the shooting on November 24. They re-opened the store later that evening. They loaded another video; we have that one. Thought we'd share it with you."

As Morris stared at the screen, his jaw dropped. He could only shake his head and repeat 'son-of-a-bitch' {his choice expletive} several times. Liz and I looked at each other and shrugged. We figured Morris knew the guy. He finally looked up.

"Collins! Victor *friggin'* Collins! I fired this son-of-a-bitch eight, maybe nine years ago; booted him out of the precinct."

"He worked out of Hermosa?" Liz asked.

"He was the blue-eyed boy at the academy; galloped up the ranks; grabbing every assignment that was offered. He was assigned to me. Very smart cop; I was happy to have him . . . for the first year.

"You want a coffee?" He buzzed the front desk. "Swazer, have Alice bring in three mugs of coffee, please.

"Anyway," Morris continued, "one morning I get this crazy tip. Seems my boy was suspected of working with some dirty cops and insurance agents here in the beach cities from Seal Beach to Inglewood.

"He, or one of his cronies, would roll up on an accident, wave off other squads, approach the drivers, obtain IDs, gather information, use phony citation books, and write up several infractions. Then, if it was the right insurance agency, the cop would call in the agent.

"Agent would arrive on scene, whistle, shake his head, take pictures, and speak to the cop, just loud enough to be heard by the 'at fault' fellow or lady.

"They'd talk about deductibles, then they'd suggest the violator pay the victim out of pocket. Agent even suggests he pay by credit card on agent's smart phone to *eliminate paperwork*.'"

The coffee came. We thanked Alice, the young, second-year officer. "Helluva complex plan, Morris. You sure this is how it went down?" I asked.

"God's truth, Alan. I can't begin to tell you every rotten piece of garbage they perpetrated on -- especially minorities with little understanding of the ins and outs of minor violations. They'd make sure the 'infractions' were under $1,000.00 to minimize the offender's reaching out to *real authorities*."

Morris seemed to be reflecting on the shameful events that happened on his watch. He shook his head . . . "And then there were the seniors . . ."

"That's enough, Inspector. We get the picture. He was a slimy dude."

"Still is, from the look of it, Gumshoe." Fox turned to Morris, "Did he go to jail, sir?"

"I turned the case over to Internal Affairs, to Delaware's predecessor, a fellow name of Percy. Collins was stripped of his badge, of ever serving in any public office in Los Angeles county, fined a hundred grand, all of his tangible holdings were confiscated, and he was sentenced to three years in prison, I believe, in Chino. That's the last I heard of him," he chuckled sarcastically, "until now."

"Well, he's back, Carl," I said. "Bradley's back as well. What are your plans for him in the next day or two?"

"Put Vern Yardley on front desk, throw Brad back in the field, playing detective once again."

"The incident on November 24?"

"First item on his list."

"Is our time with you over, sir, now that Swazer is back on the job?"

"For the time being, yeah. Mail me a bill on your letterhead. I'll send the requisition up the line. Probably take fifteen -- twenty days, maybe more."

Nodding, I turned to Fox, "Let's pop in and congratulate Bradley on our way out." We started out the door. I turned back, "Swing by anytime on your way home, Inspector."

"So, what now, Bossman? We're out of work!" Liz moaned in a mock panicky voice as we opened the side door to our office.

"We clean up the small jobs waiting for us; I think there are one or two skips you can work on, and I'll find something to do. In the meantime, we're invited to dinner at Rita's. You like lasagna?"

Four or five sheets of paper lay in the fax tray. I noticed them as I dialed Pop, and pointed. "Would you grab the . . ? "Pop! Dinner still on? . . . May I bring a guest? . . . Sure! . . . With lasagna, I'd say a Pinot Grigio . . . Ha! yeah, just for Rita, we'll bring a bottle of Chianti. Six-thirty then? . . . right." I hung up the phone and sat, smiling. Then I turned to Liz, "Be right back; need to use the facility."

"Gumshoe, hold on a second."

"Can't it wait?"

"Gumshoe." She sounded serious. "Better come here and take a look at this." She was sitting at her desk, obviously stunned, holding out the stapled fax sheets.

"Huh?" I frowned, seeing the look of concern on her face. "Now what, Fox?"

"Amy Wynne sent over a note with some pictures. It ain't pretty, Bossman."

Grabbing the papers, I read the cover sheet, and thumbed through the pictures on the following sheets. "Sick bastards!" I whispered to Fox. "I'd better call Pop for a rain check."

"I'll call; go do your thing."

Chapter 6

Amy Wynne is a friend, and a very talented free-lance photographer. She rented from Rita up until two months ago; but now rents a small bungalow in Torrance. She works from time to time on a retainer basis for Morris, covering some of the precinct's more serious crimes or suspicious fires.

While Liz and I were returning to Manhattan Beach, Amy had doubtless been heading for Ocean Drugs, having received a heads-up on her scanner.

The note from Amy was terse and sobering, scrawled in her bold hand: *Nothing left of drug store; four employees, two customers dead. Swazer's home ransacked, torched, badly damaged; mother critical, in Hermosa General; cat dead. House saved by FD. Call Morris. Bradley in shock.*

*****

"Let'em through!" Morris thundered as he waved us under the yellow tape, past the crowd of gawkers. We joined him as he was picking through the smoking remains of what once had been the Ocean Drugs. Three FD units were still on scene for mop-up duty, as well as two arson techs, but it was pretty clear the job was amateurish, carried out by gun and gasoline-wielding hoodlums.

"Bradley's no good to me in his condition. He's a

mess. His mom's in tough shape; coma, last I heard. She was dragged into the kitchen, tied to a chair and beaten up by these monsters. Same crew, I'm sure. They doused the walls with gas, but somehow, the sprinkling system soaked it pretty good, and an alarm was sounded at the fire station. One unit was on-scene within 1-2 minutes.

"Amy was already at the drugstore. She hustled over to the Swazer house even before my guys did. You saw the pics, right? Damn cat going 'round in circles on that fan blade?" Morris kicked at a glowing ember; "Over here, fellas!" he shouted to a fireman as we continued walking.

The smells were a toxic mixture of burnt plastic and smoke, with perhaps a touch of pungent, sudsy detergent. The inspector's head was obviously somewhere else, unmindful of the white powder that was covering both his and our shoes and trouser cuffs.

"Six dead, and a woman near death, Alan! And for what? Revenge? That's all I can figure. Long story short, I need you to track whoever did this brutality. Forensics should have some prints or DNA from the Swazer place shortly. I'll fax that over when I get it."

We stepped back onto the sidewalk; only then did Morris look down at the three of us, shaking his head at our soiled garb. "Damn! Sorry," he said apologetically. "Can't get that poor cat out of my head.

"Send me a bill for any dry cleaning or damage to your clothes."

"Don't worry about it, Morris. Get that forensics report to us as quickly as possible; we'll hit the road running."

"Are we going to the hospital before going home, Gumshoe?"

"No, I think we'll wait until tomorrow. I want to go back to our office and take a closer look at the gal with green hair. If you need to go home, I understand."

"Oh, Bossman, Rita said she can warm up the lasagna if it's not too late, and I'm a bit hungry. I'm for going."

"Yeah? I suppose the video can wait. Let's go buy a bottle of Chianti."

Chapter 7

A fax was waiting for me as I entered the office at 6:20 a.m. Thursday morning. I tossed my fedora, successfully, on the hat rack, and reached for the printout -- four perps had been in the Swazer home -- two identified, two not. I had enough to go on. I was just having a second cup of coffee when Morris knocked on the front door.

"You're up early, Inspector -- coffee?"

"Yeah, please. Got a message from Brad on my way over here -- his mom didn't make it."

"Damn!" I shook my head. "You're giving him a few days, right?"

"Of course. Whether he takes them I don't know. But, look, Alan -- I'm going to have my hands full tracking down Collins, or whatever he calls himself now."

"I suspect they're in league, one with the other, Carl -- else why would Collins show up at the drugstore demanding that video?"

"Oh, it all ties together, Alan. I'm sure! But Collins is kingpin. His fingerprints are all over it. And, I've been in touch with the detectives on that hospital shooting -- can't prove it yet, but his work as well. Now, I'd like you to go after those young murderers."

Morris started out the door. "Anything pertinent, I want an immediate call. I'll do the same."

"Happy to." I nodded. "Brings up another question, though, doesn't it?"

"Like what?"

"Like that whole thing with IA -- dropping the ball on the Sidney memo. We may just snoop into that as well."

The inspector raised an eyebrow, "Fill your boots, Alan, but stay safe. Something's not right about any of this."

*****

Elsewhere, 9:19 a.m.
the same day --
Thursday.

The scheduled breakfast meeting was a fiasco -- only the hostess, who called herself *Lady*, and two others. One was a suited gent in his mid-forties, whom *Lady* called *Suit*, which seemed to please him. The other was taller, a few years younger, arms and neck covered in tattoos, with the cocky appeal of a used car salesman. He was dressed casually in a checked shirt and blue jeans. Not surprisingly, she called him *Tattoo*.

"You sure they were notified?" *Suit* asked, looking at his watch, directing the question to *Lady*. He seemed antsy, as though he felt exposed.

She looked expectantly to *Tattoo* for the answer. He responded flippantly, "Yeah, Boss. I set it up a week ago, and reminded them Tuesday by text. *Smith* won't be joining us because of that incident at . . ."

"I know, but tell me about the other three. Did they answer your texts Tuesday?"

"Naw, but remember, Boss, we decided at the last meeting that our communication should stay minimal -- loose lips and all that."

Lady was miffed. "Sure, I remember! But when I schedule a joint meeting two weeks in advance, everyone should show. I made it, and I drive much further than, say, *Miss Green.* She should have made the effort; we take good care of her. She has the military stuff, right?"

Suit piped up, "That stuff is for me, right? Because I'm here to make the exchange and be on my way before noon."

"Yes. Don't worry. It's all safe," *Lady* tried to assure him.

"Call her! Do it now!" *Suit* demanded. "I don't care how safe it is, I want that stuff in my hands!"

"*Suit,* if she doesn't make it this morning I'll get the load to you within the week. In the meantime, we have plenty of firepower in storage that might suit your needs. We collected just over a hundred in the last two weeks, more coming in tonight; my squads . . ."

Lady held up her hand as a phone call came in. "Yes? Oh, hello. What? They're there now? . . . Yes, I understand, but do you? . . . do what needs doing then -- and do it now!" She lay the cellphone in the center of the table. Within seconds, the three of them heard a click, then a sharp blast. Silence.

Lady looked at the other two. "*Suit,* your guns won't be coming."

"Apparently not. I don't want your guns, *Tattoo,* I'm looking for something more than a .223. Maybe the BAR MK III with scope."

Tattoo apologized, "Sorry we lost the Army guns . . ."

"And *Green.*" *Lady* interjected, "she was a good asset."

"I'll have scouts on it before the end of the day," *Tattoo* continued. "Trucks roll every day with weaponry, easy to hijack. We'll fix you up real soon."

"If you need some savvy hombres, I can send up a couple of recruits," *Lady* assured him. "English speaking, passports, papers, everything -- fit right in."

Tattoo furrowed his brow, "We do need to recruit someone immediately to take her place, Boss."

"Let me worry about that. Just get the guns you have into hands where they will do the most good. In the meantime, two people to put in your cross-hairs: Morris, the Hermosa inspector, and his buddy, Gumshoe, that private investigator. And finally, find out why we had the no-shows. Better be a damn good reason."

"Let me take care of those two," *Suit* said. "Send me their information. I have a team for just that kind of thing. Now, If we're done here, I'll be on my way."

*****

8 a.m. that same morning

Liz came through the office side door. "Sorry I'm a bit late, but I was invited to a late night dinner last night." She winked at me, "and a nightcap." She looked around, saw the second coffee mug.

"What did I miss?" She grabbed a mug, poured from the carafe, then topped mine off. Next, she sat at her desk and gave me a quizzical look. "Well, anything important?"

"Morris. Swazer's mom died."

"Oh, crap!" she set the coffee on the fax he had laid on her desk, her face twisting into anguish and bitterness.

"Poor lady! So, what's our move, Bossman? If I know Morris, he has specific instructions for us, so we don't step on each other."

"You're right on target, Fox. He's going to concentrate on Collins -- we have his rubber stamp for all else."

"So, where to first, Gumshoe?"

"Take a look at the coaster you're using for your coffee. Prints confirm Jay Rudolph and Belinda Jefferson were in Brad's home. We have copies of CA driver's licenses for both -- pic, age, address and all. First stop, the green-haired one. Let's pick her up."

"We can't do that legally, Bossman. Find her, yes,

but cuff her and drag her off to jail? Not within our purview."

"Two things about that, Fox -- one, read the fine print of the fax: there is already a BOLO out for them, and two, Morris sat in that chair this morning and as much as told me to do what I have to do. This is what I have to do, Fox, for Bradley, for the victims of the drugstore fire. There's a few "skips" in your top right drawer that you can work on while . . ."

"No way, José! Give me a minute!"

"Take your time, Fox. We have a few things to do around here. Let's plan on being out the door by 9:15 a.m."

*****

We made it to the Torrance address at 9:35. The building at 16229 153rd Street turned out to be an apartment complex -- one hundred-twenty-seven units. Live-in manager, Ellie, about 5'4", thirty-something red-head, wearing a tank top, cut-offs, and little else. Behind her, close to the door into her unit, was a playpen with a chubby, curly-haired, year-old girl bouncing up and down on the pad.

Ellie pulled a photocopied map from under the counter, traced directions to the units on the east wing, then circled E3A -- Belinda's two bedroom unit, and handed the sheet to Fox. According to the apartment records, Belinda was unemployed, rent was being covered by a corporation out of San Diego, XTR-Management. The interesting thing, XTR paid the rent with cash!

"Ellie, now I need a key card for E3A, please."

After some consideration, she opted to join us. She opened her door a crack -- just enough to throw her voice into her unit, "Tommie, I need you."

A lanky fellow dressed in T-shirt and jeans opened the door to a wider crack. "Yeah, a minute!"

Two minutes later we were knocking at E3A. No answer.

"Police business!" I yelled. Still no answer. "Swipe the card and step aside, please," I instructed. Inside we could hear a strange scraping movement. Ellie swiped the lock; the light flashed green. The door cracked open, slammed closed and the light returned to red. I took the door card from her and pushed her aside.

Two blasts from inside buckled the door jamb and blew the lock and some metal shards across the hallway. A concussive force we all felt sent Ellie sprawling on the floor beside the spinning lock, holding a bloody elbow. Her face was chalk-white.

"Ellie! I told you to step back, dammit! Are you okay?" Pulling my weapon, I pointed to Fox. "Get her out of here!" Fox lifted Ellie to her feet and guided her down the corridor. "Call 911!" I yelled after them.

"You inside! Lay down that shotgun and walk out here, hands above your head!" I ordered.

"That's not the way it works, Copper!" a female voice responded. "I'm supposed to ask you what you want!"

"I'm not a cop, ma'am. Just a citizen asking you to comply."

"Bullshit! Why no cops?"

"Evidently, you're not important enough to send a real cop, ma'am. What can I say?" I tried to sound apologetic. In retrospect, it proved the wrong response.

Six more earth-shattering reports from that monster gun tore gaping holes in the exterior walls and the one window to the left of the door, throwing glass, stucco, and other chunks of shrapnel into the hallway. By now, tenants were lining the corridor on either side of E3A. I motioned for them all to gawk from a distance -- most heeded.

"Trust me," I yelled, "cops'll be here soon. Belinda, isn't it? Why did you and your buddies perpetrate such atrocities?"

"Instructions were, 'as much mayhem as possible'. Felt good! Power! Now where are the real cops?"

"Who else is in there with you?" Approaching sirens brought laughter from inside E3A. "Is Jay with you?"

"No one else; just little ol' me." She laughed an unearthly laugh. "And I'm lonely, Mr. Concerned Citizen. Wanna come in for a visit?" I heard a female voice talking on the phone; then, "I just called my people -- told'em the cops were here. You know what they said? *You know what to do,* they said. Bitch of a thing, isn't it?"

Then came a small calibre pistol report. I wasn't able to visit her -- point of fact, she didn't entertain or accept visitors -- ever again.

Stepping through the opening, I pushed aside the sofa the young, green-haired female had thought to use as a barricade, and entered. Belinda Jefferson lay just beyond, sprawled on the dark, wood-like, Pergo flooring -- shattered, bloody pieces of a cellphone along with shotgun next to her body, and a SIG Sauer P230, still smoking, in her left hand.

There was only time to make a cursory search of the apartment before four police officers pushed their way through the cell-phone-toting onlookers and into the unit. Officer Haruto, the in-charge guy, looked around. "Anyone else dead?"

"Just the young, green-haired girl -- and of course, the entire wall, including the door and window." I kicked at a small chunk of concrete.

"You shoot?"

"No, sir. She did it all. Both guns are hers," I said pointing at Belinda and the weaponry.

"Who are you? Why are you here? How do you know her?" His questions came as an onslaught: brusque, clipped, demanding.

"I was following a lead for Inspector Morris out of Hermosa Precinct. We were . . ."

"Aah, the gumshoe! And where is your fox?"

"Right behind you. Your officers are holding her back with the other onlookers."

"Let Ms Fox through, please," Haruto called out, then waved Liz through the small crowd to stand beside me. "Ms Fox, why are *you* here today?" *At least he was going to allow her to reply*, I thought. Wrong!

"What is the identity of the deceased? Do you have a gun? Did you shoot her? Do you have a carry permit for your weapon?"

She did handle it better than I. "Stop!" she fairly shouted at him, then proceeded to fill in all the blanks, ending with her dragging the manager down the elevator and calling 911. Haruto smiled. Turning to me, "Did you find anything interesting before we arrived?"

"Didn't really have much time. Pulled a couple of drawers. You'll find boxes of ammo in that drawer," I pointed, "and that closet has at least sixty or seventy hand-guns. The shelf above has four bundles -- I didn't open them. Drugs or cash perhaps. Looks like a stash house to me.

"Oh! there's also a bundle of interesting sub-machine guns leaning against a bathroom wall -- new army issue. She said something very interesting just before . . ."

"Where to now, Gumshoe?" Fox interrupted

Haruto and me, "don't we have an appointment with Jay? It's almost lunchtime."

"Oh, yeah, I forgot about our appointment." I laughed. "We need to go, sir."

"It's Haruto. This Jay fellow. He's not in Torrance, by chance?"

"No, Officer Haruto. He's in . . ."

"Just Haruto," he interjected.

"Right! Lennox. He's in Lennox, Haruto."

"Good. I like you two, but stay out of Torrance. Do you have a business card, Gumshoe? Just in case, you understand."

We exchanged cards. Turns out, Haruto was a police inspector -- on a par with Morris. Alas, no time to chat. We were on our way to Lennox.

Chapter 8

The last thing Belinda told me before she offed herself, *"You know what to do."* stuck in my brain. Was this young gal *that* indoctrinated? She had fired through her cellphone into her head to prevent tracing calls; probably even on the damn thing, listening to instructions from her coach while I stood outside. *Damn her, and damn him, whoever he is! Well,* I shrugged mentally, *she is no more.*

Now for Jay Rudolph -- and true -- he hung his hat in Lennox. The house was an old three bedroom, one story stucco, with old-style hopper windows, about a foot off the ground, indicating a basement.

It was listed in the name of Lydia Diller. Neighbors on both sides and across the street said they hadn't seen Lydia in months; the neighborhood consensus was that she probably sub-let the property to Jay -- and possibly three housemates -- two dudes, one female -- all in their mid-twenties.

Raymond Barnes, the old gentleman across the street who held the "neighborhood watch" duties, was quite forthcoming: "They's in an' out, in an' out, all day, ever day -- in ones or twos. An' ever coupla weeks they have a visitor," he continued. "Same one ever time. Suited-up fella, maybe forty -- all business. Got his license number fer ya, ya want it." We did.

"So what do we do now, Bossman? Pound on Jay's door and demand they surrender?"

"First of all, let's find out who the suited-up fella is. Let's call Hermosa, see if Morris is in . . . no wait! I have a better idea. Call Haruto; tell him it's the Fox. You need a favor. Ask him to pull up a DPPA on this license plate. Tell him it's important, and that you'll wait. That should piss him off."

Fox raised an eyebrow, looked at me and shook her head. "You serious, Gumshoe? Why should he assist us?"

"Aww, c'mon, Fox, play with me, here. Just want to see if he's a hard ass or has a sense of humor."

Fox dialed the number on the card. Woman's voice -- "Torrance Second Precinct -- Badge #1578. How may I direct your call?"

Fox shook her head, rolled her eyes, and handed the phone to me. I frowned and said, "Good afternoon, Officer. This is Gumshoe. We were speaking with Haruto earlier today, and need DPPA on the following license plate." I rattled off the plate number to the female officer.

"What did you say your name is, sir?"

"Gumshoe -- and tell Haruto not to worry. Fox is okay. Could I get that info, please?" I cupped the phone with my hand, making sure the officer on the other end could hear; "Belinda may have tipped them off before she offed herself. I think we . . ."

"Here's your info, Mr. Gumsh . . ."

"Just Gumshoe, ma'am." She hesitated, then threw out all the pertinent details; I jotted them down: name, address, phone number, driver's license number, even social security number. "Thanks, Officer; tell Haruto we got it from here."

I shared the notes with Fox. "Did you just ask for some illegal cop-stuff, Bossman? What's DPPA?"

"No! Well, maybe, but I used DPPA all the time when I was in AFOSI. It's a law enforcement tool; regulates the release and sharing of personal information based on DMV records. If he hadn't given it to me, I'd get it from Morris."

She pointed at the name. "Do you know the guy, Bossman?"

"Not yet, but," I glanced at the dashboard clock, "nuts! too late today, but tomorrow we take a drive to Montecito. Let's just watch Jay's residence for today; see who comes and goes."

We snapped pictures of six individuals entering and exiting Jay's home, most of whom were male, most in their twenties, just as Old Man Barnes had said.

*****

Two hours later we headed for Manhattan Beach. We were just unlocking the side door when my cell rang.

"Garrett."

"Garrett! Where are you, Garrett?"

"Morris! We're just sitting here about ready to call it a day. Why? What's up?"

"You stay right there! We'll be there in ten minutes! Gumshoe, my ass!" The inspector signed off. He sounded hot.

Smiling, I turned to Liz, "Huh! That was Morris. Wonder what he wants."

Chapter 9

The six visitors we had snapped at Jay's were now pinned to my cork board, staring at us. Fox pulled two glasses and a bottle of cognac from the cupboard while I made a trip to the loo. As I returned, I heard voices, and discovered we were graced with the presence of, not one, but two inspectors: Messrs Morris and Haruto. Neither seemed overly chummy.

"What the hell do you think you're doing, Asshole, asking Torrance police for confidential information?" I'd not seen my friend, Morris quite so riled up. And he wasn't finished yet.

"Sorry. I guess I got carried away."

"Bullshit!" Haruto exploded. "Morris told me about you, Gumshoe! Every move is calculated! I'd have your license except for my friend, here! Never again, you understand?"

"Okay, Haruto. I get it -- we overstepped our bounds a bit -- involving more than a suicide and a couple of missing guns."

"A couple of guns?" Fox looked at me with crossed eyes. "Bossman, you told me there were dozens of guns in there!"

I ignored her, "Now, Fox and I are about ready to put our feet up and discuss what we learned today -- over a glass of Martell, of course. If you'd like to join us . . ."

"Absolutely," Morris nodded and eyeballed Haruto, who affirmed, even while mouthing '*unbelievable*'.

"So who are these guys?" Haruto asked, pointing at the cork board, while at the same time reaching for the glass Fox held out to him.

"Along with Ira Sidney, these are guys -- and gals -- who frequent a house in Lennox. Fox and I, just today in three hours, watched them go in and out more than once. This guy, in fact," I pointed, "went out three times. We left before he came back. But one thing in common, as you can see: they mostly carried backpacks, some empty, some full."

"And the DPPA?" Haruto demanded, but less severely.

"Neighbor says a car is there every couple of weeks. Driver: 40ish, suit, briefcase, spends maybe two hours, then gone. I thought, with today's stake-out, we could tie it together into a nice, neat package."

"What do you think's going down, Alan?"

"Not sure yet, Carl, but the stockpile of guns at Belinda's unit in Torrance . . ."

"Yeah, what's your take on that, Gumshoe?" Haruto asked, holding out his glass for another two fingers.

"You saw that bundle still belted together in the bathroom. That's a brand-new sub-machine gun the army bought -- the APC9K. I saw the specs on it before I left AFOSI -- has a 30-round mag. Weighs under 6 pounds, can fire over 1000 rounds per minute."

"So you're thinking what, stockpiling guns?"

"Uhhh, yeah, but for what?" I raised an eyebrow.

"I need to get into Jay's house; there are other things yet to discover."

Haruto nodded his head, and thought for a moment. "I'll call Lennox. Tell them to get a search warrant. I'll ask Sarbonte to pencil you in for the visit once they get the warrant. He owes me."

"Appreciate it."

"You go, it's strictly business suits, no guns, no talking unless it's pertinent. That work for you?"

"Absolutely! Thanks. We'll be ready."

"Gumshoe?" he looked at me with a smirk.

"Yeah?"

"Then you'll owe me."

"What about our Montecito connection, Bossman?" Liz interrupted.

"One thing at a time, Fox. Just wear something suitable tomorrow."

"Send me copies of those six," Morris pointed to the board.

"Already done, sir. And you, too, Haruto. We should have all the identities by morning, right?"

"Ha!" Morris laughed, "in a perfect world, Fox."

I changed the subject. "How are you coming along on your boy, Collins, Inspector?"

"Nothing yet, but when I find that bastard I'll end his little game, whatever it is!"

"You make sure you pencil me in!" Haruto demanded. "And you two" -- he stared, first at me, then at Fox, shaking his head -- "I don't know what to do with you."

"Another short Martell, Inspector?"

*****

Friday, 6:20 a.m.

I jogged down to my office, tossed my fedora to swing lazily on the rack, quick shower, then turned the TV to the early news on channel 5. With coffee brewing, I opened the closet in my office to choose one of the three suit/tie combinations hanging there.

No fax, no landline, no blinking lights. Just the news . . . and coffee. I hate waiting. Getting antsy. I need action.

Whoa! I just about choked on a swig of coffee as I watched coverage of the previous night's Laker game against the Utah Jazz. The Laker's big man was strolling down the court, taking 3-4 steps before his first dribble. Wonder where his mind was. The sportscaster pointed and played the clip repeatedly during his airtime. And no call! Amazing!

Walking out the side door to make sure my Cadillac was safe and sound, I was just in time to see Liz pull up to the gate. The remote gave her entrance; I waited for her. Our office landline rang as she slid out of her Kia, dressed in a smart steel-gray business suit, accessorized by a shimmering pearl scarf.

"You look nice, Liz. Might be a little much for a search warrant with that scarf."

"Same thought crossed my mind, Gumshoe, but I can always pull it off -- unless you . . ." My cell rang.

"Garrett here. Yes . . . Oh! Yes, Mr. Barnes . . . Huh! Interesting. I have some people coming, but I'm not sure when . . . no, I understand . . . is that right? . . . I appreciate it . . . thanks for your call.

"That was Old Man Barnes, the neighborhood watch guy. Says a white box truck pulled up at Jay's place this morning about two o'clock. Barnes says he couldn't tell if they were 'bringin' stuff in or haulin' stuff out'. He couldn't see license plates at that time of the day either, just knew from the street lights that the truck was white."

"What do you suppose that's about, Gumshoe?"

"Dunno, but I don't like it." I glanced at my watch. "Too early to call Lennox for that damn warrant. Let's take a run over there and nose around a bit, Fox."

We were just a block and half away when we felt the concussive blast; it actually tried to lift my Caddy from the pavement. Almost immediately came the boom -- then flames shooting some seventy to eighty feet skyward.

Fox clutched my arm. "Bossman, that's Jay's place!" I agreed. It didn't take much speculation. We continued to the corner and stopped to observe.

There was no reason for a warrant; Jay's house was gone. Pieces of furniture, twisted metal, 2x4s, stucco, roof shingles, and vermiculite insulation covered the block, both sides of the street. Glass from neighbors' windows had imploded. I looked up to see Mr. Barnes standing on his porch. We walked up his drive. We could hear sirens.

"I had no mor'en walked out back and was feeding my dog; otherwise I'd a been sittin' in my rocker, starin' out that window."

"God must love you," Liz smiled.

"Not so sure about that. I just figure I dodged a bullet. My sittin' room is a shambles, covered in glass and shingles. Oh, and this stuff, whatever it is," he pointed at a semi-hard, black object six inches or so in diameter.

"Who knows, looks like a dehydrated, melted, burned, and encrusted piece of something inedible."

Barnes turned to Liz, "Is he always so flippant? This is my house! The outside is all scorched, inside will need paint. My deductible will take most of my savings. I don't have funds to cover the damage."

"Don't worry about the deductible, Mr. Barnes.

You're an integral part of this police investigation. Just keep accurate records for me so you can expense it properly."

"Gumshoe! Are you . . ."

"No sense in us sticking around here, Fox." I turned to Mr. Barnes. "Check your insurance policy or call your agent. I'll talk with the police. Maybe they can front you any money needed."

"Fox, do you have that Sarbonte's phone number?" I was looking across the street at the water streaming onto the flames. "May as well call him to cancel that warrant. Tell him to look for a white box van, probably a rental. I doubt Lennox FD will find anyone inside, but you might suggest his forensics team join them over here, just in case."

She punched the buttons. A minute later, "Ha! Sarbonte is right across the street, Bossman. He just pulled up in that white cop car," she added, pointing. "So, what are we going to do, Gumshoe, head up to Montecito?"

"No. I've been thinking about that, Fox. Let's go meet the man, then we'll head down to San Diego to talk to Belinda's property manager -- just as soon as I change into a suit."

*****

"You're giving that nice, old Mr. Barnes the money to make his repairs, aren't you, Gumshoe?"

"More blessed to give than receive, Fox. Your Mama told you that. Besides, that nice, old man was a big help. I doubt he knows how big, but he will before this is all over. Might be a big reward." I stepped into my personal office.

Fox flipped on the TV. "We don't even know what 'this' is yet, Bossman," she yelled. "Guns, for sure, but what's the rest of it? Do you have any bright ideas?"

In my office with the door closed, changing into a Navy suit, I found it difficult sorting out Liz's voice from the moderator on the 8 a.m. news. "Just a minute, Fox! I'll be right out!"

Chapter 10

"What happened back there, Bossman? I mean, there's nothing left of that house!" Fox was watching the first-hand reports from neighbors on the Lennox house explosion. No camera caught the exact instant the house lifted off its pins, but one caught it milliseconds later -- flames and glass spurting horizontally from the basement windows, followed by a rush of smoke from every opening. Then the whole neighborhood hit with shock waves and litter.

"Blast like that? C4 placed strategically in basement, gas stove in kitchen, and walls saturated with gasoline is my best guess. They emptied the contraband early this morning, left one man behind to prepare for our search warrant -- possibly with trip wires or booby-trapped door . . ."

"Wait, wait, Gumshoe! You sayin' somebody tipped them off that the cops were on the way?"

"Makes sense. Why else move out? I figure something went very wrong, and the guy will either be found in the wreckage or he split before he was turned into a grease spot."

"How about someone else slipped in, tossed a match and ran? That way the lone guy is erased and can't blab?"

"That's a plan, Fox, but I don't think so. Killer

would have waited for our warrant team to step up to the door, then send a bullet through a window from a distance." I pondered for only a moment, "No, I figure the house was rigged to blow, but went off prematurely. We were meant to be part of the debris, Fox."

A flash of realization raced up Liz's back and settled in her stomach. "Holy Cow! Do you realize we could have been on that porch, Gumshoe? We could be dead!"

"Not a pretty thought, Fox."

*****

We were on our way to San Diego to visit XTR-Management. We had done some homework on the company -- they managed only one complex in San Diego (the one with their offices), and from there they managed only three large leased properties in Los Angeles County.

"Is there a purpose to all this, Gumshoe? I mean, even going back to the Bradley shooting, the missing guns, the Delaware fax screw-up, the suicide in Torrance, the explosion today, and the San Diego and Montecito connections. So I ask again, what's it all about?"

I glanced over at her and frowned. *Okay, I thought, now you're just talking like a confused amateur, Fox!*

"That's why we're on the job. We're investigators, remember? We don't know yet what we don't know. And every twist can either speed things up or make them more confusing. But we dig and keep digging!"

"You're right. Just a little overwhelming to see that house disappear before my eyes. And to think I could have been knocking on that door!"

*****

Walking into XTR-Management, I was surprised to see it was so small. Two desks with chairs, and two chairs for visitors -- that's it. It was manned by Michelle, who seemed a no-nonsense young lady, maybe 25, with short, curly, red hair. She was taller than Fox, but had less flesh on her, and she was wearing a grass-green top, floral mini skirt.

She motioned, I sat. Fox strolled the perimeter, taking in wall coverings. One minute in, Michelle realized I wasn't a potential client. "Boss isn't in right now. He's looking at a new property in Alpine."

It took another ten seconds before I realized Michelle would be as helpful as a strip of floral wallpaper. "Oh, really? That sounds just like Jesko. I was hoping we'd have time for a few drinks while we're in the area."

"Jesko? I'm sorry, sir, his name is Camacho."

"Huh?" I flipped my notepad back a page and stared at it for a millisecond. "Isn't this 1422 Navy Way?"

"No! This is 1422 Remington Avenue. I don't know who you are, mister, but you're way off, and I'm not sure you're really lost! I think you are competitors checking out XTR."

She was a shrewd one. I stood, leaned over her desk. "Michelle! You caught me, but I'm not a competitor -- I'm a headhunter. I was told there's some pretty good talent in this outfit and I wanted to see for myself. I was hoping part of the crew would be here, but your office is small and spartan. This is it, right?"

"This is our office, yes. I can't even offer a cup of coffee, so if there's nothing more, I'll say goodbye. I have work to do."

We bid Michelle adieu, hopped into my Caddy

and headed back up I-5. The day-trip wasn't a total waste. Fox managed to pick up business cards from the four managers in the field, a brochure of the many amenities, and full-color photos of the properties they managed. From observation, she gleaned a few other interesting factoids. She made me proud.

We had names of five operatives, including one of the majors (Camacho). Fox noted they had a huge wall calendar from Wells Fargo Bank. On Michelle's desk, I'd managed to spy some interesting outgoing mail: two thick manila envelopes -- one addressed to the same bank, and the other to someone in Beverly Hills. The name on the letter was covered by other mail, but the address was plainly visible.

As we drove I called out the address to Fox. She was just jotting it down when my cell rang. I handed it to Fox.

"Garrett's phone, this is Fox."

"Liz, where's Alan?"

"Rita? Alan's right here. What's up?"

"We've been receiving death threats on the phone for the last half hour. Roland says not to worry, that it's just crank calls, but I'm scared, Liz."

"We'll be there as soon as we can. Lock the doors!" I floored the Caddy and turned to Fox, "We just poked a bear!"

Chapter 11

"We've another twenty minutes before we hit our off-ramp. Call Morris. Now! Damn, these people are connected, I'll say that for them."

"They sure are, Bossman," Liz murmured, pushing the inspector's quick-dial button, gripping the above-door grab with her right hand, "We'll be there soon . . . that's if you stay at only twenty over the limit.

"Inspector! Hi! Fox and Gumshoe, on our way back to the office -- 'bout a half hour out. Got a call . . . no, no, sir; listen to me! Somebody threatened Pop and Rita with a death threat -- yes, sir! . . . Could be imminent. Would you? . . . Thank you, sir. . . . Of course!"

"He'll send a squad?" I asked.

"That's what he said. He's close, so he, himself is on his way; a squad'll be right behind him."

Pulling my foot off the gas pedal, the Caddy dropped to 70. I breathed a sigh.

*****

Rita was sitting on the porch, Morris and Pop were sitting next to her on the white railing, and another officer was leaning against a pillar. The cul-de-sac was lined with cop cars -- I counted eight before hopping up the steps to Rita's (and now

Pop's) digs.

"What's up, Pop? What happened?"

Morris provided the answer. "Just be thankful you called when you did, Alan. Two minutes after I pulled in, a couple of units rolled up. While we were inside talking to Pop and Rita, one of those Mercedes vans came up -- you know the type -- they saw the squads and made a quick U-turn. Two more of our cruisers showed up, but by that time the van was pulling out of the cul-de-sac. Gregg, here, was in one of our cars. He'll tell you what he saw."

"Erratic driving, that one!" Officer Gregg said. "Roared around the corner. Looked like a bunch of kids -- maybe half a dozen inside. Normally, we would have hit the lights and gone after them, but we had orders to get to this property pronto."

Rita went indoors and returned with a pitcher of orange juice and some small plastic cups. As she was pouring, Morris received an incoming call. He shouted, "They're coming back! Pop! Rita! In the house; hurry now!"

We could hear tires screeching, followed immediately by what I thought must be bursts of automatic gunfire. Evidently one of the inspector's units was at the bottom of the cul-de-sac, exchanging rounds with the the van's occupants. I positioned myself behind a beautiful tree just below Rita's. I waited.

The van came into view, laminated side windows riddled with holes. Two windows missing glass had long guns poking out. The driver stomped on the brakes and cut the wheel hard to the left, trying to bring the vehicle to a screeching halt.

It happened so fast I had no time to fire safely, only time to yell, "Look out!" then watch the van, as if in slow motion. It flipped and passed Rita's, spinning counter-clockwise, skidding to a stop up the roadway. A couple of long guns bounced along behind. The van then exploded; no survivors.

*****

Darkness dropped down on Manhattan Beach. Morris, his crew, and the coroner had finished their work and were gone.

From Rita's porch, we ordered pizza for the entire neighborhood while we watched the burned-out wreck being chained up onto the bed of a tow truck. As its tail-lights disappeared into the night, a dozen extra-large pizzas were delivered -- barely enough to feed our cul-de-sac neighbors, the press, and even a few of the looky-loos who drove in from places unknown.

Finally, the news cameras stopped pointing, and the looky-loos meandered off. Fox kissed my cheek, borrowed my car, and bid me goodnight.

After walking up to *Pop's*, I threw myself into the shower, toweled off, threw on a pair of shorts, and poured two fingers of Martell. I sat, sipped, and watched the whitecaps break against the pylons, watched the pier's light poles morph into shadowy giants -- playing hop-scotch in the circles of light on the pier. Fell asleep in my chair. Long day.

*****

6 a.m. Morris woke me. "Forensics confirmed five in the van; Jay was not among the dead. One female. All under twenty-seven. Such a waste of humankind, Alan! We have identified all but one.

"I'm going to have Bradley notify the next of kin, or as many as he can find. Press is having a field day, connecting dots between the house explosion in Lennox and your cul-de-sac tragedy."

"Not sure tragedy is the right term, Inspector. More like carnage. They brought it upon themselves, almost as if . . ."

"Premeditated suicide," Morris finished my sentence.

"Yeah, something like that. Can you put a cruiser down by Rita's place for a couple of days?"

"Should be there already, Alan. Now put on some clothes and meet me in your office -- say, ten minutes!"

As I jogged down the pavement, I met a police unit with two officers patrolling, just a few houses below Rita's. I gave them two thumbs up as I passed.

*****

The trepidation I had felt with his early morning call became smiles and a shaking of my head at the old man's antics. Hell, he simply wanted a friend to chat with before the stress and pressures of the day took over. I understood.

There were times Fox and I could provide him with a morning uplift, complete with caffeine, and as comic relief some afternoons . . . actually, many afternoons.

But this morning was different: Morris brought breakfast! Fox pulled into the lot just before the last of the doughnuts disappeared. Then Morris bid us adieu, and Fox and I headed for Beverly Hills.

Chapter 12

"Why are we starting with some unknown address in Beverly Hills, Bossman? I don't understand; why not head up to Montecito, check out that suited visitor at the Lennox house?"

"How long have you worked for me, Fox? I always start at the perimeter and work my way inward. Start at the center, sure, you might cut off the head of the snake, but all the little snakelets may puff out their chests and think they can become the head snake.

"I'd much rather cut off the snake's tail; work my way up; destroy all the babies -- then you can yell at the momma-- 'Hey you! Come out, come out! I destroyed your little ones! Nobody left to help you! They're all dead!'"

Liz smiled. "Like, uh, 'Hey, Momma! you have no wiggle room left!'" Liz was obviously pleased with herself for the amusing statement. "And here I always thought you were afraid of Momma, Gumshoe."

"Not so!" I smiled. "You figure you're a Momma, Fox?"

"And a hot one at that, Bossman, red hot!"

"Let me check." I reached up, held my hand to her forehead for a moment. "Nah! Sorry, Fox. It's normal."

"Now, you see? That's your problem, Gumshoe." Fox gave me a dead-pan expression, one eyebrow raised, "You always start at the perimeter."

By this time we were traveling north on the 405 freeway. At least CalTrans was doing roadwork in the southbound lanes, so just normal morning traffic for us -- about 32mph. We were still six miles from Wilshire Boulevard, our off-ramp for Beverly Hills.

*****

The address was easy to find -- a swank multi-level residence just off Beverly Boulevard. We rang the bell. An older gentleman answered [later we would argue as to how old] -- balding, wire-rim glasses, dress shirt, bow tie, and creased, charcoal slacks. No doubt, his idea of casual.

"Yes?" His voice matched his attire -- clipped, soft, efficient.

"Here about a package you received." Fox answered before I could say a word. I frowned, but said nothing. The gentleman squinted at her queerly, but after a slight hesitation, he ushered us through to a small ante room off the main entry.

He motioned for us to sit on two of the four chairs in the room. Dutifully, we sat. I removed my fedora and set it on my knee.

"What is the number, please?"

"I beg your pardon?" I asked him.

"Your box number, sir. Normally, we forward items, but some folks -- like you, I'm assuming -- prefer to pick up here." His face showed a changed expression. "Ah, yes, I see. Perhaps I jumped to conclusions. That's why I didn't recognize you. You don't have a box here, do you?"

"No. How many boxes do you have here?" Fox asked.

"Forty-one. Sorry. I should have asked. We have nine slots left. Do you need a box? I can do that for you. My name is Carson, by the way -- and you are . . . ?"

Fox produced a business card. "Could we get a list of the forty-one clients?"

"I'm sorry, no, Ma'am. That would defeat the purpose of a mail-forwarding service, wouldn't it?"

"Not really," I chimed in, smiling as I faced Carson. "Would you not rather have a Beverly Hills address than, let's say, a Lennox address?"

A reaction, but not the reaction I was looking for. Carson raised an eyebrow and smiled. "We would never entertain mail forwarding clients from Lennox."

"Wouldn't even take their money, right, Carson? How about from San Diego way? XTR-Management, perhaps."

This time Carson was noticeably affected. He became immediately reticent to continue our conversation. "I believe we are finished here. I'll see you out."

We stood. I tipped my fedora. "No, no -- we've taken too much of your time. We'll see ourselves out."

*****

"That guy, Carson, was a fun guy, eh, Bossman? Creepy! We're going to grab some lunch now, right, and then head for Montecito, right?"

Back on Wilshire, Fox was breathing a little easier. I ignored her. "Did you see Carson's body language, Fox? I think we blind-sided him. First, you asked him for a list of clients, then I named one of them. I wonder who he's on the phone with at this very moment.

"Put a call through to Morris. Maybe he knows the top cops in Beverly Hills. I have a gut feeling that someone should nose around the details on that address. Does Carson own it? If not, who? There may be a connection -- not sure, Fox, but as I say, my gut says *tread lightly*."

As she punched in the number, she nodded her head. "I thought so, too; but my gut keeps saying, *'feed me!'*" She lifted a finger for silence as she connected with the inspector. They spoke a few moments, some small talk, and disconnected. "Morris says he knows a guy. He also says, *'don't go nosing around an ongoing investigation'.*"

"What the hell does that mean, Fox? Is that place under surveillance?"

"He didn't say that, Alan. Probably just a cautionary afterthought."

"Damn. Call him back! No, on second thought, let's go feed your gut. What do you feel like?"

*****

As I slipped my credit card on the tray, I shared my plan for the afternoon with Liz. "We're not heading to Montecito, Fox; we're going to visit Internal Affairs headquarters. They're right down the street."

"More poking around perimeters, eh, Gumshoe? Oh, yeah, I remember. You know a guy. Is this guy expecting you today?"

"We weren't sure if it would be today or tomorrow, but we've kept in touch."

The Internal Affairs Division was on Figueroa, not all that far from the eatery. We pulled into the almost-empty parking structure. "What's going on, Gumshoe? Where is everyone," Fox asked.

"Strange. This is Tuesday, isn't it? Let's find out."

There was a note on the locked front doors: *Facility closed to public. Please call 1-213 555-9876 for information.*

I flipped through my phone book and pressed a number. "Elliott. This you, Garrett?"

"Yeah. We're here, but doors are locked. You folks having a closed meeting or a party or what?"

"Not quite. Notice from upstairs. Nobody in, nobody out until we figure this new flu bug out. I'll give you a heads-up when you can visit the brass around here. What are you looking for, exactly, Garrett?"

"Oh, you know, Elliott, I just like looking people in the eye, and then ask a question they may not be expecting."

"Such as?"

"Example, hmmm. Uhh, let's see -- okay." I cleared my throat as if to start a friendly interview.

"Thanks for seeing me, Officer Elliott. That's your first name, right?"

"Yes, it is."

"What's your last name, Elliott?"

"Hightower."

"How long have you been a part of IA?"

"Six years."

"Good place to work, Officer Hightower?"

"I think so."

"What's your rank?"

"Sergeant."

"You being bribed by anyone?"

"What, sir?"

"You know, dismissing an investigation in any of the precincts?"

"Okay, that's enough, Garrett. You could get shot or physically booted out of the Bureau with that approach."

"Too strong, eh? Okay, Elliott, interview's over; but did I catch you off guard just a little bit?"

"Maybe, but totally out of line, Garrett."

"How many in the bureau, Elliott?"

"A hundred-ten last count; six separate divisions."

"All clean hands?"

"We police our own. What's this about, Alan?"

"How did Sidney get in unnoticed?"

"Who?"

My phone indicated Haruto was waiting. *Why would Haruto be calling me?*

"Sorry, Elliott, I have a call waiting I need to answer. I'll get back to you."

*****

"Haruto, this is a surprise. What's up?"

Chapter 13

"Stay away from Montecito, Gumshoe! Feds have had your 'person of interest' under surveillance for close to a year."

"What feds, Haruto?"

What was Haruto up to? Was he trying to be involved? I knew he was aware of the connection between Jay's house and the Montecito suited gent, but . . . huh! Did he follow up by calling the Montecito cops? Was he playing games? Other thoughts ran across my brain, but Haruto interrupted them.

"DEA and ATF have a joint operation going on up there. The only reason I know, Gumshoe, my cousin, Corporal Tabitha Norman, is quartered up there. I called her. Seems they all know of the guy."

"Good to know. Possible to get her phone number, Haruto?"

"I'll call her. She might call you back, but with a name like Gumshoe . . ."

"Understood. Thanks for the heads up." I signed off.

"What's a Corporal in the police department, Bossman?"

"A step up from a traffic cop or beat cop. Some supervisory position below sergeant. Probably a four-year man or woman. Serious about her career. Just a guess."

*****

Back to the office. It looked like a sheet of paper or something was stuck on the front door. Fox hopped out; I continued through the gate into the parking area and entered the back way. Fox brought the paper in through the front.

"So what do we have, Fox? Luther's *Ninety-five theses* glued to the door?"

"Haven't looked yet. Thought we'd open it together for the full effect. Feels like quite a few pages in the envelope. Do you speak Spanish, Bossman?"

"No, why?"

"There's a whole paragraph on the envelope -- see? Everything is in Spanish except six words. First, at the top, *Gumshoe & Fox*, and then at the bottom, *Be Very Afraid!*"

"Well, let's have a look inside, Fox."

Liz pulled out a sheaf of some eight pages -- a cover sheet followed by two more sheets of text, all in a mix of cut-out letters or handwritten Spanish. Then came the photos -- such horrible images! Page after page, graphic, brutal, bullet-riddled, some decapitations, some eviscerated; all with strong, bold captions, all screaming with cruel atrocity.

Fox turned her head away and stood, "I'm sorry, Gumshoe. I can't look at any more." She ran to the bathroom. I continued to thumb through the pages, more incensed with each image, at the same time worrying about the motive of the sender. *WHY*?

The photos on the last page provided the answer: glossies of Fox, Pop, Rita, and me -- all heinously mutilated, worse than the others, photo-shopped.

Now I understood. I called the one person I knew to be fluent in Spanish: Ferdig, one of Pop's firefighter buddies.

"You have a queasy stomach, Ferdig?"

"You kiddin? Naw! What's up?"

"How soon can you be here?"

Fox joined me as we waited for our translator. "Those pictures were awful, Bossman. I couldn't look at any more, and as it is, I'll probably have nightmares for a week!"

I called Morris; invited him to the pow-wow.

Morris arrived two minutes before Ferdig. I introduced both men, set them at Fox's desk and dropped the envelope in front of them. Then I crossed to the liquor cabinet, drew out three glasses and a fresh bottle of Martell. Behind me, I heard expletives and a whistle.

"What?" I asked, turning.

"Who are you messing with, Alan?" Ferdig asked. "I thought you were a simple private eye, tracking down deadbeat dads, and planting bugs in a fourteenth floor highrise, for a suspicious wife, to catch the president bonking the secretary. Damn, Boy! This is the Sinaloa boys and the remnants of the Los Zetas cartel -- and they aren't happy with you." He reached for a cognac, shaking his head.

Morris chimed in, "Gumshoe, this changes things!"

"Translate, please."

"Basically, the outside of the package says, 'Inside is a short history of anyone who interferes with our business. Gumshoe and Fox, you should be very afraid'. It's signed, T.A. Durazo.

"So then, you go to the inside. They're saying they have been marching all along the border, making inroads just about everywhere from Tijuana to Laredo, targeting and eliminating opposition. The pictures that follow are proof of their ruthless efficiency.

"The last page has photo-shopped depictions of you, Pop, and your family, Alan, with captions saying things like 'you're next'. A real friendly dossier, my friend. I don't know what else to say, except watch your back.

"But now, if there's nothing else, I think I'll say goodbye before another page is added. Good brandy, by the way."

"Of course, Ferdig. Thanks -- much appreciated. You still at House #33?"

"Naw. Transferred to Arson Unit over at #67. You'd think I'd have a little easier going, but it gets just as frantic. I thought I'd snatch a few minutes to write, but no such luck."

"Aah, an investigator! Fun work, I'm sure. And you write? What do you write?"

"Different genres -- crime, westerns, young adult; you know, just good stories."

"Good for you. I used to love Max Brand, Zane Grey, and of course, Louis L'Amour. Take care, and thanks again."

As the fireman walked out, Morris asked for a refill and cocked his head at me. "This is major league, Garrett. Those kids -- that's one thing, but we're talking the strongest cartel in Mexico -- and they have you in their sights!"

"That thought and its implications hit me just before I called you, Carl," I smiled. "I included you only to share in my good fortune."

"Where's your better half, Gumshoe?"

"I sent her home early."

"Her leg still giving her problems?"

"Her stomach."

"Her stomach? Is she preg . . . Oh! the photos! Of course!"

"She only saw a few; she didn't see the last page. I'm going to call the Border Patrol in on this, Morris. What do you think?"

Before Morris could answer, his cell rang. I went back to thumbing through the pictures, mesmerized, occasionally flirting with my Martell, when my cell phone jarred me to vigilance.

"Garrett."

"Mr. Garrett. I expected Gumshoe to answer. Is this he?"

"Yes, how can I help you?"

"Corporal Tabitha Norman, Montecito. Perhaps I can help you. My cousin, Haruto says you wish to speak with me."

Morris tapped me on the shoulder. I frowned, "Just a moment, Officer Norman, I have a cop bugging me."

"Is that Tabs?" Morris grabbed the phone from my hand; "Tabbi! Why are you calling Gumshoe? . . . Okay, no, me neither . . . we're kinda busy right now . . . sure. I'll call you back soon . . . I love you, too. Say hello to Richard. Bye."

Morris disconnected, handed me the phone, and said, "We received a notice as well. Pics of Bradley, Lucy and me, just like yours. Delivered to us an hour ago by two kids on a scooter; you know, like one'a those Vespas or some such. Taped to door and gone."

I was still nettled with Morris for hanging up on my Montecito caller. *Just who do you think you are, Inspector?* -- but I settled for, "Maybe we should get the feds involved."

"I think so, Alan. What did Tabbi want with you?"

"She was calling to, hopefully, get the feds involved."

"Well, why didn't you say so?" The inspector made a call. Five minutes later my cell rang.

"Garrett here," I said.

"ATF Eli Strom. We have a cop up here says you might need some info. Looking for a Mr. uh, a Mr. Gumshoe Fox."

Chapter 14

"Officer Strom, thank you for calling. This is Alan Garrett, private investigator. Have a little agency here in Manhattan Beach. Picked up the trail of a person of interest; traced him to an address in Montecito, and were just about to check him out when we were advised to keep hands off."

"You did, huh? Person of interest for what?"

"Guns, and murder."

"And are you Gumshoe Fox?"

After an explanation of the name and the persons involved, he was only slightly amused. "You been in the military?"

Ha! I thought, *You've been checking me out on some handheld ID device, haven't you, Strom?*

"Air Force AFOSI-- 20 years, sir."

"Who'd you serve under, Gumshoe?"

"General Maggorie, sir."

"I happen to know the general -- good man." Strom's demeanor, even over the wire, seemed suddenly, more relaxed. "So -- and, by the way -- stop with the sir. Call me Strom. So, how may I help you, Gumshoe?" *Evidently I had checked all the boxes.*

"Someone down here is playing Russian Roulette with firearms, Strom. Guns appear, then disappear; they get turned in, then picked up and back on the streets in the hands of 'not so savory' people -- mostly youngsters. We thought we had a handle on the problem, but both of our target stash houses blew up, empty. No crew, no guns.

"A top cop in our area said to stay away from our Montecito lead -- because of the DEA and you folks. Then just today we get this written warning from some Sinaloa big-shot, T.A. Durazo, that unless we back off very soon, we would become headless -- we and our families."

"Sounds like you hit a nerve. How many were directly warned, and how much firepower do you have there?"

"Seven warned. So far as firepower, who knows."

"Trust me, you don't have nearly enough. I'll send twenty. They'll be there 5 a.m. sharp, tomorrow morning. They'll be wearing chartreuse arm bands on left arms. Gimme the address."

"You sure you can spare that many?" I asked. Morris looked relieved at the news.

"Oh, yeah, we have a very fluid crew. I'm sending Rodriguez as lead. He'll direct his crew as he sees fit, and will coordinate with you and that cop, what's his name."

"Name's Morris!" the inspector cut in loudly; gave me a frown as if to say, *'cheeky bugger!'*

"Address?"

"722 7th St. in Gardena," Morris confirmed.

"Fine. I'll have Rodriguez break off seven for Gardena. And don't forget, they'll be there at 5 a.m. sharp."

"Thanks." We breathed a sigh of relief as we signed off. Help was on the way. . . tomorrow.

*****

3:15 a.m.

I sat in front of the picture window in my swivel chair -- clad only in polyester boxers -- nothing else, sipping coffee. Only light in my bungalow was the intermittent red dot on my alarm telling me that the doors were secure. Other than those giants still playing hopscotch on the pier, all was dark. I couldn't sleep. Pop was, of course, just two houses down the cul-de-sac, cuddling Rita. Unreasonable, I realized, but my bungalow felt frighteningly empty.

Beads of perspiration appeared on my forehead. There was always a comfort in knowing Pop was upstairs. But no more - I was alone, I was vulnerable, the Sinaloa Cartel was on my ass! Frankly, I was -- for the first time since leaving AFOSI -- afraid! Not just for myself -- I was afraid for Fox, for the inspector and his wife, for Haruto, Pop and Rita, Bradley Swazer. The weight of it sent shivers through me.

Get a grip, Garrett!

Something didn't feel right -- *call Fox!* flashed through my mind -- I dismissed it. Instead, I stood, walked to the coffee pot, poured another coffee, then back to the picture window to take another look down the cul-de-sac; all was still quiet. Not even a cat walked the pavement. I began to relax.

The shrill ring of my phone was like a pitcher of ice-water over my head, jarring me to full alertness. I glanced at the time: 4:12 a.m.

"Garrett."

"Bossman, are you awake?"

"What's up?"

"Something just woke me up. Sounded like a door slamming, followed by screams and a small-calibre gun. Came from somewhere above me. I'm on the second floor. I'm scared, Bossman."

"Help is on the way, Fox. Keep your weapon beside you. And remember, good guys -- chartreuse arm band -- left arm."

"These units are normally very quiet." I could hear her voice growing thin with fear. "I hea . . . Gumshoe! did you hear that?" Then, nothing! I thought I heard breathing before the phone was disconnected.

"Fox? Fox!" I tossed the phone on the chair, ran to my bedroom, threw on some clothes, pulled my shotgun from the closet and loaded it -- eight shells. I hustled back into the kitchen, set my shotgun on the counter, splashed cold water on my face, and dialed Fox.

A male voice answered. "Yeah?"

"Is Liz there?"

"Don't know a Liz, mister. Lady here is shook up, but she'll be okay. Says her name is Fox. From the looks of her place she's a momma fox separated from her kits, and none too happy. Two dead, faces scratched to you-know-what, gouged eyes, one ear bitten half off, blood from one end of the place to the other, says none of it's hers. When we pushed in, we shot two more, have one in custody. Which one are you, mister?"

"Fox works for me, I'm Al . . ."

"Oh, yeah, the gumshoe. Well, it's your turn, Gumshoe. The Fox did her part. We only mopped up after. We're on our way to visit that Haruto fellow. You gonna be good there?"

"Yeah, sure. How . . .?" *click*. The phone disconnected. So much for small talk. I glanced out the window, then called back. Fox answered. "Hi, so what's going to happen to the four dead?" I asked, without giving her the opportunity to brag.

"The fellas -- uhh, six men, one woman -- had body bags, took them along. One fellow, Bernie, stayed behind to police up here, then I'm bringing him to you. The whole team will join up at the office. Bernie figures by 9:00 a.m."

"Sounds good. I was going to suggest you get some sleep, but now . . ."

"Don't you worry none, Bossman, I'm all yours." Then she whispered, "Bernie is only seventeen -- maybe."

A booming voice came from Fox's phone: "I heard that, Ma'am." I hung up. Didn't know whether to frown or smile. That's when the door frame splintered.

Chapter 15

The door, hinges and all, hit the floor. Bursts from semi-automatic fire turned some of my walls, cupboards, and paintings to shreds, destroyed my refrigerator, stove, and coffeepot.

As the door was falling inward, I instinctively dropped behind the counter with my shotgun. I rolled to the edge, saw several faces coming through the opening, pointed and pulled the trigger five times -- my gun chambers twelve #.oo buckshot. The doorway was no longer full of angry faces.

I crawled out from behind the counter just in time to see a grenade lobbed in through the wide door opening. Without thinking, I raced to it and lobbed it back outside. The explosion was deafening, but at least ten feet beyond the porch.

In the meantime, I could hear semi-automatic gunfire down the cul-de-sac. *Pop must be under siege,* I thought. "I can't help you, yet, Pop. Hold on!" I was yelling as loud as I could -- even though I knew he couldn't hear.

Continuing to the doorway, I sneaked a quick look toward the lawn, then down at the would-be intruders who were now lying near the door. A trail of blood was leading down the walkway.

Movement in the driveway brought my gun to

the ready, but a shout stopped me. "Hey! in the house! Friendly here!"

"Show yourself!" I yelled back. Adrenaline was coursing through me.

A chartreuse arm raised. "Coming in!" the male voice shouted. "Hold your fire!"

"I'm good! Did you save the others?"

"You mean the old couple down the hill?" the tall, blond guy asked as he walked through the door frame.

"Yeah, the old couple," I repeated.

"Yeah, I think so. The old lady, anyway. Your mom?"

"No. My dad and his fiancé. Her house. And my dad?"

"Took several shots to the abdomen. Alive, still talking, but shot up pretty bad."

Racing down the cul-de-sac, with fedora in my hand, I left blondie to assess the black body bags needed, and the damage to the bungalow.

"Rita." I shouted as soon as she came into view. "Pop? How's Pop?"

"They had an ambulance with them, Alan. He's on his way to Kaiser. You okay?"

"Yeah. House is shot to hell, but biggest loss is the case of *Martell Cordon Bleu.* The other losses are covered by insurance, but when I saw the cognac spilling from the cabinet, I just had no kind words to say."

"Any news on Inspectors Morris and Haruto?" I asked, grabbing a chartreuse arm.

"We have an open line, but nothing yet. What's your cell? We'll stay in touch."

Pulling the Cadillac from the garage, I rolled it down the grade. "Rita!" I called out. "You're bleeding! You've been hit! Ride with me."

Rita hobbled to the passenger side and crawled in. "It's nothing, Alan. Just a scratch."

"Bullshit, Rita. Did you look at it? Is it a through and through?"

"Just a nick, Alan. I'm really worried about Roland. He was badly shot up! He's at Kaiser. You know how to get there? Of course you do. I'm sorry. I'm just so worried."

I let her rattle on. I was worried for Pop, too, but she was in the midst of a real episode: shock and pain. I'd seen it before, and I'd bet a million bucks her leg injury was more than a scratch. We sped to Kaiser Emergency. I jumped out and demanded that Rita stay put.

Seconds later an attendee and I ran out with a wheelchair. "Get out and get in the wheelchair," I demanded.

"Why, Alan?" She bravely exited, wincing in pain and immediately fell into the wheelchair in a faint. I shook my head at the orderly.

"Thought so. I'll catch up with her later," I told him. "I need to find my pop. He came in just ahead of us with bullet wounds. Point me in the right direction, please."

"Hallway to the right. What's her name?" he called after me.

"Rita Mason. She lives with Pop. I'll be back!"

****

Pop was already in surgery. ICU duty nurse said she'd keep me informed. As I sat waiting to hear of his condition, I called Liz. It was 6:51 a.m. After answering, Liz just listened as I gave her the news.

"I'm okay, but both Pop and Rita were shot up. They're at Kaiser right now, I'm waiting at ICU for an update on Pop. Rita thought she was only scratched, but she fainted from loss of blood. Not sure where they took her, but she's in good hands. Your teenager, Bernie Boy -- has he heard any news?"

"Phone hasn't rung a peep, Bossman. You're tied up there -- tell you what, I'll call the inspector and Haruto and report back."

"Appreciate it. You didn't even ask about me, Fox. They broke my door down, tossed in grena . . ."

"You told me you were okay, Alan Garrett!" She practically screamed. "And I believed you! Now, I'm going to make those calls, then I'll call you back with a report, after which you can tell me all about it!"

She left me with a dead phone in my hand.

****

7:42 a.m.

Still no update. *Have you ever noticed that you race against time when you're the one running, but nothing happens while you're waiting?* I finally walked out of emergency, down the corridor, and found myself in the gift shop.

There was a banner fluttering in the periodical section with the latest on the best sellers' list. I picked up a couple, browsed through a few pages of each, and placed them back. Found one that appealed: "Poetpourri" -- a group of short stories of a page or two each. Not what I'd call a best seller, but it suited my taste -- quick reads. I paid the young lady behind the counter, then sat in the hallway, reading.

An elderly woman, maybe eighty-odd, was about to enter the gift shop, but changed her mind. Instead, she stopped in front of me, leaning on one of those tripod canes. "Hello, young man, mind if I sit?"

"Of course not!" I smiled and slid over a tad to give her more space. "You are here because?"

"My husband, Randolph -- Randolph Blake. He's

in ICU. Hit and run."

"Oh! I'm so sorry, Mrs. Blake. Did the cops catch the guy?"

She frowned, looked at me strangely, "Did the cops catch th . . ." then she laughed nervously. "Aah, I see. No, Randy was the driver. He was so upset he put his foot on the accelerator. Of course, the police caught up with him, which made him even more terrified. He. . ." Tears began trickling down her cheeks. " . . . Doctors say it was a massive one; he may never recover."

She slid closer to me. "I'm Katie, by the way."

We shook hands, "And I'm Alan, Katie." I could see she was emotionally drained. Without a second thought, I wrapped my right arm around her and gently lay her head on my shoulder. It was a spontaneous action -- I suppose we both needed a hug. There was no resistance -- in fact, she breathed a long sigh and melted.

The tension release was obvious. Through her sweater I could feel her muscles relax. I held her like that for a minute, maybe more. Finally she spoke, "Randy used to do that," she whispered. "Everything's going to be okay, Katie, he would say, everything's going to be okay."

I stroked her hair lightly, saying nothing. She looked up, "Would you say that to me, Alan? Please?" I looked down at her moist, red eyes.

"Everything's going to be okay, Katie. We're going to pray about it, and everything's going to be okay." She settled back on my shoulder, content. We prayed. My phone lit up, as if on cue. "Garrett." It was Fox.

"Bossman, things aren't so good. There's no word from Morris. He was supposed to have seven feds up there, right? But there's no word. Haruto's house was invaded; but he escaped. I understand he's on his way to check on the inspector.

"Bradley's fine. I spoke with him. He didn't even go home. His house was torched, feds arrived, too late to save the house, but they put three hoodlums in body bags and three in a wagon. Swazer's on his way to Hermosa precinct. He said those were his orders from yesterday, no matter what.

"There's a crew of fifteen on their way to Morris' place, probably already there. How's Pop and Rita?"

"I'm still awaiting word. Nothing yet, but Katie and I are staying positive."

"Katie?"

"Yeah. We both have loved ones here at Kaiser. We believe everything will be alright. I'll call you back when I know." I ended the call.

Suddenly I could see Katie's mind travel to another place.

"Oh, Alan, I'm so sorry!" She raised her head from my shoulder, "I'm being so selfish!"

"Shush, Katie!" I whispered gruffly, then smiled. "Everything will be alright." We sat there for a few minutes longer, then she said, "Book any good?"

"Don't know, just bought it. Want to hear a short story?"

"Oh, yes, please! Randy used to read to me -- an hour each evening, unless other plans prevailed."

"Okay, let's see . . . aah, here's a short one."

"A line in the Dirt"

{ From Poetpourri ©2015 Myron Ferdig }

We drew a line in the dirt
Then we all took turns
There was Fred, Mickey, Norm,
Tom, and me
Didn't matter who went first
Everybody knew anyway --
Tom always won

Then we drew another line in the dirt
About ten feet away from the first
Like we always did --
Same group
Again, it didn't matter who went first
But this time it was different
Any of us could have won
We even made wagers
I won quite a few times

I was a pretty good spitter
But nobody could pee like Tom!"

Katie listened in rapt attention until the short, one-page ditty finished, then she giggled -- but said only, "That's terrible, Alan!" After a moment's complete silence, she couldn't hold in yet another giggle. "And you bought that book?" Katie was, by now, laughing. "Who writes such silliness, Alan?"

A female voice came over the PA system, "Alan Garrett, please come to ICU nurses' station. Alan Garrett."

"That's me." I said. I handed her my card. "You call me anytime, you hear?" I kissed the top of her head, she squeezed my hand. "God bless, Alan."

"Oh, here," I handed her the book. "Call and tell me if the book has any redeeming value."

She smiled. "I surely will, Mr. Gumshoe." I left her sitting there and hustled to ICU.

Chapter 16

"Let's see," ICU nurse Eesha said, looking up, "your step-mother is here, right?"

"Uhh, are you speaking of Rita Mason? I brought her here, but she's not my mother. I'm here for news of my father, Roland Garrett. But I am concerned about Rita. How is she?"

Looking at me soberly, Eesha said, "As you're not related to Ms Mason, that information is privileged. So, you say Roland is your father? May I see some identification, please?"

"You seem overly protective of my dad." I frowned, but produced my wallet, driver's license, and PI card. "Is he okay?"

"No, he's touch-and-go. But, we are using every caution to protect and care for him and Ms Mason. You see, Mr. Garrett, we received a call from the ATF advising us to use care in allowing access to the couple you're asking about."

"May I see my dad?"

"We're waiting for him. He's scheduled to be rolled out of surgery any moment now. He's assigned to ICU-12. Hmm," she frowned, "same room as Ms Mason. She may be up for a short visit -- a minute or two, but he'll be under for an hour or more unless he's some kind of miracle. The surgeons pulled three bullets out of him. Two more passed through. But you can see him."

"And Ms Mason?"

"She's already in the room. C'mon. I'll get you dressed."

"Thanks," I choked on a humorless laugh, but donned a mask, white surgeon's gown, latex gloves and followed Eesha through the double doors into the ICU.

She stopped at ICU-12. "In here," she pointed, "I'll be back in five."

Rita looked up as I opened the door. "Alan," she called out. "I'm so glad to see you. I guess my wound was more serious than I thought. According to the doctors, you saved my life. I'm so sorry about the leather seat on your nice car. It will be stained forever!"

"Oh, Rita, stop that nonsense!" I replied, taking her hand. I sat with her for a minute. "I could see you had more than a scratch, is all. And the closer to the hospital, it became more obvious.

"And, my car? Rita, if I ever worry more about my stuff than about doing the right thing, I'll be a poor example of a human being!"

"I was out of it, I guess."

"A bit. Now what does the doc say about being released?"

"Probably tomorrow, but your dad is hurt badly, Alan. There were so many bullets . . ."

"I heard. Four or five in his belly. At least they were small calibre, otherwise he wouldn't have a belly left. I'm sorry we involved you and Pop in this mess. Who knew that nosing around some guns and kids would bring out the long knives of the Sinaloa."

The door opened -- a gurney pushed in and a

trio of nurses fussed over the figure it contained. Tubes and drip bags set in place, the nurses smiled and one by one, they walked out, smiling at the two of us.

With a bittersweet smile on my face, I patted her arm, and walked over to Pop's bed. I sat with him, my hand on his. He didn't move. I felt for a pulse, found a weak one, and mouthed a *thank you, Father*. I stayed there like that, not moving, simply asking my Savior to have mercy on Pop and Rita; to bring them home to Manhattan Beach and me. Then I let go of Pop's hand, returned to sit with Rita for a moment.

"Rita, I'm leaving. I have your cell number. I'll be calling again later. Don't worry about arranging a ride tomorrow if you're released. I'll make the arrangements. Just get well." I kissed her cheek, squeezed her hand and left.

Walking through the doors to the ICU desk, I was surprised to hear, "Mr. Gumshoe!" I wheeled to see Katie seated in a chair against the back wall.

"Katie, hello! Have you been able to see Randolph yet?"

"They're taking me in at 9:00 -- just a few more minutes." I looked at my phone. *No one has called me regarding the inspector and his wife. I wonder how they are?* Katie continued, "Would you stay with me a while longer? He is still undergoing some kind of treatment, but the nurse has said he's going to survive. She also says not to freak when I see him." She burst into tears, "He's handcuffed to his bed."

"Because of the hit-and-run incident?" I shook my head. "What happened to the victim? The person Randolph ran over -- did he survive?"

"I was told he wasn't even hurt, just a frightened

kid of about sixteen. He had a trouser leg torn on something like a bolt or nut sticking out from a fire hydrant, but one of the policemen on the scene said his skin wasn't even scratched."

"And they handcuffed Randolph? Sure, I'll join you for a few moments. But if I get a call I may have to run."

Eesha came to usher Katie in to see Randolph and did a double take when she saw me. "You again?" Then she turned to Katie, "Is he with you?"

"Yes, he's a friend that I need to assist me."

Eesha shrugged, "Alright, if you're sure."

Still in the hospital garb, I waited while Katie was being outfitted by Eesha. Then through the doors we went -- this time to ICU-4, where Randolph lay on a gurney, one arm cuffed to a rail. A policeman sat in a chair against a wall, reading a magazine.

Randolph was awake -- barely. He looked with tear-filled eyes into Katie's own, and whispered, "I'm so sorry."

She, in turn, shushed him, and kissed his cheek. "You just get stronger, Randy. This was nothing more than an accident, the boy wasn't even hit.

"Randy, I'd like you to meet Alan Garrett. He's a private eye down in Manhattan Beach. He's here visiting his dad."

"Hello, Randolph," I tried to stay upbeat; Katie amazed me with her positivity. Randolph looked to be past 100 -- haggard, ashen, worn to a nub. "The lady's right, sir; do as she tells you," I smiled down at him, "Nothing will come of this," I touched his shackled arm.

The policeman in the corner looked up over his magazine and shook his head in my direction; I nodded an acknowledgement, but only smiled broader, looked at Katie, and whispered, "I need to go. You have my card. I have some friends who may be able to help clear this up should the kid or his folks try to make a fuss."

"Thanks, Alan. Be assured I will call you." Katie walked me to the door of ICU-4, hanging on to my arm. She looked up at me for reassurance. Satisfied, she squeezed my arm, pursed her lips and nodded. I bent down, kissed her cheek, hugged her, and slipped out.

Stopping long enough at the main ICU desk to shed my hospital apparel, I thanked the duty nurse. That's when my phone rang. "Yeah, Garrett here."

"Bossman, where are you?"

"At Kaiser. What's up?"

"Pop and Rita -- they okay?"

"Pop's not, but Rita and I are optimistic. How's Morris and the missus?"

"Carl and Lucy are missing. How long will you be there, Gumshoe?"

"I'm just leaving, heading for the shop. What do you mean *missing*?"

"Gone! Disappeared! Nowhere in sight! I don't know how else to describe it, Alan!"

"Okay, Fox! Take a breath! Where are you right now?"

"At the Morris place with exactly seven feds. We lost one to the bad guys. Fourteen others are already headed for our office with wagons full of black bags. Meet us there, Alan. We'll plan a rescue or whatever for Morris."

"Whatever it takes, Fox," I agreed, "whatever it takes." Cell phone told me it was 9:43 a.m. "Give me fifteen."

Chapter 17

On the way, I called Tony's Garage. Tony's a buddy who owns a body shop. I explained my bloody Caddy, asked him to pick it up when I arrived.

"No problem, boss, I'll be waiting."

Four black Suburbans were lining both sides of the street as I rolled up. Tony was sitting in a short-bed pickup out in front. He raised an eyebrow as I hopped from the Caddy. "I was going to ask if you wanted to grab an early lunch, Gumshoe, but it looks like you might be busy," he laughed as I tossed him my key.

"Yeah; rain-check, Tony." He sped off as I unlocked the door. Four armored vehicles, four more big sedans, and Fox's Kia pulled up. I wondered whether the onlookers thought this might be a major drug bust. Explanations might be in order later.

The feds clustered around one of the armored vehicles and waved me over to join them. Fox, meanwhile, went inside to make a pot of coffee. The obvious leader of the group, Rodriguez, separated himself from the pack, met me, shook hands, and we walked to the group to make introductions.

"No room for all of us in my office," I laughed, "maybe eight or ten at most."

"Not a problem, Garrett. We're going to dispatch

four *hearses* and one *paddy wagon* up to Strom in Mendocino. We just need a few minutes to regroup. May we use your facility?"

"Sure. What were the final numbers?"

"We'll go through that later, okay?" He frowned and turned to his group. "Listen up! Those of you heading back and needing a pit stop -- inside! Make it quick!" *A little curt,* I thought, then I smiled. *Garrett, that could have been you just two years ago. Nah, I was cooler than that!*

A squad of sixteen, including two women, headed toward the door. Five minutes later, one by one, they exited, each with a steaming Styrofoam cup in hand.

Once regrouped, Rodriguez began, "Today was successful for the most part, with the exception of ATF Ozzy King, who unfortunately lost his life in a firefight. We are also missing Police Inspector, Carl Morris and his wife, Lucy.

"We are pleased to report that we took out twenty-six, and have seven prisoners that will be going back to Strom. The fol . . ."

"Where's Haruto?" I interrupted. "Torrance inspector, Haruto. I got word he was on his way to the Morris place 7:00 a.m. or earlier." Fox was approaching the group with a large coffee carafe and Styrofoam cups. "When did you talk with Haruto, Fox?"

"Sorry, Bossman, I didn't talk with him," she replied, as she poured. "I think an ATF fellow told me the house had been invaded, three or four bad guys were put in black bags, and our guy, King, was killed in a firefight. Haruto was assumed to have accompanied the feds to the Morris place."

"Yeah, that was me," Anthony, one of the fellows

confirmed. "I just assumed he was somewhere in our pack. Sorry."

I whirled, "Fox," I said, taking over the coffee carafe, "get on the horn with Torrance precinct immediately! Find out where he would have taken his wife and family." I turned back to watch as Rodriguez practically tore a strip off Anthony.

"Dammit, Anthony! We don't assume anything in this unit! You're heading back to Mendocino! Whitey, switch with Anthony. The rest of you, listen up! We put tracers on a ton of vehicles around the four target areas. Right, Truck? How many?"

A big man in the front called out, "Forty, sir."

"Forty tracers. And how many moved between 4:30 a.m. and let's say 6:30 a.m?"

"Including the Kia over there, sir," Truck pointed, "seventeen. We pulled five over and eliminated four as possibles, arrested one with a shitload of weapons, trying to run."

"Which leaves eleven; we're monitoring their positions, right? Are they scurrying back to the border?"

"No, sir. Four headed in different directions, but seven headed down Wilshire to the La Brea Tar Pits parking lot west of downtown LA."

"Humph! What do you make of that, Garrett? Any ideas?"

"No, sir. Just that the Insp. . ."

"Gumshoe!" Fox called out. "Haruto and his family are safe. He couldn't reach us, but he contacted the Torrance precinct with a terse 'don't worry'. Nobody knows just where he took his family, but they're all safe. Desk sergeant says he has four kids under ten."

"Good reason to pull them out and lay low," one in the crowd remarked.

"What were you about to say, Garrett?" Rodriguez asked.

"Morris was going after a dirty cop -- a Victor Collins. There's a history between them. Put him behind bars a few years ago, but back out. Finagled his way into IA. Morris figures the Cartel, the guns, the kids, and this Victor Collins fellow -- who now calls himself Sidney -- are all tied together."

"Go on, I'm listening."

"What if those seven, along with whomever else, are regrouping downtown with a coordinator, to plan their next move? And, what if they've kidnapped Morris and Lucy?"

"Sinaloa Cartel? That's too many what ifs." Rodriguez scratched his head, "Nah! not their thing. I think they'd slaughter them on the spot. Leave them nice and messy for us to pick up pieces."

"Perhaps not, if the coordinator is Victor Collins."

"Did the seven tracers meet up?" Fox asked.

"Yeah," Truck spoke up, "And that might be a problem, Boss," he said turning to Rodriguez. "Our guys found two trackers destroyed at the La Brea Tar Pits parking lot -- and then five continued on to a coffee shop on Wilshire. One of our guys tracked them, and found the tracers in a trash can. That was over an hour ago."

"Damn!" Rodriguez breathed out in defeat. "So much for a plan."

"Yeah, one of the Sinaloa must have a scanner. A shame," Truck agreed, reluctantly.

I looked at Fox. "You thinking what I'm thinking?"

Her brain was in sync, "I am, indeed, Bossman."

Chapter 18

"Who the hell is Carson?" Rodriguez frowned, "and how does he fit in?"

Fox filled him in on the green-haired gal, the subsequent visit to XTR-Management, and their outgoing packages: one going to the Wells Fargo Bank, the other to an address in Beverly Hills. "It's just off Beverly Boulevard, not five miles from the Tar Pits parking lot." She gave him the address.

"It acts as a mail-forwarding facility from what we could see," I added. "Gentleman by the name of Carson runs it. Could be nothing, but Fox and I both felt, as we walked away, that his enterprise and clientele were a trifle shady."

"So you think we should check it out, is that it?"

"Yes, sir. I do."

"Okay. Here's what we do. Truck, who do we have tracking those seven vehicles with tracers?"

"Andrews, Valmore, and McCauliff."

"Have them nose around that address."

Rodriguez gave Truck the Carson house street number. "Send back a report on vehicles, activity, et cetera. Make themselves obvious, a show of force, but don't approach the house. Look inside cars, take license plate numbers, tell any curious neighbors we're looking for a dangerous illegal and it's best to leave the scene.

"The rest, carry on with your assignments. No, wait! Leave one wagon here. Transfer the dead from one to the other three, and hold one crew of four back. If Gumshoe, here, is right, we may need another wagon before the end of the day."

Fox tugged on my sleeve. "Gumshoe, they have this handled. Let's head to Kaiser, check on your dad and Rita."

"Can't, Fox, not while Morris is out there. Pop is in good hands right now, I can't do a thing for him, but I need to know Morris is safe. You understand that, Fox. Right? Please, God, let Morris be safe!"

Twenty minutes went by; the convoy of prisoners and paddy wagons had long since gone; no call had come from the three feds.

This wasn't getting us anywhere, I could feel it in my bones. "We shouldn't just stand around here, Fox. I'm worried for Morris."

"Then let's go find him, Bossman."

Rodriguez watched us closely, "Don't do anything stupid, Mr. Gumshoe! Wait for our three boys to call in."

"You wait, sir. Fox and I are heading out." I tossed my gear into the Kia. We headed for Beverly Hills.

*****

"Let's take another look at that map, Truck." Rodriguez growled. "We should have heard by now. Let's saddle up. How long does it take to drive the distance from where they are to just up the damn street? Call them one last time before we move out. Damn that Gumshoe!"

*****

Fox pulled the Kia to the corner. I pulled my

binoculars from its case and scanned the street, noting especially the Carson mansion five houses down on the left. No sign of the three feds anywhere. Lining both sides of the street were five sedans and a black pickup.

Strange, I thought, *residents had ample off-street parking in this section of town.* "Cruise to the end of the block, Fox. Don't slow down. See that black Suburban at the other end near the corner? Make a u-turn, come back and park just behind it."

"Bossman, Wait! Big, white pickup coming up Beverly with blinker on."

"Okay, Liz, let's argue over something. Not too loud but with gestures so if they see us, they'll just continue on, hopefully, laughing."

The monster crew cab pulled around the corner, but instead of moving along, it stopped not twenty feet away from us. Four male occupants emerged, one or two stared at us for a few moments -- *I prayed that Liz could maintain our act* -- then all four started up the street. One was tall, white, maybe forty; the others were swarthy, younger men.

"Back up a couple feet, Fox; I can't see Carson's door with that damn truck in the way."

She complied. I trained the binoculars on the door while Fox snapped several telephotos of the men and one of the pickup. Suddenly, Carson's door opened. The four from the pickup were ushered inside by a face that caused Fox to let out a yelp. The man belonging to the face stepped outside, leaned on the rail, scanned the street in both directions, then stepped back inside, closing the door.

"Bossman! did you recognize him?"

"No, Fox, who is he?"

"He's one of the three feds Rodriguez sent over here as scouts. I think his name is Valmore."

"No!" I couldn't believe what I was hearing. "I'm calling Rodriguez. Motor out of here, Fox," I added as I dialed, "in case somebody remembers us and comes for a closer look. Let's round the block, pull in at the other end behind that fed Suburban."

I tried Rodriguez' phone twice -- the line was busy. We pulled in behind the big, black Chevrolet SUV; it took only a few minutes. As we couldn't see the opulent Carson estate from here, I decided to peek inside the vehicle.

Windows were dark. I tried the tailgate with no luck. I tried a couple of other doors -- all locked. "Fox, would you hand me my duffel, please?" My bag held just the right tools for these newer vehicles: a nail punch and a hammer.

Fox continued to try Rodriguez. Just as I punched the side door glass the call rang through. The head agent picked up on first ring. "We're ten minutes out, Ma'am. Just hold tight."

"Fox!" I yelled, racing back to the Kia. "Bad guys from the house coming! Get us outta here!" Fox handed me the phone, backed around the corner and floored it, tires smoking.

"Fox?" Rodriguez shouted through the phone. "What the hell's going on?"

"Fox recognized one of your guys, sir," I shouted back. "Turns out, he's a bad guy. I just broke into your SUV. Your other two men are in it. They're both dead, sir."

Chapter 19

Fox stared at me, incredulous; Rodriguez was silent for a few moments, then bellowed, *"SHIT! Were gonna clean'em all out, the slimy bastards! Where are you right now, Gumshoe?"*

"You must have remote anti-theft on your vehicles, because as soon as I broke the glass three or four came boiling out of Carson's place, guns drawn. Fox and I are on Oakwood Avenue, but we're about to circle back. We'll meet you wherever."

"Okay, let's see. Aah, coffee shop comin' up on left hand side of Beverly, corner of Vista. Come down Vista, cross Beverly, we'll be inside for a pit stop."

"We're only 3-5 minutes away. Be right there." I relayed the message to Fox. She had just passed Vista. She wheeled around and within three minutes she guided the Kia next to the fleet of SUVs. We stepped inside. Waiting were sixteen faces, all filled with anger.

"You're sure our boy is a traitor?" Rodriguez reached for the film Fox had taken. She shrugged her shoulders; then along with ten pairs of eyes, she and I watched the chief fed as he studied the collection of photos from the camera. Finally, he looked up, "It's Valmore, people -- no question about it."

He punched a tab on his cell. "Gimme Strom."

There were two minutes of silence, during which time Fox connected a thumb drive to the camera and transferred the photos to the fed's phone. "Confirmed, sir. Sending pics to your phone right now . . ." Another moment of silence while the person on the other end studied the situation. Then, "My thoughts exactly, sir. Call you when it's over."

Rodriguez dropped his cell into a shirt pocket, looked at the troop of agents gathered round him, "Head count. We all here? I guess still a few in the loo. Here's our objective: Garrett, here, figures members of the Sinaloa Cartel, along with some local terrorists are holding his buddy, Inspector Morris and wife.

"Strom wants arrests and extraction as quietly as possible. We knock first, use whatever force necessary. If Morris is there -- great. Arrest everyone, sort them out later. Understood?"

"No search warrant needed?" Fox asked, frowning at me.

I shook my head as Rodriguez replied, "Not with your photos, ma'am. Gives us reasonable cause to knock the door down should it become necessary." While he was talking, the others emerged from the bathroom and joined us.

"Aaah, I see we're a full squad. Let's roll. Garrett, you lead. When we get to the corner, we'll make the turn, you park where you did before." I nodded. Rodriguez continued, "Give us a minute or two before you approach."

*****

"Street's coming up, Bossman, but I don't see that white crew-cab."

"You're right. I don't either, Fox. Don't see the other vehicles that lined the street either. The fed

97

suburban is missing as well. Pull over and wave Rodriguez down. We need another conversation."

I jumped out of the Kia and waved my arms. The entire fleet double-parked, flashers on, while we discussed this new wrinkle.

"Place could be booby-trapped like the place down in Lennox," I warned.

"That swanky place? Won't happen, Gumshoe. But if it makes you feel better, I'll take just two men to the front door and knock."

"I have a better idea, sir. We have a fix on the fed vehicle through ATF headquarters, don't we? Have Strom locate it, we'll probably find them congregated nearby."

"Good idea, Garrett. Truck, call HQ. Get coordinates for Gumshoe, here. Monte! You and Ribera come with me."

The GPS tracking key for the black Suburban was just being uploaded into my cell phone as I slid into the Kia's passenger seat. I was watching Rodriguez mount the front porch of the subject estate when a deafening explosion rocked and splintered the entire neighborhood.

Chapter 20

Truck was beside himself; covering his face with his hands, shouting epithets, screaming, "NO! NO! NO!"

"Truck!" I yelled. He turned and looked in my direction, pure panic on his face. "Call Strom! Do it now! Give him a report!" I turned to Fox. "Let's go Fox, we have a GPS to follow."

"We can't just walk away from this situation, Bossman!"

"We can and we will, Fox! We can't do anything for what happened here. If Morris is dead, he's dead. If he's alive, our best chance to save him is to follow the Suburban! Now drive! Take a right at the next corner."

Fox shook her head, let out an epithet that wasn't worth challenging, and turned the corner. Ten seconds later she adjusted her rear-view. "We're being followed, Bossman, looks like some of the fed crew decided to break protocol and join us."

"Bless them. I have the feeling we'll be happy they have our rear-ends before the sun goes down, Fox. Let's hang a left -- see if they continue to follow."

"Company's still with us, Bossman, and the GPS says were almost parallel with the ATF Suburban, just a couple of streets over, maybe three blocks ahead, heading north. Shall we move in behind it?"

"No, just let it take the lead to wherever we're heading. Good on gas?"

"Half a tank. Our boys are right behind."

The ATF Suburban stayed in a straight line north-northwest to the 405, continued to the 118 toward the coast. We followed. After twenty minutes it was obvious they would hit the 126, cut left to the 101. We continued a few cars back. I doubted they had seen us.

My cell phone rang. "Mr. Garrett, sir?"

"Yes. Who's this?"

"Agent Tipton, right behind you. They're heading for Montecito, sir. What's your plan?"

"You boys should have the plan. I'm assuming you've kept Strom informed?"

"Oh, hell, yes. He figures we should have intercepted them by now."

"Here I thought we were simply on a cattle drive, Tipton. Pushing them up the trail for your boss."

"Right behind you, Mr. Gumshoe." He laughed as he hung up.

Ten minutes later, when they should have hopped on the 126 onramp, they pushed on through a half mile and turned left onto Foothill Road paralleling the 126.

"We need to pull back, Bossman. They'll spot us as soon as we take that left turn."

"You're right, Fox. Gotta rely upon the GPS for a half mile or so. I see overpasses both ends. Let's use the cloverleaf and kill some time."

We slowed to a crawl as we crossed under the 126, pulled onto the onramp, then completed the figure eight, following the ATF van at a distance. Somehow we lost the black Suburban. I dialed them. "Where are you, Tipton?"

"Stopped for gas right here at the intersection. Don't worry, we'll catch up."

Fox kept the Kia at a slow crawl as we trailed behind, heading west along that frontage road. Map showed no turn-offs until a small gravel spur called Arroyo Park Road, heading into the wilderness, probably eight miles, then east a quarter mile before heading back south. According to the map the road ended short of Foothill Road by no more than a quarter mile.

"What the hell?" I frowned. "They're heading up that gravel road, Fox!" I looked a second time from the map to the GPS signal.

"We going to follow them up there, Bossman? I don't like it. Could be a trap."

"Agreed. We'll find out soon enough. The road can't be more than a half mile ahead. Let's speed up a little. Has Tipton caught up yet?"

Fox adjusted her rearview mirror. "Not a car in sight."

We continued on until graveled Arroyo Park Road loomed immediately before us. I glanced behind just as Fox confirmed, "We're on our own, Gumshoe; how many you figure?"

"In that big van? Probably seven, eight, minimum, and probably mostly hardcore."

"Wonder if our Mr. Carson is among them. He seemed the genteel sort."

Some two hundred yards up the hill there was a dirt shoulder --wide enough to park off the gravel. I pointed. "Pull over, Fox. Let's proceed on foot from here."

Fox pulled the Kia over. "You're not serious!" She was incredulous! "We're going to charge up this road on foot, chasing seven or eight Sinaloa Cartel members, exposing ourselves to who knows what! Bad idea, Gumshoe!"

"Stop it, Fox! Look at the map and the GPS! The road hooks around to the right, ends up probably little more than a football field away from our car." I traced a line from where we were to the end of the road. "Now," I continued, "that ATF van is still on the move, and I think it will continue to road's end. So should we follow the van, or jog through the woods and greet them?"

Fox frowned at my logic as she studied the map. Finally, she sighed and shook her head, "Sometimes I hate you, Bossman!" she blurted out as she exited the Kia. "I don't have proper boots! How am I supposed to go hiking in these?" she pointed at her gray loafers.

"Oh, well, c'mon, let's go! Your shotgun and my rifle are on the floor behind us."

I hopped out, opened the rear door, and grabbed both weapons. Shouldering my SRM-1216, I handed Fox her AR-15 rifle, then assisted her up the slight ravine into the scrub brush to the northeast, hoping I had calculated correctly.

*****

We heard the music long before we reached them -- a small group of Mexican picnickers enjoying an afternoon get-together at the end of the road. There were six adults along with seven or eight youngsters of various ages gathered around a fold-up table. Three cars were in a semi-circle headed back up the road.

Fox and I surprised them, shouting, "Coming in!" and dropping in on them like two lost hunters. The adults approached us cautiously, the kids openly curious. Realizing we were no threat, the ladies offered to dish up plates for the two of us, inviting us to join them. We declined.

Fox settled herself on a flat rock near the table, removed her shoes, and while chatting with the ladies, rubbed her aching feet. Meanwhile, I motioned the gents aside.

"Mexican Cartel crew is on its way here, fellas. Not sure why they chose to drive up here, but it's for no good reason, of that I am sure. Best if you finish your picnic and be on your way."

"We've been here since this morning, Mister," one of them assured me. "We were just talking about packing up when you came.

"Ladies! Children! Time to go! *Andale!*"

The entire group sprang into action, with only the slightest of questioning from a few of the children. I was impressed at their response. The men answered by saying they would explain later. Fox handed each of the women a business card, and bid each a goodbye with a pat on the shoulder or a squeeze.

The men stood talking among themselves as women and children piled into cars; then the three approached me.

"Mister Garrett, we have a plan to assist you just a little. We'll put all the families in two cars, then José, here, will take you two in the third car. Then we can drop you off when we see the car that's coming in our direction. Otherwise, you may be sitting here all day. If no one is coming, we drop you off at your car. Sound good?"

"We don't want you involved in our problems, fellas," I told them. "But if you see them, wait until all three of your cars have safely passed them, then call the number on our business card, give us a head's up."

"We can do that. Good luck to you." The families climbed aboard their own vehicles and started down the graveled road, leaving Fox and me sitting on the flat rock at road's end.

*****

Two minutes went by, then five. No car, no phone call. Fox looked at me as she put her shoes back on. "How long should we just sit here and try to relax, Bossman? It will be dark in four hours." I glared at her using my best sarcastic smirk!

The day flashed before me in *Technicolor*. How does a body relax after the last eight hours we've traveled through? Early morning shootout, hospital visit to Pop, explosion, chase, and now sitting on a gravel road waiting for a Suburban filled with Mexican thugs and a traitorous ATF agent.

My thoughts were interrupted by Fox's phone.

Chapter 21

Fox's demeanor changed from mildly apprehensive to abject horror as she listened to the caller. "Yes, please!" she said and hung up.

"José's coming back to pick us up, Bossman. There are three or four dead people in the middle of the road about a half mile from here. No Suburban, no other vehicles in sight."

"Are our Mexican friends okay?"

"So far. But all three picnickers have backed around the corner to save the children from viewing the dead."

"Good plan. Where in hell is Tipton, Liz? Those guys should have been right behind us."

"Maybe they missed the turnoff to the gravel road, Bossman."

"That's bull!" I said as José's car came into sight. "Here's our ride. C'mon, Fox, jump in. Let's see who the victims are, and let's pray they aren't Morris and his missus. This just doesn't make sense, Fox."

Normally, I could put the pieces together, nod my head, and say something like, *just as I thought*, but this time I was at a loss.

José pointed. "Just ahead. Please hide the bodies so our kids don't see them." Fox assured him as we exited the car. José made a three-point turnaround and headed back.

So we walked -- gravel crunching beneath our shoes. "You're going to buy me a new pair of shoes after this," Liz grumbled. "I should be home making spaghetti."

"I make a good spaghetti," I remarked. "do you mix the sauce in, or spoon it ov. . ."

"Bossman! Look!" Liz let out a cry as we rounded a curve and almost stumbled upon the first of the three dead, lying face down in the bloody gravel. I rolled him over. Lieutenant Tipton. I remembered him from the early morning shootout. He'd been stabbed several times -- throat and heart areas. No wallet, cell phone, or badge; couple of bucks in his pocket along with keys and pocket knife.

"Now I understand why he didn't pick up his phone," I looked up at Fox, "he had some cartel boys acting as ATF agents riding with him."

"The scum!" Fox hissed and moved to the second body as I called Truck.

He picked up on first ring, "Truck here."

"Yeah, Truck. This is Garrett. Pull up your GPS on two vehicles, please. Tipton followed us out of Beverly Hills. We lost him as we continued to follow the black Suburban; wound up in the hills near Highway 101.

"We just found some bodies on a gravel road. One is Tipton's. We can see other bodies -- haven't examined them yet -- probably the dead agents I discovered earlier in the ATF Suburban near the . . . Please, just listen, sir! Yes, I'm sure. Definitely Tipton. On a gravel road out near the coast. We'll photograph them all for the record. You have some other dirty agents on your team, not just Valmore."

Fox startled me, "I guess Carson was of no more

use!" she said, standing over another body, twenty feet farther down the road. "Knew too much, poor fellow." She grimaced as she photographed the body.

"Truck, I'll get back to you. Get that GPS information for me." I hung up. "Anything in his pockets. Fox?"

"You check, Gumshoe. I rolled him over. I think it's him -- not really sure, but that's as far as I go."

"Fine! I'll be there in a minute." I dragged Tipton's body into the chaparral beside the road, wondering if all women were squeamish. Then I trotted to have a look at Carson. That's when I changed my mind. Not many men could look at what I saw without losing stomach contents.

"It is him, isn't it?" Fox was leaning over me, one hand on my shoulder.

"Yeah, it's him. Help me drag him into the brush; then we'll take a look at the third fellow over there. *Together*," I added sternly.

A fourth body lay just beyond the third. We determined they were the two I had seen earlier in Beverly Hills in the black SUV. Both had been executed. We checked and photographed as before, then dragged them away from the roadway.

I continued on. "I'm going to take a quick look around the next curve before we call José, just to make sure there aren't more bodies."

"I'm staying here, Gumshoe. Call me. I'll call José."

*****

Rounding the bend in the graveled road I discovered two more badly-disfigured bodies. They were lying alongside each other, and again, lying face down, bullet through the back of the head.

As before, I turned them over. The clothing on

both bodies was torn and dusty, arms and legs were scratched and bloody. *What happened here?* I photographed, then pulled them into the chaparral, where they remained, hidden from view. I was still puzzled by the excess damage to both. I recognized neither.

The hillside sloped appreciably downward at this point; I was careful to ensure the bodies didn't roll down the gully. As I was pondering the horrific events Fox and I were witnessing, my cell rang.

"Garrett."

"Mr. Garrett, Eli Strom here. I understand you found evidence of more corrupt ATF agents. Can you support that accusation?"

"Certainly, sir." I went through the events of the last two hours, and finished by sending him photographs of the six bodies we had come upon.

"There may be more, sir. We haven't walked the entire roadway. I'm walking it right now. In fact, I found the last two just before you called."

"Keep me posted. Regarding the GPS signals, I added Tipton's Suburban. You should be able to pull it up on your screen. Matter of fact, looks like it isn't moving, Garrett, so it's just off the pavement. The other vehicle is no longer on your road; it's heading west toward the 101. I'll send two intercepts and ask for a CHP assist. We'll drag their asses down before the day's out, the sons-a-bitches."

"Thank you, sir, appreciate it. I'll keep you posted. By the way, our road is actually two inches of gravel." Strom laughed. I signed off and quickly pulled up the GPS tracker.

"Found two more agents, Fox," I called out. "Pulled them into the bushes. Looks like they were in a war; torn clothes, bloody from head to foot.

"Strom called. GPS shows Tipton's vehicle is somewhere ahead. Call José. Tell him to come ahead. I'm going to continue walking. Oh, and call for a bus to pick up these bodies, Fox."

No more than twenty steps further, I noticed clumps of weeds, dirt still attached, along with bits and pieces of twigs in the gravel on the ravine side. Then I saw the Suburban -- in the gully, some thirty feet below -- on its side.

A clear picture formed in my mind. These two agents had somehow survived the tumble down the hillside and managed to crawl up the embankment. *Yeah*, I shook my head, *only to be shot!* I shook my fist and shouted in disgust, "You bastards!"

Chapter 22

José's SUV came into view, with Liz riding shotgun. She motioned for me to climb aboard, but I shook my head. I walked to José's window. "Do you have any rope, José?"

"No rope, Mr. Garrett, but Manuel has a winch on his Forerunner. Is there a problem?"

"Come with me," I said. Liz joined us at the ravine's edge overlooking the crashed vehicle. "I'm not thinking of pulling that Suburban up, just curious to see if anything of value is in it that we should retrieve before 'looky-loos' find it and scavenge it."

José nodded his head. Walking back toward the line of vehicles, he passed his car and continued to the Forerunner. I watched as he spoke to the driver, then as he came back, slid into his SUV and continued up the road about forty feet. The Forerunner pulled over allowing the third vehicle to pass, then Manuel guided his car to my side.

"How far down is it, Señor?"

"Take a look. Thirty feet maybe?"

Manuel hopped out, glanced over the side. "A little more. My winch is fifty-three feet. We can reach it, no problem. Here, take these." I took his gloves gladly, grabbed the hook on the winch, and as he fed the cable, I repelled over the side.

"Keep more tension on that cable, Manuel! This is tougher than it looks!" Flash-flooding had created ankle-breaking gullies, running downward in all directions through the chaparral. Manuel slowed the winch cable. Much better! I descended to the Suburban. Then came a shock!

"Fox," I yelled, "get some paramedics out here on the double! And a heavy-duty wrecker! It's Carl and Lucy! He's alive. Not sure about her! Any of you fellows have a crowbar?"

"Hook the cable to the axle, Señor," Manuel yelled back, "I'll join you."

*****

The car had rolled at least once as it went down, ending on the driver's side. The roof had buckled somewhat, windshield was hanging half out, cracked into a million pieces but held together by the laminate sandwiched between the layers. No other glass had been broken; I could only guess the two dead agents had either jumped or been thrown out before the Suburban came to its final resting place.

The three families above discussed their situation, then two packed vehicles disappeared, leaving Fox and Manuel alone above.

Manuel joined me, repelling down, using the cable. Together we examined the vehicle, the gas tank, the windows, the passengers. We could see and hear Morris groaning. I could see what I thought was Lucy's dress or nightgown beneath him. I detected some movement. The old man seemed to be lying on top of her; hopefully, most of his weight was against the rear passenger door.

Offering little resistance to the forks of Manuel's crowbar, I broke the rear window to gain access to the passenger compartment. Small chunks of tempered glass were sent flying.

"Do you have any water, Manuel?"

"Si, water, beer, and cola in the back of my van."

"Fox!" I yelled, "send down some water. Trunk of the van!"

After a few moments Fox yelled, "Got it! Two bottles coming down!" She tossed the bottles to Manuel, who caught each one easily. He handed one to me. I crawled through the opening, and slid forward toward the two inside. There was a double-roll of paper towels in the back. I grabbed the package and carried it forward.

Fortunately, the roof cave-in was over the steering wheel; the rear seating compartment showed little physical damage.

The inspector was aware. When I touched his shoulder he tried to turn, but only cried out softly, panted, and lay still.

"Don't try to talk, Morris. It's Alan. Lie still, old man. Help is on the way. We'll get you and Lucy out of here."

Lucy was in bad shape. I took a hard look at what I could see of her; there was some movement at her ribcage. Both she and Carl were battered from the roll down the hill; who knew what more they had suffered at the hands of the hoodlums.

Ripping open the towels, I poured water on a pad of three towels, and patted Morris' face, head, and neck. Then I lifted the bottle to his lips. He did little more than wet his lips, but at least he wet his lips.

Next, I turned my attention to Lucy. She was unconscious -- at least that's what I hoped. Her head was tucked into Morris' stomach. He whimpered as I moved his arm to apply a cool towel to her neck and shoulders. I thought I detected a reaction, but couldn't be sure.

Manuel poked his head in the rear window. "Señor, I hear sirens. Help is coming."

I reassured Morris that emergency vehicles were arriving on-scene, and I would be back. Then, in turn, Manuel and I, using the cable, walked back up the ravine to the road.

*****

Coroner was the first to arrive. I directed her wagon to the first body -- Tipton's. "Who moved the body, and why?" she asked. I explained to her satisfaction; we moved on to the other five. As the lady was leaving, with her six filled body-bags in the back, Fox bummed a ride to our Kia. On their way, they met a fire truck and two paramedic rescue vans. Fox jumped into the Kia, followed the newcomers to the rollover.

*****

Four paramedics and one fireman joined me, using Manuel's cable to descend to the crippled van. The fireman unhooked the cable and yelled up to Manuel, "We got'er from here, friend! You can be on your way!" I waved and thanked him.

"Keep my crowbar. I have your card, Gumshoe!" he answered with a laugh. "I'll be calling you! Good luck!" With that, he was gone.

*****

The driver of the big, red ladder truck shouted, "Any easy place to turn this rig around?"

"About a quarter mile ahead," I yelled back. "Terrain's flat both sides. Shouldn't be too soft." I hadn't seen the heavy-duty tow truck. As it arrived, the fire engine moved further up the road.

The tow truck pulled into place. The driver, Mike, jumped out, looked over the bank. "Fifteen-minute job!" he grinned.

"Two injured inside," I barked at him, "friends of mine!"

"Oh! Got it!" he shrugged, "half an hour! Set my hook on the front axle. I'll lift and drag'er around maybe 30-40 degrees. Then you fellers can do your work and not worry about rolling down any more. I'll be real gentle. Don't worry."

He ran his boom out over the Suburban, the fireman hooked the front bumper and stood back. The cable lifted the vehicle about 8-12 inches. Next the tow operator slowly drew the boom back, swinging the Suburban around so its windshield faced the gravel road.

"Okay, fellas, she's all yours. Keep my cable in place so she don't slip and run further down!"

The fireman used a knife to cut out more of the windshield. He reached in and unlocked the driver's door.

Meanwhile, the two paramedics topside lowered two gurneys. We pulled them into place beside the car. The driver's door was damaged, but the fireman, by standing on a tire, wrenched and bent the hinges back.

Next, he dropped through the opening and pushed the front seat-backs forward, providing more room for the paramedics to work. Then he crawled out through the rear window.

Morris came out first. A splint ran from fingers to the shoulder of his left arm. His left leg was wrapped from the middle of his thigh down. His neck was in a brace. But he was alive. I said a quick prayer of thanks as the gurney was set on an air mattress.

The two paramedics went back inside. After a few minutes one of them called up a list of items needed to move Lucy. A large bag slid down the ravine, I carried it to the medics.

The gurney was placed at the edge of the door opening, and after a painfully-long three minutes it slowly disappeared inside. Another eight minutes went by before we saw it emerge. The fireman and I held it firmly while one of the paramedics crawled out to take charge.

Next, Mike took over. Using the boom and four slings, Morris and Lucy were, one by one, lifted and swung out and over the road, then lowered into the able arms of the two waiting paramedics. Then the boom came out again and lifted the two medics and me out of the gully, leaving the fireman alone with the wrecked ATF van.

"Great job, fellas," Mike commented.

"Thanks, and you," the three of us agreed. We shook hands, the rescue units drove off. I breathed a prayer of thanks, hopped into the Kia with Fox, and waved goodbye to Mike and the firemen.

We followed behind our injured friends, leaving the clean-up to the pros.

"Glad to see this day end, Bossman," Fox said as she shook her head and blew out a "whew."

"I'm right there with you, lady," I agreed, "and the day isn't over -- at least for me.

"We won't know the status of Carl and Lucy for a couple of hours, so I'm going to see Pop and Rita. Then I want to check on *Pop's Place*. Maybe have a couple doubles of Martell before I walk up the hill -- last I remember, the kitchen and door had just been slaughtered by a semi-automatic long-gun."

"We'll go together, Bossman."

"Thanks."

Chapter 23

On the way, I called Kaiser. Pop was awake, but seems he was worn out from the multitude of visitors and bouquets. Firemen are definitely a close-knit group! I spoke with Rita for an update. "What can I say, Alan. Three bullets in his stomach. He's been trying to walk out of here ever since he woke up."

"Tell him we'll see him later. The inspector and his wife are at Cedars-Sinai Medical Center. They were kidnapped from their home, and taken out of town; then the van they were in was pushed over a cliff and rolled over. It's a long story; I'll explain later. We're going to stop someplace, have a bite to eat, then stop to see them. We'll swing by to see you later, Rita."

"That'll be fine, Alan. Give them our love."

There was a Norm's on La Cienega, close to the medical center. We stopped there for a bite. Huh! The 'bite' was more like a feast! Then we waddled out, climbed into the Kia, and drove to Cedars-Sinai.

"Sorry," the security at the door told us. "No visitors allowed. Covid 19."

"What?" I asked. "We were in a hospital this morning, visiting my dad and his fiance; how can this be?"

"Ruling just came down," the fellow with the badge said. "You might not be able to get back in. It's a statewide edict. Our management discussed the situation, wondering if we should wait until tomorrow, but decided to start ushering visitors out of here at 4:30 this afternoon.

"I was assigned to turn visitors away at the entrance. We're even taking temperatures of all staff -- get this: you walk outside ten minutes for a smoke, you get tested before you can walk back in."

"Can you ask the front desk for us on the condition of Mr. Carl Morris and his wife, Lucy? They were brought into emergency as victims of a vehicle rollover."

A young attendant at his side volunteered to check. She came back with news that they were both being prepped for surgery. "I'm Nadine. I'm on 'til midnight. Give me your phone number; I'll call you." Fox handed her a card. "Are you related to the Morrises?" Then she giggled as she read the Gumshoe and Fox names on the card.

"Carl is a police inspector from Hermosa Beach. Lucy is his wife."

"Oh! What happened?"

"Sinaloa Cartel tried to kill them. Fortunately, we rescued them. Appreciate any news you might give us; doesn't matter what time. Also, please call us when the visitation ban is lifted, Nadine."

"I promise."

*****

6:35 p.m.

"Where to, Bossman?"

"Covid 19! Damn! I knew it was a thing, Fox, but I didn't think it was as much a health threat as these folks are telling us. I think we should head for Kaiser to see Pop and Rita."

Fox nodded. "I agree. Let's hope they won't shut us out tonight."

The commute traffic had thinned out; we made good time. There were poster-sized signs on the entry doors:

<u>NOTICE – No visitor entry as of 8 a.m. this date until further notice. No exceptions. All Staff: check in at Front Desk.</u>

The date was the following day. A sigh of relief escaped me as Fox and I mounted the steps and entered. Desk pointed to the elevator. "Sixth floor," she called after us. Elevator took us to the sixth floor. Nurse's station gave us the room number for Pop: 621. Rita was in 602.

The nurse on duty laughed. "Busiest room on the floor. Is he a celebrity?"

"He thinks so. What's his prognosis?" I asked.

"If he takes it easy, he should be able to head home tomorrow, by ambulance, of course. He was shot in the stomach three times, you know. Only bed-rest; use of wheelchair to the bathroom for a couple more days.

"The lady, Rita, was sutured for a gunshot wound, required several units of blood, but resting nicely. She should be able to go home tomorrow, as well. Just watch for infection. We're assigning a nurse for them. I understand they are a couple."

We opened and walked through the doorway into Rm 621. Walt was visiting Pop. "Tell this guy to go home. I'm fit as a fiddle, son. I don't need flowers and candy and all this other crap! Look at this room. Looks like a funeral parlor. I need to go home."

I shook my head, smiling. "Hold on, Pop. Walt is just showing his love," I chastised him. "Soak it up! Tomorrow you'll be home and it will all be forgotten in the hub-bub of day-to-day life."

Yeah, Pop was Pop. I remembered the time when I found out that Pop had gone into a burning commercial hi-rise to rescue three young sisters trapped in a unit. He came out, not only with the three teens, but with a severely burned, old, gray cat in his arms.

That old, gray cat became our old, gray cat, and lived eight more years before she succumbed to her ninth life. I named her Harriet, simply because she had very little hair. The three teens suffered smoke inhalation; Pop came out no worse for wear. He visited the teens every day for a week. Tough old bird, my pop.

"Oh, I suppose," Pop continued. It's just that firemen have been coming in and out of here all day. Wears a fellow out. Have you seen Rita yet?"

"Going there in a few minutes. Glad you're out of here tomorrow; this new Chinese flu or whatever it is, is predicted to be a real killer. Hospitals are forbidding visitors from gaining entrance."

"Make sure she's going home with me, Alan -- oh, and thanks for getting her here like you did. She lost a lot of blood."

"No problem, Pop." I kissed his forehead and headed for the door, Liz right behind. Walt said his goodbye to Pop and stepped out with us.

"You can't go home tonight, Alan, it's been shot to pieces. I have a crew working on it -- new entry, new cabinets, appliances -- should be ready by tomorrow afternoon, late. Rita's bungalow took a couple of hours. Our guys finished up mid-afternoon today, then started on *Pop's Place*."

Fox piped up, "Stay with me, Bossman; my place wasn't damaged." Walt raised an eyebrow, looked at each of us, but said nothing.

We shook hands, said our goodbyes, and went to look for Rm 602 and Rita. She was raring to go, but said she'd wait for Roland.

"I've been waiting for that man for fifty years. I can wait one more day. Maybe he'll take me for a hot fudge sundae on the way, and discuss how blessed we are. Thank you again, Alan, for saving my life."

"You just continue to take care of my pop, Rita."

"I promise."

Fox and I were smiling as we walked out of the hospital. God is good!

*****

"So, Gumshoe ... my place?"

"No. Been thinkin' about it, but I'm going to the office, Fox, have a double Martell, probably take a run on the beach, back to the office for a shower, and another two fingers of cognac. Then perhaps I might need a place to crash."

"I'll join you."

*****

Fox left the Kia at the curb; we entered the office. All appeared as we had left it -- a miracle. I glanced out the side door. Parking lot was empty except for a small package wrapped in brown Kraft paper. Someone had tossed it over our fence. Odd! I bent over to read the note scrawled on it: *Ferdig -- Enjoy!* I laughed, picked it up, brought it in.

Fox already had the cognac poured. "What's that?" she asked.

"Looks like our arson investigator left a present. We'll open it later." I savoured the taste of the cognac and continued, "Let's just thank our Creator for His protection surviving the ordeal of this long day."

"Amen . . . and, Lord," added Fox, "please heal the inspector and his wife, along with Pop and Rita, and continue to protect us."

Chapter 24

Fox was a better sleuth than jogger, but she trotted along the beach for about forty steps before dropping to her knees in the sand. "I'll be here when you return, Bossman, but hurry. I'm cold."

"Suit yourself, Fox," I panted, trotting backward, facing her, "but I'll be a while. Why did you agree to jog with me?"

"I thought, maybe we'd have a romantic stroll along the water, you'd have your arm around me -- you know, the stuff movies are made of."

"Yeah, the Harlequin stuff. Books to template. Ten pages in and you have the plot: gal moves from big city to rural America. Sits in cafe alone having a danish and a cup of green tea, bumps into a stranger who just happens to be a rich bachelor: a playboy, a yachtsman, a doctor, a son of a Fortune Five Hundred CEO, take your pick . . . sets out to wrangle him.

"Twenty more pages skimpily clad at pool party, first slobbery kiss; twenty more pages things turn steamy, next six pages X-rated. Then becomes complicated with competition: fangs and claws come out . . ."

"Stop, Gumshoe! I saw that movie, too. I'm thinking of *Sleepless in Seattle* or *Lady in Red* -- you know, a feel good movie where . . ."

"Whoa, Fox! I'm talking books! You know, use of imagination to tell a story! And you switch to movies! You want to talk movies, fine! I'll pick something like *It Happened One Night* or *The Quiet Man.* Yours are good, mine are better."

"Not so, Bossman! I started this exchange with a romantic movie on my mind! Rewind your brain! *You* switched to books!"

"You're right!" I laughed. "My bad!" All this time I had been jogging in place. "See you." I turned and sprinted to the first marker, some two hundred yards down the wet sand. Then, hands on knees until my heart-rate came down to a reasonable rate, I sprinted back and sat next to her.

"That was spectacular, Alan! I didn't know you were a runner!"

"I run to think and ease stress, Fox," I looked at her, panting, "mostly to ease stress."

"Humph!"she laughed, elbowing me. Then she leaned so she was nose to nose with me. "There are better ways to ease stress and get sweaty, Bossman."

"Now you tell me. I'm going back to the shop. I need a shower. Come along if you'd like."

"If it includes the shower and another Martell cognac, I'm in.

"Feel like a burger, Bossman?" my shivering subordinate suggested.

"Matter-of-fact, now that you mention it, I'm starving! Half-pounder with . . ."

"I know. Mushrooms, garlic fries, and a hot fudge. Half hour?"

"Make it an hour. I have some phone calls to make."

"Plus," she squirreled a sly eye-roll, "we have a shower on our schedule. That'll take an hour . . .

won't it?"

"Elizabeth!" I shook my head. "Have you gone to page sixty already?" I pulled her into my shoulder and we laughed our way to the office.

Chapter 25

Liz was singing a strain from, I think, *'City of New Orleans'* and blow-drying her hair as I toweled down. As I was brushing my hair, my cell rang. "Garrett."

"Gumshoe?" a female voice . . . sounded young.

"Speaking."

"Mr. Gumshoe, it's Nadine at Cedars-Sinai, you know, it's about your police officer friend, Carl Morris."

"Oh, yes! Thank you for getting back to me. How is Carl? And how is Mrs. Morris?"

"They're both still in intensive care, Mr. Gumshoe. I haven't seen them, but I heard it's touch and go. I don't work tomorrow, but my girlfriend will be here. Her name is Zuzu. I gave her your phone number."

"Zoozoo?"

"Yes, spelled Z U Z U, just like it sounds. She promised to call."

"Thanks, Nadine." I hung up. *Damn Covid! I should be there!* I punched a number on my cell.

"Ready for that burger, Bossman?" Fox had just emerged from the bath.

"Yes. Call it in. I'm calling Bradley to make sure he's okay. Then I'll check on Haruto."

Bradley Swazer picked up on the second ring.

"Garrett! Are you okay? Where's Morris? I've been worried sick. Haruto says you have good instincts, so not to worry. Says you'll show up with some corny jokes, say it was a fun day, and offer a snifter of Cordon Bleu to all the ATF crew that came down this morning."

I didn't laugh. "Is Haruto with you, Swazer?"

"I'm with him. My house was destroyed early this morning; I couldn't reach anybody else, so I called him. He invited me to join him and his family in a 'safe house' of sorts in Long Beach."

"Put him on, would you?"

"Fine, Mr. Garrett, but first, do you know anything about Morris's whereabouts?"

"Yes, Brad, he and Lucy are in Cedars-Sinai up in LA in bad shape. We can't visit because of this covid thing. You have wheels?"

"Yeah, I was able to escape -- pulled out of the garage into the alley and floored it while the house was in flames."

"We'll swing by Hermosa in the morning. Let me talk with Haruto."

"Good evening, Gumshoe. You and the young lady okay?"

"Yes. Tough day, and afraid it's just the beginning. We tore a strip off their hides today, so I think they will lick their wounds, regroup, and bring it in spades. We need to be on the alert."

"What happened, Gumshoe?"

"We put about forty of theirs in black bags, and about six of ours, including our ATF lead. I suggest you and Bradley do your thing tomorrow. Let's meet at my shop at 5 p.m. tomorrow. I'll go into detail about today, and we'll make some plans."

"Is Morris really in hospital, Gumshoe?"

"Yes, and it's not good. Word is 'touch and go'."

Haruto signed off with, "See you tomorrow." As he was hanging up, a white Prius pulled up with a *Shellback Tavern* sign on the side.

"Burgers are here, Fox."

*****

Fox kept fingering the Kraft package from Ferdig as she spooned caramel sundae into her mouth. "May I open this, Bossman?"

"Of course, Fox. I doubt it's anything for my eyes only. Just don't get caramel on it. That stuff is sticky!"

She tore the paper away and tossed it on the floor, like a little kid on her birthday. "Three books, Gumshoe! Look!" She held them up for me to see; I glanced up -- then took a double-take -- I recognized one of them.

"Toss me that western, Fox. I'm sure I read that on the plane ride to Miami!" I thumbed through the first few pages; "Yeah, *A Ranger's Tale!* That was a good story. I finished it, then gave it to Maggorie's kid, Paul." I placed the book on her desk. "What else is there, Fox?"

She picked up one with a ship on the front. "*A Lad From Sardinia*," set it down and lifted up the last one. "*Cowboy Justice On The Border*."

"Another western. Let me take a look at it, please."

The first page told me I was wrong. Words like Mexican Cartel, hardened Oakland cop, Nogales Police Department told me this was a contemporary story. "Looks like it's worth reading, Fox . . . if I ever have the time."

"You read that one, I'll read this one," she said, holding up the ship, "if I ever have the time." We both laughed.

"I'll have to let Ferdig know I've read one of his books -- he'll be pleased. Now I'm going to retire for the evening. Suggest you do the same. I walked into my private office, drew the curtains, shut the door, lay back in my swivel chair, and closed my eyes. Three minutes later I opened the door a crack, tiptoed out to see where Fox had ended up, thinking she was asleep, either in her chair or on the carpeted floor . . . or, possibly waiting in hiding for me. But . . . she was gone! As was her Kia! So much for games . . .

*****

6:10 a.m.

Coffee was on, I was going through the necessary chores of a private eye: sweeping the floors, emptying the waste baskets, jotting down messages from the answering machine, and I was just beginning to clean the john when Fox unlocked the side door. "Good morning, Bossman. You're up bright and early. How'd you sleep?"

"Like a log."

"Logs don't sleep . . ."

"Exactly!" I moaned, "that's how I slept!"

"Ha! Serves you right! I slept in a huge bed, all by myself, and I slept like a baby."

"Yeah, I know, you cried all night."

"Cute, Bossman. Carry on," she added, "toilet bowl brush is under the sink."

"I know, I know. Grab some coffee; we have a long day ahead."

She patted a sheet of paper sitting on her desk -- an itinerary. It started with 'clean the bathroom', and ended with 'call Zuzu at Cedars-Sinai'. She studied it for a few seconds. "One down, Gumshoe," she smiled.

I reached for the desk phone to call Swazer, but was preempted by a ring on my cellphone -- Tony's

Garage. *Awfully early to be calling,* I thought.

"Have I reached Gumshoe and Fox?" a perky, voice asked.

"Tony's Garage? Is this Rosalee? Hi, Honey, this is Uncle Alan. Haven't talked to you since you were, what, six? Your birthday party, right?"

"I think so, yes! I'm fifteen, now. A Gumshoe is a detective, am I right? Are you a detective, Uncle Alan?"

"A private eye. You working for your dad, now?"

"One day a week. Job experience, Dad calls it. It's okay. Your Cadillac is ready. Shall we bring it by?"

"No, we'll swing by and pick it up. That way I get to see you."

*****

We started out of the parking lot when a car horn slowed us to a stop. It was Swazer. "Hey! Where are you off to?" he asked. "We were supposed to get together here, weren't we?"

"Sorry, Brad," I answered, "didn't expect you so soon. We're on our way to pick up my Caddy. Park and join us."

During the jaunt to Tony's, I explained the previous day's adventures, and trials. I asked that Swazer go on with me to Kaiser to pick up and transport Pop and Rita home, or at least get a fix on their discharge, while Fox returned to our office.

"We'll have breakfast somewhere on the water, Fox. Pick a spot." Little did I know breakfast would have to wait.

Chapter 26

Fox was already speeding away after dropping us off. Tony seemed anxious. He insisted we have a cup of coffee with him and his daughter. We entered his office; his daughter followed.

As Rosalee poured coffee all around, I smiled up at her, remembering the bright eyes, shiny black hair, with its cute ponytail. Now I noted a flash of worry in those, now, almost woman's eyes.

"What's going on, Tony?" I asked.

"It's probably nothing, Alan . . ."

"Dad! Tell them!" He wasn't fast enough to suit her. "Uncle Alan, the word on the street is that Dad's shop is going to be torched and that his life is in jeopardy."

"Sorry," Sergeant Swazer broke in, "who's the 'word' you speak of?"

"In my business, I have a lot of friends, some shady, some on the up and up," Tony shrugged. "The *word* is a group of my friends who watch everything going on in Gardena, Lennox, El Segundo, and up to Inglewood.

"Look, Alan, this isn't the only chapter of little groups gathering information 'on the street'. Might be a local barber shop, a neighborhood coffee shop, or a neighborhood pub. Point is, a few buddies warned me to stay away from whoever owns the Caddy, because it might be 'detrimental to my health'."

"May I ask, who these buddies are?"

"Sure, Alan. My pal, Pedro Alcinces. Pedro was in this morning, spotted your wheels, and gave me the heads up. That's why I had Rosalee call so early. I want the car gone. No charge, I owed you a favor."

"We'll go, Tony. Just one more question. How do I find Pedro?"

"He runs a catering truck. White one. Parks and sells tamales, burritos, and such. On Crenshaw usually; sometimes Rosecrans or Western. Watch yourself, Alan. Good meeting you, Sergeant Swazer."

*****

Twenty minutes later we found Pedro and his white van on Crenshaw Boulevard. He was just setting up for the morning coffee crowd and not too pleased when he noticed my crystal-coat, cherry red convertible pull up behind his rig.

"Pedro," I called out as we exited my machine, "we were told we might find you here. A couple of questions and a cup to go, please."

"Tony, right?" he growled.

"Yeah, what did you say to him that scared him out of his shoes?"

"After I closed up yesterday afternoon, I was in a pub talking to the boys. Some cop, a Commander Sidney from downtown, walks up, flashes a badge, starts askin' about a red Cadillac -- you know, had we seen one, and if so, where. Says the owner is posing as a lawman and needs to be apprehended. Hands out cards, says there's a reward. Then he moves on to other tables.

"Last night I swing by Tony's to set up an

appointment, I see yours. It matches the description this guy gives us. I start to call this cop, Tony says 'hold off'. I tell Tony to get it out of his shop, fast."

Swazer showed the badge on his belt. "Do you still have the card, Pedro?" he asked.

"Sure." He pulled the card from his van's visor and handed it to the sergeant. "Tony convinced me you weren't the criminal that other cop, Sidney, suggested."

Brad handed me the card. I shook my head. "Let me just say be very wary of Sidney. He was fired from the police force about two months ago. He's a swindler, murderer, and more."

Awfully brazen of him to walk into a bar impersonating a police commander, pass out cards and ask for assistance, I thought. *I guess the bigger the hoax, the more believable.*

"What pub, Pedro?"

"The Robin's Nest, just off Rosecrans."

We ordered strong, black coffees with lids, thanked Pedro, hopped into the Caddy, and headed for Kaiser.

I explained to Swazer that Sidney was, in fact, one Victor Collins, a slimy criminal Morris had jailed years before.

"But he's the IA officer that came into our precinct, ordered me to sit at a desk over that shooting! Why didn't Morris tell me?"

"Morris was in the dark until he saw a mug shot of Sidney; then he made it his job to arrest him again."

"Are you saying this was a coordinated attempt to stop the inspector from pursuing Sidney -- or whatever his name is?"

"And perhaps you and me and a few others. Not sure. Working on it, Brad, working on it."

"Turns my brain into knots, Mr. Garrett, I can't make sense of any of it."

"It's there somewhere," I said as we pulled into Kaiser's short-term parking. I called the desk. "Here to pick up Roland Garrett and his friend, Rita."

"Rita's last name, please."

"Hell, I don't ... oh! Mason. Rita Mason." A blue sedan pulled into a parking spot across from us and down about three cars. My suspicious cerebrum began bouncing thoughts off my skull. I mentioned it to Bradley. He looked over his shoulder.

"Yeah, I see it," he nodded.

The desk was saying, "Let me check."

"Fine. May I come in?"

"No."

We waited five minutes. No answer. Eight minutes. I hung up and called her again. I turned to Swazer. "Keep an eye on that sedan, Brad. No one has exited the . . ."

The desk attendant came on, "First you hang up on me, and now you're talking to someone else!" *At least there was a lilt to her voice.*

"Sorry, Miss. I was . . ."

She ignored my babbling. "They'll meet you at the Plaza South Wing. The entry is just beyond the emergency entrance. Follow the signs. I'll make sure they are there."

"Thanks, Miss." Back to Brad, "Maybe those guys are like us, just phoning in for instructions, but somehow, it doesn't feel right."

"I agree," Brad nodded.

We backed out of the spot, far enough for a head-count inside the sedan, then shifted into a forward gear and slowly continued in the direction of the emergency entrance.

"Three," Bradley confirmed my count. "All males. Looked young. I didn't see Sidney."

"Maybe it's nothing," I said, glancing in my rear-view. I relaxed for a moment, began looking for signs to Emergency and the Plaza South Wing.

Swazer tapped my shoulder. "Looks like they're following, Mr. Garrett. Just pulled out, heading this way."

"I was afraid of that. There's a parking garage ahead, Bradley. I'm going in. If they follow, we'll make a quick decision."

"Gotcha, Mr. Garrett. You say when."

Slowing at the gate, I grabbed the ticket; the lift gate let me pass through. I put my foot on the pedal, we accelerated in and up the ramp to the second level. Tires squealed on the ramp below us.

"I'm stopping now!" I said, braking to a stop, diagonally, partially blocking the lane. Both Swazer and I pulled our weapons and hopped out, crouching between cars on either side. We waited.

Chapter 27

The blue sedan slammed on the brakes, my heart pounded as I waited for the crash, but it stopped inches from my Caddy. Swazer was already standing at the passenger window, demanding the three exit. I dashed to the driver's side and yanked the door open.

The driver was reaching for what turned out to be a KEL-TEC PLR-22 from his belt -- a nifty semi-automatic pistol that fires a .22 LR round -- in fact, twenty-six of them before reloading. He gave it up willingly . . . with my Beretta pressed against his temple.

Brad had the passenger door open. "It's over, fellas," he was saying to the other two. "Hands where I can see them."

There were x-rated retorts from inside, but no fireworks. I yanked the driver from the car, threw a handcuff on his right wrist and the other cuff on the rear door handle, then walked around to assist the sergeant with the other two.

They came out willingly, but vocally with 'You don't know who you're messing with', and 'your ass is fried, man', and other expletives. I held a gun on one of them as Swazer put the other on the ground, frisked him, and cuffed him, hands behind his back.

"Don't move!" he told the one on the ground. "You have another set of cuffs in the Caddy, Mr. Garrett? Zip ties, anything?"

"Maybe!" I smiled. "Be right back." In the Caddy trunk I carried my tackle box. I opened it. I had stringers, mono-filament line, 18, 24, and 36" steel leaders for deep-sea fishing the big boys, and a few other things I could jury-rig to make do.

My smile broadened as I envisioned my new "improvised handcuffs." I chose a stainless leader with a treble hook fastened to one end. *This ought to work*, I thought, holding it up to examine my invention. I walked back, satisfied.

Two cars, one after another, came up the ramp. I waved them through. The first one stopped, rolled his window down, and wanted to know why we had blocked the roadway. I smiled, and explained that three punks were in custody in connection with theft and firearm possession. That satisfied him. He had enough room to go around. The second car followed suit.

Brad had the other two miscreants in the back seat of the blue sedan. "Not a peep out of either of them, Mr. Garrett. Just young punks."

"Yeah, with weapons." I opened the rear door. "You!" I pointed to the young kid with no cuffs, "get out here, now!"

"Screw you, Cop! I want a lawyer. You're supposed to read me my rights, yeah? You ain't done anything right, Pig!" He turned to his cuffed buddy, "Right, Dog?"

Grabbing his arm, I twisted it and jerked him out, making sure he would still have use of it once free of the sedan. "Kid," I whispered in his ear, "I'm only saying this once. I'm not a cop. All your lawyer bullshit talk doesn't mean anything to me. You and your two friends will tell us what we want to hear, then we'll decide whether to take you for the long ride or not. Now, put your other hand behind your back!"

He was probably fifteen -- already blubbering. Without a word his hand came around. I threw a slipknot around one, drew it tight, twisted the line and created another slipknot and pulled both arms together. Then the line went over the top of the two arms and between his legs, coming up in front. I had just enough steel leader to hook the treble hook to the front of his shorts, in a precarious position. Movement on his part could be painful.

The third teen -- the one I had handcuffed to the door handle was shouting expletives at the top of his lungs, echoing throughout the garage. He was the driver, probably seventeen or eighteen. Time to deal with him.

As I approached, he tried to kick me in the groin, but lost his balance and fell, jerking his handcuffed arm in torturous pain. His face turned to chalk; he was going into shock.

"Damn," I said. "I'm sorry, son. You need a doctor right now." I turned to Bradley. "Swazer, take those two to lock-up in Hermosa. Use their sedan. It'll create an issue, I'm sure, but we'll sort it out later. I'm taking this one to Emergency.

"Oh, Brad," I added, taking the handcuff off the door handle, "take my contraption off Pretty Boy in there and use these on him instead. I'm taking the folks home."

"No. Keep your cuffs," he called back, "your nifty contraption works just fine." I laughed.

"I'm following you, Mr. Garrett. I'll make sure you're okay before I leave."

I called for hospital security. When connected, I

asked that they meet me in front of Emergency to take an injured delinquent off my hands. They met us on the steps, accompanied by a nurse with a gurney -- the poor lad, by this time, was unconscious.

Swazer flashed his badge to the two hospital cops, gave them his card as we delivered the boy to them -- one Terrence Crawford, according to his driver's license.

"Who's responsible for him?" one of the security guards asked.

"Obviously, no one," Brad said with appropriate sarcasm. "I'll have an officer here within the hour. When you're finished with him, we'll take him to Hermosa; put the tab on the Hermosa Beach PD."

*****

"Where have you been?" Pop asked. All of them were wearing white masks. "The nurses thought you abandoned us."

"Been a little busy, Pop. Hi, Rita." I hugged each of them, in spite of the two nurses trying to keep us separated. One handed me a mask.

"You put this on immediately! You want to keep everyone safe."

Removing my fedora, I smiled and slipped the mask over my nose and mouth. I wasn't about to offer an opinion contrary to the wisdom of professionals. I had my own ideas, but this was not the time or place. Besides, masks have a place.

"You okay to travel, Pop? You look a little pale. You need another day here?"

"Just get me home, son. I can think of no better place to spend my time than a hospital bed."

One of the nurses turned to the other. "Sounds

awfully ungrateful from a man who came in here with three bullets in his chest, only able to walk out because of the skills of this hospital's surgeon and staff!"

"Yes, ladies, I'm grateful to all of you, especially the nursing staff," Pop responded. "I'm simply not one to lie in a small, cramped room, staring at the ceiling -- with staff coming in and out, checking this and that, all day long.

"Getting well, to me, is sitting on my own porch, relaxing, breathing fresh air, with perhaps an occasional friend popping by."

"Well, all the best to you both. Please make sure you wear your masks when you're out in public!"

Rita hobbled into the Cadillac's back seat with only a wince; Pop took more time, but fortunately, the big door opened wide, giving him easier access to slide in. He smiled, "Put the top down, Alan. I want to be *Toad of Toad Hall* for an hour."

So, thanking God for His mercy, I transported Pop and Rita home in my convertible.

Chapter 28

We started up the cul-de-sac; Rita breathed a sigh. "Alan, two things: the doctor told me I would have bled out had you not insisted on rushing me to Kaiser when you did. I am forever grateful."

"And the second thing?"

"Would you assist us up the steps and inside, please?"

"Of course," I smiled, "but all the bad guys are gone, Rita. Look! Two unmarked cop cars, one near the corner and one up closer to *Pop's Place*."

"I'd just feel better, Alan. Getting shot by hoodlums in my own home is a bit unnerving."

"Not just a little bit, my love," Pop said, assuring her with a smile. "That was very nearly all-out war. Are Carl and Lucy going to make it, Alan?"

"Hope so. Lucy looked especially bad. A young hospital aide is supposed to call me when she hears anything definite, probably not until tomorrow."

"I hope we ripped them up!" Pop said, wincing in pain as he exited my Caddy.

"Over thirty-five body bags worth, Pop, so yes, I think we did. We lost a few feds as well." I went through the previous day's fight from start to finish: Sinaloa, the DEA, the explosion destroying the Beverly Hills mansion, and ending with the episode on the gravel road.

It wasn't the time to mention the questioning by *phony Supervisor Sidney* of the whereabouts of a red Caddy, or the talks with Tony and Pedro about my wheels; nor did I mention the three youths there at Kaiser. There was time for that sometime down the road.

As I ushered Rita through the door, I could see the lines of anxiety disappear from her face; Pop glanced at me as he followed, mouthing a silent "thank you" -- then he became serious.

"Walt tells me our bungalow has significant damage, son."

"Haven't even seen it yet, Pop. Walt has a crew working on it. Says they'll wrap it up tomorrow, so I'll wait.

"We dodged a bullet, for sure," I laughed. "A grenade came through the door, but I tossed it back out just in time. I think it took out a shrub or two, but I was a trifle preoccupied at the time. I'll pick you up tomorrow evening, we'll go see it together if you like."

"For sure, Alan."

"See you, then." I gave them hugs and walked out, waving to the cop in the unmarked car as I drove to the office. Liz met me at the side door. Her attitude was less than cordial.

"Not sure if the Ritz-Carlton held our reservations for breakfast, Bossman," she raised an eyebrow and cocked her head as she made the statement.

"Plans changed. Sorry." *What's up with her?* I thought.

"You coulda called." *Still chilly.*

"Fox! I was a little busy!" Her tone was rubbing off, and I answered in kind.

142

"Did you pick up Pop and Rita?" *Why was I being grilled?*

"Yes, I did. They're home." Then it hit me. She was still scared silly from our episode yesterday. I stopped her, put my arms around her and held her close.

"Fox, I'm sorry I left you alone all morning. We went through a traumatic experience yesterday, and I shouldn't have left you in our office by yourself all morning."

"You should have called."

"I'm sorry."

She gave me a wistful smile, "You should have called," she repeated, with almost a pout, snuggling against my chest. We stayed that way for probably 45 seconds, then she looked up, smiling. "Did Haruto call?"

"No," I frowned, "what about?"

"He was wondering where Swazer is. Says he has a spare room in case Brad needs a place to stay while he's homeless. I told him Brad was with you."

"He had two cuffed hoodlums in the back of the kids' sedan last I knew, headed for Hermosa lockup. Let's go sit. I'll tell you all about it, Liz."

Fox opened the cabinet, pulled out two snifters, the Martell Cognac, and poured.

*****

Haruto walked through the door at exactly 5 p.m. Fox poured a Martell, set it on the desk in front of him. Sitting heavily, Haruto breathed out an audible sigh, and lifted the glass, nodding to me in appreciation.

"I spoke with Swazer earlier. Understand he's swinging by here as well. Any news on Morris?"

As if on cue the phone rang. It was Zuzu. "Mr. Gumshoe?"

"Speaking. What's the news?"

"About your friends, sir. The gentleman is out of ICU, but the lady isn't in good shape . . . may not make it."

"Were they shot?"

"Yes, sir. Both have bullet wounds to the head, but hers are more serious. I have the charge nurse here with me. She can explain better." She passed the phone to Sonia.

"Sonia, tell me," I said.

"Mr. Gumshoe . . . Gumshoe, is that right?"

"Call me Alan, Ma'am. How are Carl and Lucy?"

"How are you related to the patients?"

"I'm their closest thing to a family, Ma'am, his best friend. He's a police inspector, I'm a private investigator. We work many cases together. I found them in a ravine."

"Fair enough. Carl has bullet wounds to the neck and forehead. In addition, he has two broken ribs, left arm has a compound fracture, and bruising from, I'm guessing, a car accident.

"The bullet wounds are not life threatening; he will end up with a new part in his hair. I suspect he'll be with us over the weekend and perhaps Monday as well.

"The wife is far more serious. She's scheduled for surgery at 8 p.m. to remove a bullet. It went up through her jaw, lodged just above her ear in the temporal lobe of her brain. Very delicate surgery.

"In addition, the accident has broken several bones and crushed her right shoulder. If she pulls through, she will probably never again have use of her right arm."

As I thanked Sonia and Zuzu, Swazer came through the front door. I hung up, filled them all in, then looked at Swazer. "Load is on you for a few weeks, Brad. Morris will be out for some time."

"Yeah. Got the picture," the young sergeant replied. "I am also aware this isn't simply gang warfare; we're looking at a very coordinated effort to disrupt order here in Southern California."

"Well said," Haruto chimed in. "Gentlemen and lady," he tipped his drink toward Fox, "We have a snake's den somewhere close by -- we need to turn over the rocks until we find its hiding place."

"And cut its head off," Fox added.

"So, any ideas? Leads?" Haruto asked.

"Two or three." I nodded. "The real estate company, XTR-Management, down in San Diego; the suited gent that made monthly trips to Jay's house -- we have the license number of his car. . ."

"License number, humph! We have his name and social security number!" Haruto said, his eyes throwing daggers at me.

"Oh, yeah, forgot," I smiled. "Then there's the fake IA guy, Sidney -- or Victor Collins. I don't know how far Morris got. Do you know if he had any notes on him, Swazer?"

"No, but I'll follow up on him."

"I'll take XTR-Management," Haruto volunteered.

"Okay, Fox and I will coordinate with Strom and see if we can put the screws on the guy in Montecito."

With that, we topped off our cognacs and wished each other good snake-hunting.

Chapter 29

The day couldn't go by without calling Strom. I called his cell. The call went to voice mail. *Strange -- it's only 6:30 p.m. Almost banker's hours,* my brain rattled off. I left a request to call me back. Now what?

"You coming home with me, Gumshoe?" Fox asked.

"No, I think I'll take a stroll on the pier; see how my fishing buddies are doing; maybe stop at Barb's and have a beer and one of her juicy beef franks -- smothered in shredded cheddar, chopped onions, and relish -- join me? I'll buy."

"I think I will! Thank you, Bossman! Let me use the little room, then grab a sweater."

A little voice told me to grab a jacket along with my fedora -- should have listened. I grabbed my fedora.

*****

Fox was wise to wear a sweater, I decided, as we neared the end of the old Manhattan Beach pier. Sure, this is Southern California, but we were still living in January -- and the sun would soon be dropping off the edge of the Pacific. I had goose bumps on top of goosebumps!

Three fisherman were hunched over the end of the pier's railing, lines out, bundled up in Alaskan garb, hoodies or collars drawn up covering neck and ears. But they looked up, smiling as we neared.

"Alan! Good seeing you!" Willie sang out. "Bite's on! We caught seven between us; three nice keepers! And we've only been here, what, twenty minutes, fellas?" They all agreed. "Joaquin is big winner so far," Bardy piped up. "Got hisself a Yellowfin, 7 1/2 pounder."

Joaquin smiled, "You should bring your gear down here, Alan. Get a fish on, it'll warm you up. You look like you could use a warmin' up."

"Aw, his girl is gonna warm him up later," Bardy laughed, jabbing Willie in the side, "ain't that right, miss?"

"Hey! knock it off, Bardy." You're out of order with a comment like that. This is my partner, Fox. We're taking a stroll, then going to Barb's for a hot dog."

"Sorry, miss. Enjoy your walk."

"Enjoy your fishing, fellas," Fox said, squeezing my arm. We turned and walked to Barb's.

We bought two of her famous 8 inch franks to go, walked back to the office, spread out our dinner on the front desk, pulled two Bohemia beers from the fridge to wash them down, and had just taken our first bite when the phone rang.

"Garrett here."

"Yeah, a problem, Mr. Gumshoe Garrett. Ha! You are a problem. I'll need to deal with you, soon."

"Who is this?" I demanded, but the caller was gone. I frowned, took a bite of my frank, and chewed.

"Fun call," Fox agreed, staring at the look on my face. "A woman! Now what are we going to do?"

"We should stick with our plan, Fox. Enjoy our hot dogs and beer. Maybe I'll call Pop. You want to stay in town tonight?"

"I want to stay where I feel safest, Bossman, and that's with you."

I made the call. "Pop, it's Alan. Do you have room for Liz and me tonight? . . . half an hour. Thanks . . . no, just tonight. Thanks, Pop." I turned to Liz, "Finish your dinner, we're going up to Rita's afterwards."

Chapter 30

Pop and I stayed up chatting in the kitchen, while Fox followed Rita, disappearing down the hallway to the spare bedroom. Moments later Rita reappeared.

"She's having a shower, will be back out in a few minutes. I suggest we all retire early tonight. None of us have had much rest in the last few days. Liz tells me you received a veiled threat from a woman, Alan! Do you have any ideas as to who that might be?"

"A few remote possibilities, Rita. Nothing really substantial, but I'm working on it."

Pop took Rita's suggestion and bade us goodnight. I could see that he was still feeling the pain from his recent ordeal. I was so pleased seeing his mental and physical strength after the trauma of his experience.

Rita, meanwhile, was busily making up a bedroll for me in the living room. She came into the kitchen. "I'm leaving you, Alan. I'm glad you're here, especially tonight."

Liz popped her head in the door. "Going to bed, too. Thanks, Rita." She blew me a kiss and walked out.

"You don't know how much better we feel with you being here, Alan," Rita continued, "now, go to bed. Get some sleep!" She kissed me on the cheek and left me alone in the kitchen.

After rinsing my coffee mug, I set it on the counter, then headed for the living room. *Who was that mystery woman? Was it Lady?* I had no idea. The only name and face that came to mind was the receptionist, Michelle, at XTR-Management in San Diego. *Can't be*, I told myself.

Lying on the bedroll, I was too tired to sleep; tried pulling every female I knew out in the open to examine, but to no avail. Finally, after half an hour, I drifted off, fully clothed. Within the hour a wrinkled, toothless, old hag leaned over me, smiling. Then she pulled herself on top of my chest, squeezing the breath from me. Her words echoed through my brain: *"You are a problem, Mr. Gumshoe Garrett. I'll need to deal with you, and soon."*

Jerking awake in a cold sweat, I filled my lungs with air, looked around, and realized where I was. *The infamous old hag! I'd heard of her but I'd never met her before!* Sleep was now behind me. I walked to the office, made a pot of coffee, and waited for the sun.

Chapter 31

Haruto was the first to call. "XTR-Management offices were closed. Sign on the door said leave a message in the mail slot or call 555-xxx-xxxx for assistance.

"Just a message about rentals available and a notice of rent due," he informed me. "I'm heading for their complex in Alpine this morning just to snoop around. I have an appointment with the resident manager at 9:30. I'll share what I find."

As he was hanging up, Liz pushed through the side door, grabbed a mug of coffee, and plopped down in front of me.

"Couldn't sleep?" she asked.

"Something like that."

"That woman on the phone got to you, huh?"

"Actually, her mother. Scared the crap out of me."

I gave Liz the Reader's Digest version of my nightmare. "Really weird -- but, I've heard of her, Fox. When I was in AFOSI I ran into a few fellows who told me of such experiences right down to the face; happens when you're overtired. Google it, Fox."

*****

Strom called, not five minutes later. There was

consternation in his voice. "I know you called yesterday, but I've been busy, as I know you have. Before you ask -- No! We did not intercept the Suburban. They switched cars just before they hit Highway 101. We found the Suburban just yesterday afternoon in a ravine. In view of the recent explosives used by our enemy, we approached it with caution, found a bomb; our bomb squad defused it."

"Damn! So we haven't gained a thing, Strom! They may have hit Route 101 and gone south!"

"Could be. Sorry, Gumshoe."

"What's the word on our fellow in Montecito? Do I have the green light to go after him?"

"Coordinate with LaRusso, the DEA chief. I've asked him three or four times to put the screws on that bastard, Trujillo. He drives around in his Rolls like he's untouchable."

"Is he?"

"Who?"

"Trujillo. Is he untouchable?"

"What are you suggesting, Gumshoe?" Strom's voice rose considerably.

"I'm wondering why he wasn't apprehended or at least taken in for questioning." My volume matched his.

"How do you know he wasn't?" Now we're practically shouting through the phones.

"My sources," I answered, hotly.

"Listen, Gumshoe! Don't ruffle LaRusso's feathers. He doesn't have a sense of humor."

"Neither do I when it comes to the events of the past few days. You lost three or four good officers; I almost lost my dad and his partner in a firefight; a police inspector and his wife are in Cedars-Sinai Hospital, fighting for their lives; and a surge of other horrific acts of violence have been committed in our communities."

The more I talked the angrier I became. Suddenly I realized it -- *tone down your decibels, Alan,* I lectured myself. "Give me LaRusso's number, Strom," then I added, with some temperance, "please."

"I have a better idea, Gumshoe. Come on up. We'll see him together."

"We'll be there tomorrow."

"First time I've seen the 'no-filter Garrett', Bossman," Fox laughed. "I'm proud of you!"

*****

Thursday, February 6

The drive to Santa Barbara was smooth and uneventful. The combined DEA/ATF forces had appropriated adjoining offices on a southeast corner of the local government pavilion -- on W. Figueroa between Anacapa and Garden, where you could find almost everything you need: police, mayor, courthouse, city hall, and city attorney.

Across the street were county offices: the fire department, and the public works yard with its trash trucks, road graders, snowplows, and various other pieces of rolling equipment the city might require. There were even some Cal-Trans vehicles behind the chain-link fence as we rounded the corner.

We pulled into parking lot D as directed by Strom. He stepped off the veranda and walked to my convertible to wave and introduce himself.

"Gumshoe! Good to meet you. And you," he reached in to shake Liz's hand, "you're the Fox, right?"

Fox answered, "I am, indeed. He says he's my boss, but don't believe everything you hear."

"Gotcha! I like your wheels, Gumshoe." He

turned and waved to the fellow sitting in one of a half-dozen plastic chairs on the veranda. "LaRusso! Come on over!"

The two men couldn't have been more different. Elias Strom was tall, muscular, with dark, wavy hair, and spoke with carefully chosen words. Paul LaRusso was heavy, bald, of average height. His speech was impulsive, words flowing from his mouth in a rapid-fire staccato manner. Reminded me of the cigar-chewing lawyer in an old movie -- without the suspenders.

"What's this I hear about you hoping to have an interview with Trujillo," LaRusso started, reaching into the Caddy for a handshake. That right?"

"Pretty much, sir. I think he's responsible for a string of murders and mayhem in the Los Angeles area and I want to look him in the eye and put the accusation to him."

"Yeah, *mano a mano*, eh?" LaRusso smiled. "Maybe it is time, eh, Strom? Let's go inside -- call my source -- see if Trujillo is in the neighborhood. If he is, maybe we'll drop in on him."

Fox and I followed the two feds inside. LaRusso ushered us into his office along with Strom. He made a quick phone call.

"Well, boys," he smiled, nodding at Fox, "and girl -- we're in luck. Trujillo is in. I just got the green light to call on him. Strom, you good with this?"

"I've been encouraging you to go after that slime for six weeks. Give us ten minutes. We'll have a few guys gear up. We'll smoke his ass."

"Or," Fox frowned, "we should at least get some answers to our questions."

I bit my tongue. Questions flooded my brain as well, but not for Trujillo. I checked the time. It was 11:48 a.m.

Chapter 32

"Papa! Company!"

"Who is it, Maria?"

"Three men and one woman, Papa, and some more behind them. Maybe ten."

"Tell them I'll be a few minutes."

"Should I let them in, Papa?"

"No! I can't imagine what they want, but I'll be down in a few minutes; tell them to wait."

*****

The four of us stood at the door for ten minutes. Finally, Fox announced the obvious. "He's gone, Bossman. Slipped out the back. Let's go home."

LaRusso and Strom turned to their men. "Didn't anyone check around back to see if he decided to run?" LaRusso asked. No one spoke up. LaRusso shook his head, "Elite team, my ass! Damn bunch of rookies!" he exploded, scowling at Strom.

"Hey, Asshole! Where were your men?" Strom fired back. "I, at least, pulled together a crew!"

"Huh! Obviously, to no avail!"

Fox and I shared a look, bid them adieu, and left them to argue over the incompetence of the other.

*****

"Since we're in downtown Montecito, let's find a

nice little place to eat, then hit the road for home, Bossman."

"Whatever," I answered. "I'm so disgusted with those two 'experts', Fox! They've been sitting on Trujillo for how long, now -- close to a year?"

"How about Tre Lune?" Fox pointed. "Looks good to me. Stop there, Bossman. Stop!"

Her words broke through my thoughts, and I pulled over to the curb. "Sorry, Fox; I was thinking. What did you say?"

"I said let's stop here for lunch, then go home. Leave those experts to figure out their next brilliant move."

"How about we enjoy a nice lunch here at the -- what's this place? -- the Tre Lune, then do some private-eye-type stuff? I think my camera's in the red bag in the back seat, next to my rifle. Let's go have lunch. Couple of phone calls to make, Fox."

*****

In my shirt pocket I kept a little address book. Thumbing through it, I found the name I was looking for. "Is Corporal Tabitha Norman in, please? Thank you."

"Who is that, Bossman?"

"Haruto's cousin, remember? . . . oh," I held my hand up. "Yes, Miss Norman. You probably don't remember me, but I'm Alan Garrett, private eye . . . yes, that's right . . . my associate and I are in Montecito having lunch at the Tre Lune. We'd love to have you join us . . . just coffee, then. That's fine . . . we'll spot you. You wear a uniform, right? . . . good. See you soon."

My next call was to Bradley Swazer. He promised to check on Morris a couple of times a day.

"Mr. Garrett, hello! There hasn't been much

change, according to your friend, Zuzu. The chief is still in ICU, Lucy is barely hanging on, sir."

"Any problems in your area, Brad? Any messages that sound ominous?"

"No, sir. All is quiet. Why do you ask?"

"A brief, threatening phone call I received from a female. She made a statement then hung up before I had a clue as to who she is. Wish I hadn't answered it; might have had a voice to work from if she'd left a message."

"Don't beat yourself up, sir. She might not have left a message."

"Probably right. Stay safe." We ended the call. Fox had looked at the menu; the young waiter was waiting for me. I glanced at the menu.

"Hmmm," I grimaced, raised an eyebrow at Fox as if to say, *no hamburgers, huh?* ... "Okay, I'll have the Bresaola con Rughetta and a glass of La Braccesca-Antinori Toscana."

"I'll have the same," she said, and closed her menu.

"Coward!" I laughed.

"Oh, oh, here comes the fuzz," Fox whispered, as a female officer walked in.

Standing, I waved the newcomer to our table. As I did so, I whispered back, smiling, "You're dating yourself."

*****

After the formalities of meeting, shaking hands, and discussing the beauty of Montecito, I asked the Corporal what she knew of the Jaime Trujillo family.

"Jaime? You must mean Manuel."

"Whichever one has a daughter named Maria."

"Neither one. Manuel lives by himself on Greenaway, and Alejandro is an old man -- has no children. Lives on Gard Avenue."

"No, no, no, no. This Trujillo lives on Greenaway Drive, but his name is Jaime. I have a driver's license and it shows Jaime in black and white. Do you know him?"

"Must be Manual -- nickname maybe. Everyone in town knows him; drives a metallic blue Porsche; always drives a few miles over the town speed limit; comes to a rolling stop at stop signs; flaunts moving violations -- must have piled up two dozen tickets or more. We know him."

"What does he do for a living," Fox asked.

"I don't know; we've been told by the feds to keep our hands off, as their team has him under surveillance."

Allowing Tabitha a chance to sip her coffee, I then asked, "Don't they share information with your department?"

"As I said, we were told *hands off*. Why? What's happening?"

"Two things for now, Corporal. We accompanied the feds to the Greenaway address just before noon today. A young girl, Maria, answered." We detailed the high points of our visit, noting Maria never allowed us entrance, identified the male as Papa, and 'Papa' avoided us by way of a rear sliding door.

"Long story short, Corporal. You probably heard about the buildings that were blown up last week in and around LA County. We had firefights in several communities that resulted in over thirty deaths, involving dirty federal officers and the Sinaloa Cartel."

"Vaguely, but we had our hands full with our own issues," the young officer informed us. She explained, "We had a local teen go missing last

Tuesday. Found her body Saturday -- dumped on a treed hillside -- raped and bludgeoned to death.

"In the middle of that tragedy, we had an unrelated three-hour car chase, complete with gunfire. Fifteen year-old kid. High on something and wielding a gun. Shot by one of our cops. A shame. Basically, both good kids. Everyone here in Montecito knew them. Just kids. We've never had anything like it before."

"Where was Trujillo?"

"Home. He led one of the search groups for the girl, both Friday and Saturday."

A real Poster Boy, I thought.

"Have a favor to ask. Fox and I will stay in Santa Barbara tonight. We are going to spend this evening on a Greenaway stake-out. We would appreciate it if you would join us. 6:oo p.m. It's dark enough I think. I'll spring for dinner at someplace nice here in town, then we'll go there directly."

"What do you hope to find?"

"A good reason to acquire a search warrant."

"I'm game, but what about the fed?"

"Another reason for the stake-out."

Chapter 33

We rented a Ramada room with two queen beds. Clerk told us where to find a car rental -- I wasn't about to do a stake out in a cherry-red Cadillac. Enterprise had six cars available: a couple of luxury cars, two midsize, a Nissan, and a Prius.

We chose the Prius and drove back to the Ramada, where we unloaded my tools from the Caddy to the Prius.

"Let's do some sightseeing, Fox. The motel clerk recommended the Santa Barbara Courthouse, just down the street. Architecturally magnificent, so he says."

"Sounds good -- that Moxi Interactive place sounds like fun as well."

"It sure does. From the brochure you picked up, looks like we could spend a full day there."

*****

We were not disappointed. We spent over an hour at the courthouse, walking the grounds, viewing the elaborate Moorish design. The building itself is three stories high, with a great hall on the second floor, often rented for weddings and other private affairs. Murals, floor to ceiling, covered its walls, depicting historical events in Santa Barbara and its surrounds.

From there we headed to The Moxi Interactive Museum, which turned out to be a favorite. Two hours of science experiments later, we returned to the Ramada, vowing another trip to the Moxi at some future date. What a fun place! But for now -- 4:52 p.m. -- it was time to prepare for the evening's big event: the stakeout at Trujillo's on Greenaway.

In the room, we freshened up; then motored up the hill to Montecito and Officer Norton's condo. She was waiting, dressed in a charcoal, tweed pantsuit, green backpack over her shoulder. She tossed the pack in ahead of her and hopped in.

"Different ride than earlier. Did you two use both vehicles to come up here?"

"Nope," Fox laughed, "Bossman, here, decided the Caddy might be too conspicuous, so we rented this one. Where to?"

"*Los Arroyos,* back down San Ysidro and hang a right on the Highway. Nice setting on the water. Always good food, always busy, and good prices -- and, I made reservations for three."

"Good thinking."

"Maybe not," she laughed, "we have only three minutes to get there. I'd better make a call. If you speed, I'll have to arrest you."

She called. "Lacey? Tabitha. Don't sell my table, we're on our way. Be there in five." She turned back to me, "Told you they were busy."

Chapter 34

"Tabitha! Haven't caught up with you since, I don't remember when. Where you been hiding? Who are your friends?"

"Two Sherlocks from LA up here following a case. I met up with them earlier today and they invited me to join them for dinner -- I suppose, so they could pick my brain," Miss Norton laughed.

"He can pick my brain anytime he wishes," Lacey giggled to Tabitha, flashing me a grin. "I gotta go." She left us to serve her next table. Moments later she was back, "Come to think of it, I may have overheard something that might be of interest."

"Like what?"

"Like a big, orange Ford van stopped at a carwash last Thursday, two men aboard. They spent almost an hour cleaning inside and out.

"Our busboy works part-time at the carwash. Wasn't working that station, but said pinkish water was flowing down the drains. He said it was blood; we just laughed at him."

"How coincidental," Fox rolled her eyes, "a girl's body was found in the hills recently, right?"

"That's a stretch isn't it, Fox," Tabitha frowned.

"Small town," I raised an eyebrow and cocked my head. "Is your busboy working tonight, Lacey?"

"No, he's either home or at the carwash. Gotta go, or I'll be fired," she winked.

"Fired, hell," Tabitha laughed, rolling her eyes at us, "she's fifty percent owner."

After a satisfying dinner, I announced, "Time for our stakeout. Potty break, anyone? Might be a long night. Oh, yeah, cell phones off."

*****

Number 41 Greenaway was quiet when we pulled up at the opposite curb. It was completely dark. Not even a porch light. Tabitha scanned the property with her night vision binoculars. "Nothing yet," she whispered.

"Police issue?" I asked indicating her binoculars.

"No, these are mine. Made by Vabsce. It's a combination, with a video camera. I do a lot of hiking and a bit of camping. They're great. Unfortunately, no audio. My next ones will have audio," she informed us.

"Camera have a red laser light?" I asked.

"Uh, sure does, why?"

"Make sure your next one can be used for spying. Costs a few more bucks, but worth it. Can't use it tonight. But, not to worry. Whatever I record, I'll share."

Tabitha chatted on for another perhaps ten minutes, mostly about her job, her uncle Haruto, and living on the Santa Barbara coast. Fox added a comment or two, while I only grunted in assent.

An hour dragged by. Twilight became blackness. Talk was reduced to occasional whispers, occasional whispers to silence.

Only the occasional vehicle drove past, brake lights at corner, left turn onto Geranium Drive; I frowned. All four or five had turned left. Processing that piece of information, I wondered if we were going to have any success in our "low-percentage gambit." Another thought -- *great legroom in the Prius.*

Just shifting in my seat, I spied a newer orange van pass us. It stopped at the corner, then turned left onto Geranium.

"Did you ladies notice that van?"

"I did," Tabitha piped up. "Orange -- several people inside."

"Every car that's come up this road takes a left at the corner, Bossman. I think we're staking out the wrong address."

"So do I," Tabitha said.

"Agreed. Change of plans!" I smiled. "Is everyone game to hang a left and follow those vehicles?"

"Sure," Tabitha said exuberantly. "There are only fifteen single family houses up there, no apartments. Should be quick."

"We find the van and other cars in a driveway -- what then, Bossman?"

"Take down license plates, take videos of any people we see, then boil down what we've discovered, if anything."

"I'll take care of identifying the vehicles through our DPPA system," the young officer volunteered.

"I trust you, Tabitha, but I'm growing more suspicious of everything that's coming out of the feds encamped in this area. I think we should send our findings to your cousin, Haruto."

"Your investigation, your decision. But let's first see if we have a case."

"Good idea," Liz agreed. I pulled away from the curb.

We traveled up Greenaway, then turned left onto Geranium, a much narrower road. Didn't have far to go -- only about six address numbers up the road.

Eight cars lined both sides of a long driveway. At the end was an elegant, white, two story with Grecian columns.

Two men were standing on the front balcony, engaged in heated conversation. A woman sat in a lounge chair, face hidden by a flowering Camelia in a large planter.

Walking up the front steps were three women and a gent. I drove slowly, Fox pressed her thumb on the video, capturing as much as she could.

We continued up the hill to the road's end. Fox passed my night-vision equipment to Tabitha. As we made the turn coming back down, we saw headlights of another vehicle coming up Geranium. I drove a little faster so I would be forced to pull over to allow the newcomer the road. I timed it perfectly, almost in front of the target driveway. And as hoped, the car turned into the driveway.

"Recognize anyone?" I asked Tabitha.

"No, but I was able to video both car and driver as they turned," she said, breathlessly.

We remained there for two minutes, capturing as much as we could of the scene, then continued down the hill to the Ramada.

* * * * *

"There must have been nine or ten cars there, and the same number of people outside. Yet, you recognized no one, Miss Norman." I shook my head as I unlocked our motel door. "I find that very head-scratching in such a small community.

"Call your uncle. We'll send everything to him for some DPPAs. Tell him to hurry because it's for Gumshoe; might give him a giggle."

Haruto received Tabitha's call warmly. After the

greeting, he told her, "I just downloaded your attachments, Tabitha. Haven't opened them yet. I have other problems to attend right here in Torrance, but I'll have answers for you sometime tomorrow morning.

"Tell Gumshoe our inspector friend, Morris, has been transferred to a therapy rehab, The Edgewater. Still no word on the wife. And tell Gumshoe, *don't push!*"

She hung up. "I'm really pumped," the young Corporal said, excitedly. "I can't wait to see what Uncle comes up with!"

With the promise to stick around Santa Barbara until noon the following day, I laughed, "Let's meet up and see how we should interpret our findings."

We drove her home, then it was back to the Ramada.

*****

Fox and I were enjoying a second cup of coffee at the beach Friday morning when Tabitha called. "Where are you?"

"Enjoying breakfast at Lucky's. You have news?"

"Don't leave! I'll be there in ten minutes!"

Chapter 35

"We were right!" Tabitha exclaimed as she approached our booth. Fox scooted over to give her room to sit. "Uncle Haruto gave me a detailed review of all the vehicles, and identities of six of the people in our videos. He has a few still to run through facial recognition equipment -- says he may have more for us later, but . . ." she stopped to catch her breath . . .

"Coffee, please," she smiled to a passing waitress. "Anyway, you two, we have uncovered a big deal, including the Sinaloa Cartel, and a dirty DEA agent!"

Two women at an adjacent table turned their heads and whispered something; I held my hand up, and patted toward the floor. "Keep your voice down, Tabitha," I cautioned, "little birds fly through open windows to sing to kings."

"Sorry," she whispered, nodding her head, "Book of Proverbs . . . but it's really exciting!"

"Let's go back to the motel," Fox suggested. "We can discuss everything . . ."

"Right!" I interrupted. "Like, what are we going to do with the information?"

"Yeah!" the young officer raised her voice again. "We need a plan!"

"Finish your coffee!" I laughed.

Chapter 36

She picked up on the first ring. "Durazo! Good meeting last night. Several faces I hadn't seen in months."

"Yes, and thank you for the cargo, my dear. I can use all you deliver, especially the newer ones. Too bad about the load you lost."

"Not just the load, unfortunately. We lost a valuable asset two weeks ago. She knew too much. As you're aware we must be careful; we had to elimi . . ."

"Yes, I heard. T told me last night."

"T told you? I keep telling him to zip his lip, unless it's need to know."

"No harm done. He was actually apologizing; promised to make up for it within the month."

"Not more locals, I hope."

"No worries. My border people are expecting a fresh supply by the weekend. Van should be halfway to Arizona by now."

"I like the way you think. Junk's on schedule. I checked this morning. If all goes well, should be coming through just about now."

"Thanks, T.A. Next time I hold a meeting, are you going to make it?"

"Santa Barbara? Probably. Los Angeles, probably not -- especially if Los Zetas is invited. Timeo might be a friend of yours, but not mine. Like I keep telling you, I can provide everything you need -- young stuff as well as junk. Why not drop him, *mi precioso* (my beautiful one)? We'll take good care of each other."

"No, Durazo, I need to spread my resources around. Supply chain -- you understand."

"Sure, I understand, but you'll live to regret it -- mark my words! Los Zetas are on the way out -- the Sinaloa will soon be the major supplier for all of the U.S."

"So you say, *mi precioso!*" she laughed. "On a more serious note, your crew certainly misjudged your adversary the other day. That private detective and his girl were here yesterday, snooping around. L led them on a wild goose chase, but that won't last long. I understand he's quite the sleuth."

"Si, we'll use more care next time. I thought fear would dissuade them, but Strom sent reinforcements. I lost thirty-nine, including three that bled out on the way back. It won't happen again.

"I must go. Talk again soon. *Adios por ahora, mi corazon.* (Goodbye for now, my sweetheart.)

When her call ended, she felt a momentary surge of panic. She closed her eyes and took in three deep breaths through her nostrils, filling her lungs, then releasing each one slowly. "Better," she smiled.

Chapter 37

"Here's a thumb drive of Uncle's DPPA results," the Corporal declared, handing it to Fox. First two columns show driver's license and owner of each one, with Uncle's typed notes in a third column.

"Notice four SUVs have California plates, but the vehicles don't match. Uncle says cops up here should watch for those plates and bust them.

"Notice, too, the orange van, according to Uncle, belongs to XTR-Management secretary, Michelle."

"And look at this, Bossman," Liz looked from the screen to me and back again, "Michelle's last name is Camacho. What's your guess -- wife or daughter?"

"Or sister," I smiled.

"And, we're not done!" Tabitha continued, excitedly. "Page two, Uncle identifies some of the people who attended last night's soiree. He made stills of some of the video clips. Take a look."

The first clip was of the three on the balcony: woman, as yet unidentified, the two men, Los Zetas leader, Timeo Banderas, and the Sinaloa Cartel west coast general, T.A. Durazo.

Haruto made a comment on the next still -- a face in the crowd heading inside: *"Gumshoe, I think you will agree, this is Jay. You have his snapshot on the board in your office."*

"Wow, Gumshoe, he is good!"

"Yes indeed, that is Jay!" I agreed.

"Here's another, and you won't believe this one," Tabitha announced. Standing at the door, looking back and pointing was none other than LaRusso! And, as Haruto observed correctly, the next clip shows the finger was pointing to Trujillo, who was responding in kind!

The thumb drive had three more stills: DEA agent Valmore; Michelle, the XTR-Management gal; and [as they say] last but not least, none other than Ira Sidney, the crooked Internal Affairs employee, a.k.a. Victor Collins.

"Well, one thing is for sure," Fox said, "Michelle is not the woman on that balcony -- wrong clothes, wrong hair."

"And, whoever she is," Tabitha agreed, "she's up there alone with the cartel big shots."

"Which makes the lady up there high up in the chain of command," I concluded. "Too bad her face is turned away from the camera. But, you definitely have enough for an arrest of a dirty DEA officer, Tabitha."

"I sure do. I need to run this flash drive by my chief. We'll do it on the Q.T."

"Do you trust your chief, Tabitha?" I asked.

"Certainly!" then she hesitated, "I think so." She looked at us, "I don't know who to trust anymore."

After a moment I said, "I think we can trust Strom."

Pulling my cell phone out, I looked at her. "With your permission?"

"Of course."

* * * * *

Fifteen minutes later we were in Strom's office.

"That slimy bastard!" Strom stood and walked the floor, shouting. "You were right, Gumshoe! You tagged him! How could we have missed him as the piece of crap that he is?"

"So, who do we see about an arrest warrant for a dirty fed?" Tabitha asked.

"Leave it to me," Strom assured her. He turned to me, "Does Valmore know we're on to him?"

"Not sure, sir, but probably. I really don't know how he couldn't."

"Got the picture, Alan. We have some dirty agents. I know Federal Judge Halder. The corporal, here, and I will bring them to justice. You two can head back to LA. We'll have a search warrant for that Geranium house before day's end. My bet is we'll have a successful search." Strom turned to Tabitha, "Won't we, corporal?"

Haruto's cousin looked up at me, smiling. "We absolutely will, thanks to Gumshoe and Fox."

We shook hands, hugged Tabitha, told her to keep in touch. Back to Manhattan Beach.

* * * * *

A few faxes and phone messages were waiting for us when we returned to the office. One call needed my attention:

"Mr. Garrett, I have the figures for the repairs to my house. You said I should let you know, so I'm letting you know. This is Raymond Barnes."

"Fox, bring our check book. We're heading to Lennox."

Chapter 38

The next morning we received a call from Haruto. Fox picked up and put the phone on speaker.

"You two made quite an impression on my cousin. All she talked about was Alan this or Liz that! She did, however, give me a message to forward to you."

"Why didn't she call us, I wonder," Fox frowned.

"She said she did, but you didn't pick up. I was next on her list," Haruto laughed. "Anyway, she tells me, she and a team of feds raided that Montecito house last night. There was a shootout with four casualties. But, and get this!" Haruto said, almost excitedly. "A huge haul was recovered! In one room alone was a stash of almost two hundred fifty hand guns! In a room dow . . ."

"Two hundred fifty hand guns?" Fox burst out, unable to contain herself.

"In a room downstairs," Haruto cleared his throat and repeated, "were bags upon bags of a popular brand of kibbles -- you know -- dry dog food. Tabitha says they brought in a sniffer dog. The dog kept going downstairs. Agents opened four of the bags. Each fifty pound bag had a liner of kibble, but inside was a heavy plastic bladder -- filled with pure, uncut cocaine."

"How many?" Fox came alive with curiosity.

"You sitting down?"

"Tell us!" Fox practically shouted.

"Four hundred!"

Now I was interested. "Haruto! That's a haul! Figure 25% kibble, that leaves 75% cocaine! More than 35 pounds in each bag!"

"I already did the math, Mr. Gumshoe. Figures are as follows. I figured 20% kibble, so a little different, but about eight tons of cocaine."

"That must be a record!" Fox said excitedly.

"No, sorry," I informed her. "Bigger haul was in 2005 on a freighter . . . about thirteen tons of cocaine, along with tons of other substances. But this is still huge."

"How is it that you know all this, Gumshoe?"

"I was in on that bust. I'm sure there have been bigger, but your cousin is making history today -- very exciting!"

"You said there were four casualties -- may I as . . ."

"Yes, you may ask. DEA chief LaRusso, and an agent named Torres; cartel members, Sanchez and Barrios -- and before you ask, Tabitha has no idea how."

By this time, Fox's jaw was resting on her navel. "What! How can that be, Bossman?"

"Maybe Tabitha will let you know, Fox. My best guesses are -- in no particular order -- A. less paperwork, B. so family wouldn't lose pension, C. so DEA saves face, D. couldn't reach a judge, and E. to clean up your own messes. Personally, I like the last one, but they would all qualify."

"That's murder, Bossman! I'd rather think they went in with guns drawn and were shot by the Sinaloa!"

"Do you really believe that, Fox?" Haruto's voice had a tinge of sarcasm.

"Not really, but I had to make the case for the right side of the law."

"Trust me, Fox, Haruto and I have seen it up close and personal. There is the right side of a situation and the wrong side of a situation. A few days ago LaRusso sent thugs to kill you and me. Had that happened, he would only have smirked and raised a glass in celebration.

"Last night justice was served! Faster than some would like, but I celebrate, because LaRusso was on the wrong side of right, and is no longer in the picture."

* * * * *

"So, Bossman, what are your plans for today?"

"I was going to track down Morris for a visit. I think we need a break from the excitement of the past few days. But first I should pick up Pop to take a look at *Pop's Place*. We haven't seen it since Walt and his crew made the repairs. You want to come?"

"No, I have two skips to track down, and there are faxes we haven't yet answered. I'm content to stay here. You run along, come back soon, but not without lunch."

"Tacos?"

"Tacos will work. We have some Bohemia. I'll put a few in the fridge."

* * * * *

Pop's Place certainly looked different. New everything from front door to the laundry room, and especially the kitchen: cabinetry, appliances, tile floor, and lighting. All new. I smiled. Pop said he always wanted to upgrade the kitchen . . .

He and Rita came down to the shop with me for lunch. On the way we picked up a dozen tacos, along with some rice and beans from El Sombrero #1, close to the pier. Tasty!

During lunch, Fox said, "Your friend, Katie, left a message for you, Bossman. She says thanks. The boy and his family dropped all charges." Everyone around the desk looked at me expecting an explanation.

"Lady I met at Kaiser." I explained the short visit and the situation with Katie and her husband, ending with the reason for the phone message. "I made a phone call which helped her husband avoid jail. He's probably going to lose his driver's license, but small price to pay. He suffered a massive heart attack, but he's still with us."

Liz shook her head. "Is this going to result in another $17,830.00 'so-called' police payout for assistance, similar to your friend, Old Man Barnes?"

"You worried about a paycheck, Fox?"

The rest of that exchange had to wait -- the phone rang -- Inspector Morris.

Chapter 39

Morris and Pop must have been cut from the same cloth, as evidenced by hospital and rehab stays. The inspector was ready to take up his pursuit of Victor Collins. He had informed Swazer that Collins was one of two shooters in the woundings of him and his wife, and the killing of Tipton on the graveled road. So, when my cell rang I could tell he was less than calm.

"Garrett! Come pick me up! I need to get back to work!"

"Hi, Inspector, good to hear your voice. How are you feeling?"

"Sore as hell, but not enough to slow me down much."

"You're kidding yourself, Carl! You have a broken left arm and two bullet holes in your head. You're better off staying there for a week or so, bring your body up to match your mind," I said, shrugging my shoulders to those sitting around me, listening to Morris.

"I don't even know what that means, Gumshoe. I just know I can't lay in this bed any longer. Nobody tells me anything, I don't know how Lucy is doing. Word around here is that no visitors are allowed at all. What's that all about, Garrett? Damn! This place is like living in an alien country."

"Last I heard, Lucy is in a medically induced coma. We're all praying for her, but to tell it straight, sir, she's in very tough shape."

"I need to see my wife, Alan. Come pick me up, please."

"I'll pick you up, Carl, but you'll never get in the hospital's front door. Closest you'll get is *Pop's Place*. You can have my bedroom, I'll take my old bedroom upstairs."

"Just pick me up. We'll talk!"

"I'll bring Pop."

* * * * *

The Edgewater Rehab wouldn't allow our entrance, but Morris put up such a fuss that they finally caved to his demands for release. We met him at the front steps. Aside from his arm in a sling and walking slightly bent from the broken ribs, he looked like the angry man that he was.

"What the hell is this covid everyone is so stressed about, Alan? Calling it a pandemic! Huh! We have a pandemic of drugs, guns, and illegals running across the border. Can you take me to see Lucy, please?"

"Sure! But you won't be able to get in," I said, shaking my head. "Best we can do is ask Zuzu to check on her condition."

We had barely pulled away from the curb when my cell rang again. It was Swazer. *Huh! How did he know I was picking up his boss?*

"I called the office before I called your cell, Mr. Garrett. I have some information. Let me say hi to the inspector, first."

* * * * *

"You're sure that's what he said?"

"Positive! Soon as I shoved him in a cell he teared up. I suppose he realized the seriousness of his predicament. The older one, Angel, just kept spitting at Deputy Yardley, but the younger one, Luis, melted when I asked where they got their guns."

"Yeah? What'd the punk say?"

"Says from the trunk of a car. Says I should have seen the trunk; says it was half-full of guns."

"Where was this," I asked.

"Near the Home Depot on Aviation Boulevard. He says the homeless have set up an encampment there -- tents and such."

"Been doing that for over a year all over Southern California," Morris chimed in, "but the guns are new. Thanks for the call, Brad."

"Wait! What am I supposed to do? Send a squad to go from tent to tent?"

"We're on our way to Cedars-Sinai," I chimed in. "Come to my office tonight. 7 p.m. Bring Haruto. We'll talk. This is a really important piece of information in the gun angle to our investigation."

"Waste of time to go to Cedars-Sinai, Inspector," Swazer tried to convince Morris. "Better to call that Zuzu nurse. She'll give you an update on the wife."

"I'm going, dammit!" He turned to Pop and me, "You'll take me, won't you?"

Chapter 40

Swazer was right, of course. Morris and I mounted only the second step heading toward the front entrance of Cedars before a security officer met us with the announcement I knew was forthcoming. Morris was drained, emotionally as well as physically. The security fellow and I assisted him back to my Cadillac. We sat in the police parking space; I called Zuzu.

"Sorry, Mr. Garrett. There has been no change. She is still in a coma."

"Gimme that phone!" Morris demanded. "Miss! Lucy Morris is my wife. I need to see her! She means everything to me. Don't you understand?"

"Yes, I do. But the rule is, no one gets in!"

"Who made up such an insane rule?" Neither she nor I had an answer.

"C'mon Morris, you're worn out. Let's head back to my place. You can stay as long as you need, build up your strength until you feel comfortable driving and manning the Hermosa precinct."

Chapter 41

We caught a break! Finally! Hopefully, our teenage brat, Luis, would continue to provide more answers regarding the free guns.

First things first. Morris called Cedars-Sinai once more. He spoke with Zuzu, only to find that Lucy's condition hadn't changed in the last hour -- no great surprise to anyone except Morris. A duty nurse promised to let him know the minute there was any change.

Carl settled into my bedroom; he knew his way around *Pop's Place*, having been there many times in the past, but he was impressed by the upgrades.

"Run along, Alan. Just keep me informed."

* * * * *

Swazer was inclined to send a squad of several officers from each of the local precincts to seize any and all handguns that may have been doled out to the various homeless encampments. Haruto thought Strom and the ATF should be involved. Fox and I agreed.

"Are the boys still in lock-up?" I asked Swazer.

"Luis's parents came and picked him up. Angel's parents told me to keep him. They say he's no longer a part of their family. I kinda feel sad for him, but I'll make a decision tomorrow, probably send him over to *Juvie* for detention. No sheet on him in the system.

"And I was notified today by Kaiser that I need to send someone to pick up that Terrence kid -- the one with the out-of-joint arm. They want him out of there by 10 a.m. tomorrow morning. His parents don't want him either."

"Sounds like really good parenting," Bradley said, sarcastically. "You wonder what kind of role models the dad and mom are."

"All three were living on the streets, right?" Liz asked. Bradley nodded.

"Fulfillment of Isaiah, first couple of chapters, Fox."

"Refresh my memory, Bossman, a little foggy."

"Says something to the effect that kids will disdain all authority, like that Angel kid; they just look daggers at you. Either shoot you, blindside you as you're walking down the street, knife you, or spit in your face. We're raising a generation of little thugs."

"Thankfully, not all of them," Swazer smiled.

"Enough to be concerned, especially as a father of four," Haruto growled. "All mine are under ten. I know the value of keeping a careful eye on them."

Haruto called Strom, asking for an ATF crew to join us, going from tent to tent, retrieving errant guns. Of course, he agreed. A second Martell bottle was opened.

"Big day tomorrow," I said, lifting a glass. "Begins with interviewing those two delinquents."

Chapter 42

Fox and I, using copies of pages from an old Thomas map book, spent the evening marking out pockets of homeless encampments and stretches of sidewalk tent cities. By 8:30 p.m. we had listed more than forty areas to cover. Then she dropped me off at *Pop's Place* and drove home. I checked on Morris, had a quick shower, then tiptoed upstairs.

* * * * *

At 9 a.m. the following morning, while Swazer and I headed for Kaiser, ATF Chief Strom's crew of twenty officers arrived at my office. They split into teams of two each. Liz doled out the maps, after which nine teams disappeared. The tenth team stayed behind to make a journal of finds and direct reassignments as needed. My office became the headquarters for the day.

Haruto and a crew of officers joined with the San Diego police chief who had procured search warrants for the XTR-Management main office as well as the complex in Alpine. They, too, would share their findings with the ATF "HQ" in Manhattan Beach. It would prove to be a busy day.

* * * * *

Kaiser security staff members were waiting with

Terrence Crawford in the lobby as Swazer and I rolled up. They wheeled him out the door, demanded that we wear the masks they provided before we put the lad in the back of the squad car. We complied.

Terrence remained sullen but compliant the entire trip to the Hermosa Precinct. At one point, however, he did mumble an apology for having evil intentions while stalking my Cadillac. *Maybe the beginning of a conversation?* I was hopeful.

"What happened to Luis and Angel?" he asked as we pulled into the police parking lot.

"Luis went home to his parents, under a 10 p.m. curfew -- which, we're told, will be strictly enforced. Angel is still with us. You'll see him in a few minutes. But you will both be leaving us tomorrow for separate facilities.

"Angel is slated to go to a youth camp in central California; you to a juvenile detention center in Chino until you're eighteen, which is next month, right?"

"Uh, yes, sir. March 1."

"Work with us, son," I said. "We'll send the cartel and the criminal element running. Perhaps a name or two. It will go on your sheet in the plus column."

"I don't know nothing, man."

"You'd be surprised, young man," Brad smiled. "Questions sometimes trigger a memory or thought. We just never know what's in that brain until it's tapped." Brad took the cuffs off the youth and set him down in the interview room. We sat across the table. Swazer started with the questions.

"Who gave you the guns?"

"Some older dudes."

"Two men?"

"Four of them; one was a skirt."

"Any names?"

"I think so, but I don't remember. Angel might."

"Did they speak Spanish?"

"No, only English -- oh, one said amigo."

"Were they old or young?"

"I don't know, forty I guess. About my dad's age."

"What kind of a car?"

"Small, gray, 4-door, started with H. Maybe a Honda."

I took over the questioning. "Terrence, what were you supposed to do with the guns?"

"Protect ourselves, shoot anybody we didn't like."

"Anybody?"

"Yeah, anybody."

"Did they give you ammunition with the guns?"

"Yeah. Shells were in a shoe box. You could only grab one handful each."

"Have you shot anybody?"

"No."

"Would you?"

"Yeah, I guess, if I was mad enough."

"Do you realize you would go to jail for a long time if you had?"

"Yeah, but I thought I'd break out real quick."

"Maybe Angel and Luis, but not you, Terrence. You would go to a regular prison, like San Quentin."

"You're kidding, right?"

"Not kidding, Terrence. Serious stuff."

"Is Angel here? Can I talk to him?"

"As I said, Angel is heading to a mid-state youth camp. Could be picked up any time. But, sure!" I assured him. "Sergeant Swazer, Would you bring Angel in, please?" Bradley punched a number and asked the jail deputy to bring the kid up from the cells.

Angel arrived moments later, hands cuffed behind his back, and a tight-fitting mask over nose and mouth. He scanned the room, then settled on Terrence, staring at him, but saying nothing.

"How come he's not talking?" Terrence asked me. "Something the matter with him?"

"He stays that way until he stops cursing and spitting." I shrugged, "When and if he decides to be more mature I'll remove the mask and the gag, and even uncuff him. But until that happens . . ."

"I told them as much as I can remember, Angel," Terrence broke in, "you know, in the Home Depot parking lot." He repeated the answers he had given to the questions from Brad and me, and each time he received affirmation from Angel.

"You more mature today, Angel?"

Angel nodded his head.

Brad pulled the mask off Angel's face, and after asking once again, removed the gag from his mouth - - a meek, very different Angel. Cuffs came off next. "Sorry I was such a jerk," Angel began, "I've never been in a jail before. Kinda scary. Terrence is pretty much right, just a few corrections and additions. They spoke English. The dudes were average height, the skirt was almost as tall. They used code names. One of the dudes was *Tattoo*. He said the *Suit* would be happy with their work. The skirt laughed and said *the Suit* was an A-hole."

"Did the skirt have a code name, Angel?"

"No. Oh, they called her Lady a couple of times, like, '*Okay, Lady that does it for this place. Let's move on*', but I guess that was because she was a skirt. Oh, and the car . . ."

"Oh, yeah!" Terrence interrupted excitedly, "I just thought of something. The skirt gave Tattoo a paper and then she disappeared."

"What do you mean, she disappeared?" Swazer asked.

"She left in her car, a black one."

"Right," Angel agreed, "we never saw her again, did we? Anyway," he continued, "her car was a black Honda Accord. It had one of those temporary paper plates, so it was brand new. I think the first three numbers were B36."

"That's really helpful, fellas, and I mean that. Thank you!" Bradley said and I agreed.

"What's going to happen to me?" Angel's eyes searched Swazer's face for some sympathy.

"I was going to send you up to a youth detention camp," Swazer shook his head and ran his fingers through his blond hair, "would your parents take you back if I put in a good word?"

"I think I burned that bridge. They're going through a divorce, mostly because of me. My dad walked out the same night I got that gun. I was thinking of taking it home and shooting him, but . . ."

"And now?"

"I want to think about my future; take life and my studies more seriously -- in short, grow up."

"Can you do that without direction?"

"I think so, sir, I'll try if the police will let me."

"Here's what I think," I cut in, "perhaps Sergeant Swazer will see it differently, but I think six months in a camp will teach you more than a public school would."

"Like what, sir?"

"Tough love. Keeping your bed made, policing your personal area, perhaps being part of a team -- clearing brush for fire prevention, policing public areas, or along highways -- those kinds of things. It will give you a sense of pride and satisfaction you won't get in a public school."

"Actually, I do agree," Bradley piped up. "One other benefit is a less opportunistic environment for screwing up. Six months will go by so fast you'll wonder where the time went. You'll mature, son, be a "big brother" influence and example for friends like Luis and others."

"You really think so?" Angel asked.

"I know so!" Brad told him, enthusiastically.

"When will I go?"

"Right after lunch."

* * * * *

The sergeant put out a BOLO for a new Honda Accord, black, paper plates starting with B36 -- the DPPA showed four vehicles with paper plates starting with B36. All were sold in Inglewood. None were Hondas.

Chapter 43

Heading back toward Manhattan Beach, I left Swazer with the executive decision regarding Angel's next few months.

Fox decided to call, just as I was turning into heavier than usual traffic, so I let it go to 'messages'. I couldn't quite understand the gist of the call, but she sounded excited about something. *She always did have an overactive imagination*, I laughed to myself as I changed lanes from the fast one back to the right shoulder so I could listen to the message. It was only a ten minute drive, but what the heck.

'Gumshoe! Come home quick! Fire!' Her message was terse and sounded fearful. I called back.

"I'm on my way, what's going on?"

"A Molotov cocktail was just thrown against the door, and another over the fence at my Kia. We put out the fires, no damage, but scary! It just happened, Bossman -- only seconds ago."

"Did you catch the culprits?"

"No. We saw the car drive away -- it was a silver sedan. Oh! And Bossman?"

"Yes?"

"Eighty-nine guns have been picked up at last count, and they've covered just a little more than half the target spots!"

"And it's only noon, Fox! That's exciting isn't it? I'll be there in just a few minutes. We'll have lunch at *The Shellback*."

"Already done, Bossman, just get yourself here. Lunch should pull up in fifteen minutes, that should give you just enough time to wash your hands."

I pulled back into the Valley Drive traffic headed toward Manhattan Beach. Then, as I hung a left onto Manhattan Beach Boulevard, I spotted a silver Honda sedan roaring up the hill. As we passed, we were so close we recognized each other -- I was staring at Ira Sidney! I wasn't sure of the passenger, but I thought I remembered him from my corkboard: Jay Rudolph.

A check in the rear view -- lights and normal rear plate -- 8HTL655; next I heard the squeal of brakes -- definitely the hostiles. They weren't finished with their day's violence.

I hung a quick right on Morningside Lane and a left on Center. Halfway down the block I flipped a U-Turn, and reached for my SRM-1216. Then I waited . . . and waited . . . and waited. When it was apparent I had lost them, I reversed the Caddy once more and proceeded down Center toward the shop.

The sting of broken bits of tempered glass hit my cheek before I heard the report of the bullet going through the left and right rear passenger glass. A little slower and I'd not have lived to -- as they say -- tell the tale.

Could I make it to the office before I faced the bad guys again? I doubted it. I floored it down Center, stopped mid-block once again, grabbed the SRM-1216, and hopped out. I leaned against the hood and swept eyes up and down Center. I called Fox.

"Sorry, but I'll be a bit late. That silver Honda

and I are playing cat and mouse. Don't eat my burger."

"Where are you, Bossman? I'll send the ATF fellows."

"I'm at . . .Oh! Forget it! They're here!"

The Honda was coming up Center at a snail's pace. They had raced down Manhattan Beach Boulevard as far as Highland, turned right and back up Center. They had seen my Cadillac and stopped for a time. Now it was crawling up the hill once again.

When it came within range of the 1216, I stood and fired one blast, aiming for the front tires with the .oo buckshot. I had loaded it with a 2-3/4" load -- nine brass balls -- powerful and deadly.

I yelled, "Throw your guns out and surrender yourselves, Ira!" The response was semi-automatic gunfire. The sedan sped up and kept coming. I moved to the rear quarter-panel, and then to the trunk where I had a clear vantage point.

Holding nothing back, I sent eight quick shells through the windshield. The Honda lurched forward, then rammed a two-yard trash dumpster and jolted to a stop. By this time, gawkers were spilling from commercial and multi-residential buildings to view the short, but deadly skirmish.

The Honda's passenger door fell open, an AR-15 was tossed to the sidewalk, and a bloody Jay Rudolph emerged, hands in the air. His face and clothing, saturated, crimson. He, himself, was crying -- asking for mercy.

"On the ground, Jay!" I called out a second time, holding my weapon at the ready as I approached. I looked inside the cab of the Honda. There wasn't much left of Ira Sidney. I popped the trunk and whistled!

For a second time, I called Fox. "I'm coming home, Liz. One prisoner. Please send one of the ATF guys over here to gather up guns and ammo. Call the coroner as well, and a tow truck to remove the Honda. Might as well call Amy Wynne. The whole town saw the gunfight; they'll want to see it in print, with pictures."

I walked around my Caddy, shaking my head. It was going to need some body work and touch-up paint for sure, but it was mechanically sound. I shrugged, *Back to Tony's Garage.*

Chapter 44

"That's what I'm telling you, Bradley, I crossed paths with the silver Honda between here and your office. They chased me, there was a gunfight, Ira Sidney -- or Victor Collins, whatever his name, is dead. Jay Rudolph is in custody here -- I'll bring him over, or you send a unit over and pick him up."

"No, I'll swing by, Mr. Garrett. We can interview him together. Have you given the inspector the news about Collins yet?"

"No. I'll run home, pick him up and bring him to the office. He's just up the hill."

"Good. I'll see you in a few minutes. Both teens are gone, by the way. Angel is headed for a facility in Pine Grove, way up in the boonies, and the county picked up Terrence ten minutes ago -- tried to negotiate a youth camp stint for himself, but it failed."

Next, I called the inspector. "You did what?" he exploded with enthusiasm. "That's great news! You're sure it's Collins, Alan?"

"Positive. I'm coming to pick you up if you're well enough."

"Of course I'm well enough. Come get me!"

* * * * *

Swazer wasn't yet there as Morris and I entered the office, but Amy was.

"I took a dozen pics, Alan; not much left of the fellow in the driver's seat. You sure it was this Ira Sidney?"

"Oh, yeah. We passed each other on the boulevard. Got a good look at each other. They came after me, not the other way around, by the way."

"I'm not writing the story, Alan; only the pics!"

"Sorry, Amy. Guess I was a bit abrupt."

"May I see those photos?" Morris asked.

"Sure."

Morris shook his head. "Damn! son, you'll need DNA to verify the identity. I mean, I believe you, but you could have left a little more of him in one piece. I want to make sure that little weasel is gone for good."

Swazer joined us. Liz tossed him a *Bohemia*. He glanced at the photos, shook his head and turned to Morris. "Hi, Boss. How are you feeling?" Without waiting for an answer, he continued, "Have you heard the latest on Lucy?"

"I'd feel much better, Brad, but they won't even let me go in to see her!"

Morris spied Jay, sitting glumly in a chair, hands cuffed behind his back. "Who's that?" he asked.

"Jay Rudolph," I answered. "Blows up houses, provides guns to teens and the homeless, trying to incite chaos. We have some questions for him, but thought you might have a few as well, so we waited."

"Good! By the way, how is my precinct, Sergeant? You taking care of things?"

"A little exciting, but nothing compared to what you went through, sir. And the precinct is still in good order."

"So, tell me what happened. I can see by your faces something huge happened," Morris said, going from one face to the other.

"Not so, Morris," I said, "we simply made an inroad. Maybe Jay will be of some help."

"Then let's grill him -- see what he knows. Get it on record."

"I demand an attorney!" Jay screamed from across the room.

"Yeah, yeah, yeah," Morris mumbled, "I'll get you an attorney. Brad, call the district attorney's office. Get him a deputy defense attorney from their pool. Have him or her meet us in Hermosa at," he looked at his watch, "three o'clock okay, Alan?" I nodded. "Tell them 3 p.m."

"No!" Jay yelled. "I want a phone! I'll choose my own lawyer!"

"Fine, Kid. You have money for a retainer?" I asked.

"Huh! Don't you worry about that."

Switching Jay's cuffs to the front, I set him at the desk, and pushed the phone close to him. He fumbled with it and dialed a number.

"You have a lawyer?" I was surprised.

Liz piped up, "Push the green button so he can get an outside line."

"Oh, yeah, I forgot. Hardly use it," I said.

"I want some privacy," Jay growled.

"No privacy, Jay," I countered. "Just tell whoever you're calling that you need your attorney to join us at Hermosa Police station at 3 p.m. At that point your attorney/client conversations are privileged. Now make your call." I turned to Swazer. "Take him to Hermosa, lock him up; we'll be there by 2:45."

Chapter 45

We chatted with Amy for half an hour, then she drove off on another assignment across town -- more specifically, Morningside. A shooting.

Once she was gone, Morris shook his head; "Okay spill it. What was that green button bit? You've never used a green button to get an outside line. Did you tape him, Alan?"

"Nope," I smiled, "Fox did. She reminded me about the connection."

"Right! Blame me," Fox frowned. "It's come in handy a time or two, Inspector."

"But you understand," I added emphatically, "you're not to know. That would be against the law, you being a cop and all."

We listened to the recording:

Jay - "Let me speak with Lady."

Male - "She ain't here. Message?"

Jay - "I need a lawyer. Hermosa Cop Shop - 3 p.m."

Male - "Got it. Anything else?"

Jay - "Tattoo's dead."

Silence on the other end for 30 seconds. Then the voices continued:

Male -- roughly - "Get ahead of it. Otherwise, you know what to do." Call ended; disconnected on the other end.

We all looked quizzically at each other. "Wonder what that means?" Morris finally asked.

"Not sure, but reminds me of something 'Green Hair' said just before she offed herself. Think I'll call Swazer. Make sure the kid has nothing hidden in his pockets."

* * * * *

We arrived at the Hermosa Precinct just before Jay's defense attorney. Morris spent a few minutes greeting everyone, and receiving hugs and huzzahs for his quick recovery. Then he ushered us into the precinct conference room.

Assistant district attorney James Silva was already sitting at the table, briefcase on the floor beside him, yellow writing pad in front of him. He looked up and smiled as we were being seated.

Moments later Jay's young lady attorney walked through the front door. She was wearing midnight blue from head to heels -- business suit and gloves. The necklace and earrings were of Lapis Lazuli. The outfit set off her long blonde tresses beautifully.

"Sorry I'm late; short notice," she shrugged apologetically. "My name is Laura Billings."

"You're not late, Miss Billings," Sergeant Swazer assured her. He introduced her to everyone sitting around the table. She exchanged business cards with Silva, Swazer, and Morris.

"Perhaps you can bring me up to speed on reasons you've detained him. Of course, I'll speak privately with him," she smiled, "but I don't know the history of the young man."

"Jay Rudolph," I spoke up, "is a demolitions expert. He was instrumental in blowing up two stash-houses, one in Lennox and one in Beverly Hills." I laid out photos Liz had taken at both locations, clearly showing Jay's presence, then the "after" photos of the remains of the buildings.

Swazer took over. "He's part of an operation that provides guns to teens and the homeless, trying to incite chaos.

"Just today, he and one Ira Sidney tried to gun down hired investigator, Alan Garrett."

"That would be me," I raised my mug of coffee.

"A firefight ensued," Swazer continued, "Sidney was shot and killed, Jay was apprehended. Here are photos of the car after it was stopped." Swazer set several graphic photos in front of the young attorney, three of what was left of Sidney, two of the trunk full of guns, and two of my Cadillac with the side strafed and windows shot out.

"What am I looking at?" Miss Billings asked.

"These are pictures," Attorney Silva explained, "of the aftermath of that gun battle."

Swazer took over once again. "I just got off the phone with ATF Chief Strom. His agents have been making a sweep of tent cities and sidewalk homeless encampments in the Hawthorne area, confiscating unlicensed weapons.

"As of fifteen minutes ago, they have amassed 158 guns -- most distributed by your client from the trunk of that silver sedan you see in the photos in front of you, verified by the recipients in taped on-scene debriefings."

"So you say, gentlemen. Looks like you, Mr. Garrett, destroyed half of the other side's argument."

"Ridiculous! They were warned repeatedly," I scowled, "Sidney just kept coming; I shot him with my semi-automatic. Jay rolled out of the passenger door crying like a baby, tossed his gun out, and begged for mercy.

"Scores of guns were in the trunk. I cuffed Jay, called Amy, a police photographer, to work the scene. I waited until she arrived, then Jay and I returned to my office."

Morris broke in, "We're holding him on charges of attempted murder, arson, possession and distribution of stolen guns, and possibly more as more comes to light. The photos are yours to keep, by the way."

"Oh! And one other thing," assistant district attorney Silva cut in, "one of Strom's agents was shot by a 'crazy' who was given one of those guns. Your client had better pray he pulls through. Otherwise, Jay will have *accessory to a homicide* added to his crimes."

"I'll see my client now," Miss Billings smiled, "and thank you for the background."

*****

Miss Billings returned from the jail area twenty minutes later. "Thanks," she smiled, tapping her attaché case, "I'll be back in a day or two." She walked out.

"Nice girl," Swazer said.

"Can't be more than twenty-three, twenty-four," I surmised. "Pretty though."

Morris spoke up, "Yeah, while you two are pulling your tongues off the floor, Silva and I are going to interview this young hooligan for ourselves."

Chapter 46

"Swazer!" Morris shouted from the doorway leading to the jail cells, "Get that girl back here! Now!"

I was already halfway out the door looking for the blond by the time Swazer jumped to his feet.

"What's the problem, Inspector?"

"Our Mr. Rudolph is dead, Sergeant! That's the problem."

Not quite hearing his words, I guessed the worst, as I hustled back in. "She's gone, Morris. I ran to the parking lot -- no movement at all. She kill him?"

"Don't know yet. Sending him down to our forensics team. We should have the cause by tomorrow. Call her number, Swazer."

"Don't bother, I just did," Silva informed us. "Area code is 916. It's in northern California. Number is a funeral parlor in Willow Creek. They've been in business fourteen years and have never heard of Laura Billings.

"A well-dressed hit-lady, gentlemen. Gloves should have given us a clue."

"Damn!" Morris shouted. "Brazen little Bimbo! Right in front of us all!"

"Oh! No Bimbo, sir," I shook my head, "brilliant! She was stone-cold brilliant!"

Assistant D.A. Silva smiled, "I suppose we all have a bit of egg on our faces, gentlemen; one of us should have been more alert to the area code."

I said nothing. She hadn't given a card to me -- at least that will be my story and excuse to Fox.

Silva said his goodbyes with, "Hopefully, you'll catch her license plate on video camera -- better luck next time." He walked out the door, smiling and shaking his head.

Chapter 47

Morris waited for him to leave, then he turned to me. "We still have the phone call from Jay to his contact, so perhaps all is not lost, Alan."

"Perhaps," I agreed. I called Fox. "Things okay there?"

"Yeah; what's up, Bossman?"

"Any calls come through on the land line?"

"No. It's been quiet."

"Trace that call Jay made. I'm sure it was a cell phone. See if we can get a fix on it. I'll be back shortly."

"Did Jay break? Did you get some good info?"

"I'll be back shortly, Fox. We'll talk then. Just get that trace going."

* * * * *

Back in Manhattan Beach. Fox met me at the side entrance, all excited. "Gumshoe! The call was made to a cell phone somewhere in downtown Los Angeles. With the help of a couple of apps and our guests, I was able to triangulate it to a five block area -- Broadway to San Pedro and Hwy 101 to W. 3rd Street."

After greeting the two ATF fellows, I turned back to Fox. She had prepared for my return by drawing a circle on the white board, and sketching locations of the four perimeters. She turned to me brightly and pointed with a pencil, "Somewhere in that area."

"Great!" I laughed. "The very heart of the city. At least a million people live or work in that neighborhood every day."

"Sorry," Fox said, obviously miffed at my reaction to her findings. "It's the best I could do, Bossman."

"No, no, Fox. You did great. Just making a comment. We'll find him. We'll find her, too. Now, what's inside that circle, Fox?"

"There's Koreatown, Starbucks, City Hall, Police Department, Little Tokyo, among others.

"But you haven't told me. Were you able to pull good information out of Jay? What did he tell you?"

"Jay's dead, Fox."

"What? How?" Fox was incredulous. "No one was watching him?"

One of the two ATF fellows looked up from tallying the confiscated guns. "That doesn't sound good," he whispered to his buddy, who nodded. They both stopped what they were doing and listened.

"Either suicide or assassination," I continued. "Not yet determined. We'll know by tomorrow. Didn't get an opportunity to question him. It happened while his attorney was with him."

"What did the attorney say afterwards?"

"Goodbye," I grimaced. "Then she walked out and disappeared." I explained the visit in detail -- Miss Billings' attire, especially the gloves, and her refusal of coffee. "We have a phony business card, and no DNA. The boys are scouring video cameras in the vicinity of the precinct for a license plate; we might get lucky."

As Fox was trying to absorb my story, the desk

phone rang. She was still staring at me with *'squinty'* eyes and open mouth -- but managed to answer. "Gumshoe and Fox Agency."

"Fox, Haruto here. Is Gumshoe around?"

"Yes. But I'm here, too. What's up?"

"I understand Gumshoe fatally shot Ira Sidney and took Jay Rudolph into custody. I need to . . ."

"Jay is dead, Haruto. Probably by a 'hit-lady' to keep him from talking."

"Where did she come from?"

"Jay's attorney. Fellas are still working on it. Why? What's going on, Haruto?"

"I just got word that Jay is the son-in-law of T.A. Durazo. He has family on the water just below Ensenada in Baja. Very wealthy family."

By this time, I was standing beside Fox, listening to the conversation. I heard only the last of it, that Jay's parents were wealthy.

"What about Jay, Haruto?" I asked.

"He's Durazo's son-in-law, Gumshoe. I don't know anything more, but I fear there will be consequences. Be on the alert."

"How did you come by that, Haruto?"

"I was just walking into an XTR-Management Properties office. The manager, Norm, wasn't aware he had company. Michelle was on the phone with him. The fellow had obviously just turned in his expenses and she denied a big chunk of it.

"He threatened to go to Ira Sidney. It turned into a shouting match. I heard her scream, *'Sidney is dead! Shot by that private investigator! T.A.'s son-in-law is in jail as well'.*

"Norm turned and saw me standing there -- hung up immediately. Must have really embarrassed him that I had overheard. I pretended ignorance, but he knew, I'm sure of it."

*****

"Where are you now, Haruto?"

"Thinking about coming into your shop. The ATF boys still there?"

"Yeah. Come on -- do you mind picking up Morris on your way through?"

"No problem. Be there within the hour." We hung up. The desk phone rang again, almost as soon as I had hung up.

"What did you forget, Haruto?" I laughed.

"Not Haruto, Mr. Gumshoe Garrett. Durazo. I would like a meeting -- just the two of us. No guns, no microphones, no lieutenants, just you and me."

"Sure, Durazo, sure. So the great Sinaloa general would like a rendezvous with a simple private eye from Manhattan Beach, California." I rolled my eyes at Fox. "Who is this?"

"Really, Mr. Garrett, this is T.A. Durazo. We have done what we have done. I have some misgivings for some things I have done. One of them is lashing out at your family."

I decided this was the real deal. T.A. Durazo was, indeed, on the line. Where was this conversation headed?

"I have a beef with you, okay, fine," Durazo continued, "I should try my best to destroy you, but not your father or his fiance; I have a beef with the inspector, fine -- but I should not try to destroy his wife."

"You have my attention, Durazo, or whoever you are, but I see no advantage in meeting with you. Hell, we could meet on Skype for that matter."

"No! Face to face. Perhaps over lunch someplace public, your choice. You have been an honorable adversary. I wish to look you in the eye and tell you what I will do to you, should you continue to annoy me.

"You are like a mosquito buzzing around my head. First, my forehead, then my arm, then my neck -- and like a mosquito you have taken my blood! First it was almost forty of my loyal soldiers, then two of my fellow warriors in Santa Barbara.

"Even more recently you took out one of my generals, and now, last of all you have taken away part of my family -- the father of my grandson! Do you hear me, Gumshoe? My daughter's husband!"

By this time he was shouting. I envisioned spittle flying from his mouth into the phone's speaker. I actually felt a moment of emotion.

"Durazo!" I shouted back. "Stop! I have no apologies for the death of either your son-in-law or his traveling buddy, Sidney. They would have killed me without a second thought; and yes! I shot Ira Sidney, but I did not kill Jay Rudolph. I gave him a choice. He chose wisely. Now, I . . ."

"Face to face!" he shouted. Then he quieted down to almost a whisper. "You destroyed my blood, Mr. Gumshoe. My blood."

"I'll meet with you, Durazo. Let me just say, however, that you have no compunctions destroying lives, sending tons of Fentanyl across the border, destroying young girls' lives, murdering vacationers trying to enjoy a week in your country. You, on the other hand, cry like a baby when it comes home to rest in your household. Tell me when and where -- I'll be there."

"Tomorrow morning, 10 a.m. Barb's on your pier." He hung up abruptly, before I could caution him that he would be trapped on the pier should law enforcement be informed. The feds in the room heard. I decided to call Strom.

* * * * *

"Chief Strom, Alan Garret, here. Please hear me out before you say anything." He only grunted. I continued, "I just had a phone conversation with T.A. Durazo. He called me. He apologized for sending his troops to destroy innocents in his war with oppositional warriors like Morris, Swazer, or me."

"Such as your dad, Swazer's mom, and Morris' wife?"

"Exactly! Today I put an end to Ira Sidney and arrested Jay Rudolph. That was okay with Durazo, but later today Jay was murdered. Durazo thinks I did it, and accused me of *killing his daughter's husband without a fair trial.* I haven't corrected him . . ."

"So Rudolph is his son-in-law. How did he die?"

"We're not sure, but we think assassinated by his own attorney. But, sir, all that aside, we set up a meeting -- just him and me. For whatever it's worth, I intend to honor that meeting. He wants to *'look me in the eye and tell me what he will do to me'.* I intend to look him in the eye and do likewise, and of course, tell him how his son-in-law really died. Theoretically, we walk away as wary opponents without bloodshed.

"In case something goes awry, our meeting is to be on my turf -- the Manhattan Beach Pier. I want hands off for our meeting, but I wouldn't mind some ATF guys standing around as I walk back to the beach. Okay I'm done -- talk."

"Are you out of your mind, Mr. Garrett? I'm supposed to stand by and watch the trapped Sinaloa kingpin sit down with one of ours, take a bite out of a fish taco, threaten to cut our guy's tongue out, have a sip of tea, slap a twenty dollar bill on the table, and walk away? Did you think of putting the left side of your brain into gear before you made that agreement, *Mr.* Gumshoe?

"I can't let you do that, Alan. The man is a monster. He will have a half dozen goons sitting next to him waiting to slit your throat and throw you over the side into the surf at the snap of his fingers. You won't have time to discuss the weather."

"I have friends as well, Elias. Some even go fishing!"

* * * * *

Haruto assisted Morris through the front door just as my call to Walt ended. Morris nodded to us, and walked immediately into the bathroom. Haruto leaned over and mumbled to me, "Long day. The Old Man's worn out, Gumshoe."

"I think we all are. Let's have a Martell and call it a day."

"What? No review of the day, or tidbit to share?" Haruto raised an eyebrow.

"Ask me tomorrow morning when my left brain hemisphere tells me I should be very afraid. I have a date on the pier with the head of the Sinaloa, and hopefully, a dozen or more fishermen from Firehouse 33."

Chapter 48

At 6:30 the following morning, between bites of toast with peanut-butter, Morris called Cedars Sinai for an update on Lucy. Still no change -- on life support; induced coma; no visitors. One look and I knew . . . *The inspector certainly needed to stay busy.* At 7:15 Liz swung by to take him to the Hermosa station.

Now, with a third mug of coffee, I stood in front of the antique Griffith telescope. From here I could see some landscape where the dew line was being penetrated by the warmth of the morning, but the area on and around the pier was still swaddled in a blanket of the cotton-like stuff.

Turning to the few faces still on the corkboard, I muttered, "It's always like this; should be lifting soon."

At 7:55 a.m. my phone rang. "Garrett!" Morris sounded excited. "Garrett, we have news!"

"It was suicide!" I suggested flippantly.

"No. Has nothing to do with that, Alan, though I'll get to that in a minute. Lucy is awake, asking for me! My Lucy is going to make it, Alan!"

"That's fantastic, Morris! Can we go see her?"

"No! The sons'a-bitches tell me I can't even come through the front door, let alone her room! Can you imagine that, Alan? Wakes up, get's off all the machines and wants to talk with me, and can't."

"Yes, she can, Chief. Get her a smart phone so you can see and talk with her."

"Smart phone, eh? That's a good idea. She has a phone in the ro . . ."

"Who called to let you know, Carl?"

"That girl, Zuzu. She called me."

"Okay. We'll buy two good smart phones this afternoon, and deliver one to Zuzu or whomever is on duty at Cedars."

"Today, right?"

"Of course. So what about Jay?"

"Assassinated. Probably the same soup used for lethal injection: tranquilizer, potassium chloride, and something else, I forget. I can look it up if you need to know."

"No need, I'm familiar. Pavulon. Causes paralysis -- whole concoction works in 3-4 seconds. She wanted it quick so she could file her nails for twenty minutes before walking out."

"Only took two little needle marks in the neck, like fangs."

"Okay, Inspector, I'll pick you up around 2 p.m. Wish me luck," I said walking toward the Griffith.

"Why do I need to wish you luck, Alan? You afraid of something?"

"Yeah. Vampires, Inspector. Vampires!"

* * * * *

8:53 a.m.

The Griffith was telling me a story -- three fishermen were jigging almost directly across from Barb's, one more was thirty feet further toward the end of the pier and a group of four more were stationed at pier's end. Two of them I recognized as part of the regular crowd of old-timers, two were new to me.

As I watched, Walt showed up, an arm around his wife, two rods in the other. His wife was carrying a medium-sized tackle box. They were wearing dark blue pea-coats, strolling and chatting like the lovers they were. Choosing a spot close to a scaling station, they anchored themselves.

At 9:20 an entourage of six walked up the pier. I watched as they approached Barb's. *This is them*, I thought.

Facing the cork board, I lifted my mug, "The game begins. Oh, sorry, Jay," I said, pulling the pin from Rudolph's forehead and setting his photo on the desk face down, "You lost the last game. Sorry."

Chapter 49

February 22.

What are you going to say to T.A. Durazo in a face to face, Alan? I was looking in the mirror. *Saturday is as good a day as any other,* I shrugged. *Might even be enjoyable.*

Sure, I was nervous, who wouldn't be? One of the most wanted, most powerful, and most insidious men on the continent. A villain, murderer, rapist, trafficker of children and women, drug pusher; and I agreed to a meeting under a white flag . . . sanctioned by an arm of the Federal Government.

After a short trip to the loo, donning my fedora, taking a longing look at my Beretta, and one last look at my tongue in the mirror, I slung my jacket over my shoulder and trotted down to the pier.

* * * * *

Barb's was midway on the right side of the pier. She had four tables scattered in front. Two of them were occupied: one with a husband and wife and two children, and right next to them was a lone fellow I judged to be Durazo. In his late thirties, short, swarthy, clean shaven, heavy black coat. I walked to the table. "Durazo?"

He shook his head and pointed to the small group of three fishing over the opposite rail. Two were firemen I recognized, the third was a stranger.

"Cunning Hyena!" I whispered to no one in particular, and walked across the pier.

"You are Señor Durazo?"

"And you have lied to me, Mr. Alan Garrett," he said, almost pompously. "These men and the two there," he pointed, "are obviously your companions. We said private; just you and me!"

"And I can say the same thing of you, Mr. Tomas Antonio Durazo," I replied, matching him decibel for decibel. "The four in a group closer to the end of the pier, the two at the very end, fishing close to two real fishermen who have been coming for years, and, of course, your goon sitting at our table. Don't try to disparage me. We are both in tenuous positions -- but my friends are armed with treble hooks. What about yours?" His demeanor reduced substantially.

"Now, let's go sit and talk face to face," I pointed to the table across the pier, "and tell your bodyguard to get lost."

* * * * *

I ordered and paid for both of us. Durazo said he would trust my judgment; he did insist, however, on paying as he had invited me, but I out-bid him by saying that it was my turf and that I must pay. I ordered black sea bass with creamed avocado, topped with mango salsa.

Between bites, during which he continued to nod his approval, he pointed his fork at me, restating his phone threats: cutting my tongue out, pulling my beating heart out of my chest, etc, etc.

He was perhaps my age, two prominent cuts along his left jaw, right eye damaged from some past altercation, dark brown hair and eyes, impeccably dressed in a light gray suit, starched white shirt,

213

amber cuff links, highly polished shoes. No tattoos. I found that interesting as I studied the man.

"You don't find that frightening at all, Mr. Gumshoe?"

"No. I could take you out with two taps to your eyes or one to your forehead at 200 yards, or sneak up to within three yards and put a dagger through your throat before you even knew I was in your home near Ensenada, Durazo."

"You know abou . . ." His left hand went to his neck. He rubbed it vigorously before dropping it to his lap. *That's a tell!* I thought. The family sitting in the next table moved to a far table to avoid, I believed, being drowned in testosterone.

Durazo continued -- asked me why I had to destroy his *'blood'*. "You already had him in custody!" he reminded me with vehemence.

"I didn't! We didn't! We were about to question Jay, he demanded an attorney. He called a number from my office, we all met at the Hermosa cop shop, his lady attorney arrived, we allowed them privacy as per protocol. She left, we went in to grill him. Found him dead!"

"What's this?" I handed Durazo a copy of the coroner's report. He had lost some of his attitude. After studying it for a moment, he looked at me. "Homicide? By the lady?" I nodded. "By his own attorney?" I nodded again.

"What number did he call? You must have it, Mr. Garrett."

"Yes, I have it. But we've tried to find who he called, where it originated, and tried to find her, as well, but she disappeared."

"Who, the lady attorney?"

"Yes."

"Give me the number, Mr. Garrett. Good choice

for our meal. Thank you." He gave a whistle to alert his troops to leave.

"Stop sending drugs, weapons, and women across our border, Durazo; who knows, we could be friends!"

We didn't shake hands. Turning around, Durazo walked backwards up the pier for ten feet or more, then smiled.

My friends gathered round. "We're not going to stop them?" one fireman asked.

"No. I gave him my word," I said.

"Who won?" Walt's wife asked.

* * * * *

Several fishermen accompanied me back to my office. As we walked, I called Fox, "On your way back, please pick up some donuts and bagels, say for about a dozen. See you in about twenty?"

"Who's there, Gumshoe? What have you been up to while I've been in Hermosa? Did you send me away so I couldn't talk you out of something?"

"Donuts and bagels, Fox."

Chapter 50

"You did what?" Fox exploded. "You sat down with that murdering piece of excrement and had breakfast together? Don't you dare move!" she pointed a threatening finger, "I'll be right back!" Heads turned as she ran to the bathroom.

"Is this the wrong time?" Walt asked. Guffaws followed.

Several murmured their opinions, pro and con, of my rash move. As Liz reappeared, the front door opened. Three suits walked in: ATF commander Elias Strom, followed by the two ATF fellas who had tallied recovered guns.

"So this is what the federal ATF satellite office looks like," Strom chuckled, looking around the cramped space. Fox tossed a paper towel in her trash can and frowned at him while walking toward her desk. Strom stopped her. "Hello, Fox," he smiled, holding out his hand.

"Director," she said, "to what do we owe this honor?"

"Ask your boss, young lady. He did something today that I would never have the, uh, gonads to do."

Strom walked over to shake my hand as Fox responded strongly, "Huh! Gonads *and* stupidity. Rambo and Rocky! Great combination, sir!"

"Good to see you, Strom," I smiled. "I appreciate your men standing down while I entertained Durazo."

"I forget, Mr. Garrett," Strom said, taking my hand, "what was accomplished by your meeting?" His demeanor changed: he became real serious real fast. "I don't like standing down with a dog like Durazo in my sights, so let's make something clear; I did it because you've been an integral part of our eradication effort. No more standing down, Gumshoe."

"Got it, sir." I understood immediately why he was here. It could be an embarrassment to him and the ATF to let it be known that Durazo was on the pier.

"Listen up, everyone!" I rapped my empty coffee mug on Fox's desk, "What happened this morning on the pier goes no further than this office. Got it, all of you firemen? No further!

"What I did today in the eyes of the Department of Justice, including the ATF, was immature and reckless; achieving nothing and possibly giving Sinaloa commander Durazo bragging rights that he was able to sneak under the noses of ATF agents, conduct a meeting on the Manhattan Beach Pier, and spirit away again, undetected.

"If that translation gets out, heads might roll, so keep it under wraps. Got it?" As everyone agreed, I ushered Strom into my private office.

"Did you follow him, sir?"

"You bet your ass we tailed him, Garrett. He and three of his henchmen scrambled out of a green Honda Accord in a downtown Los Angeles parking garage. He was wearing a brown trench coat and brown shoes. The Honda made a three-point turn and exited; we picked them up a few blocks away.

They're on their way to our lock-up."

"And Durazo?"

"Durazo and two buddies entered an elevator and pushed every button on a twenty-one floor government building. The other guy jumped on the second elevator and probably went all the way to the top."

"So you lost them?"

"Afraid so, for the time being. They tied up the elevators on the northeast wall of the building. We don't know where he ended up. The building is almost fully leased."

"Okay, so I goofed up by joining him on the pier; you goofed by losing him in a building. Sounds like an impasse. What building is it?"

"On Figueroa. Filled with government tenants: local and state, everything from dog catchers to building inspectors, Police and Fire Administration, Regional Highway Patrol, Arson Investigation, Internal Affairs, LA County Attorney, Regional State Attorney Office, on and on. It's a large complex."

"Aside from protocol, we really did have an informative meeting. We went through the usual: *'I'll drop you into a vat of battery acid. Oh yeah? Well, I'll feed you to my pet sharks'* . . . etc. But then I told him of Jay's phone call and the subsequent assassination of that young man.

"Durazo's attitude changed abruptly. He became genuinely concerned."

"Well, he should. Jay was his son-in-law."

"Yes, sir. But I believe more than that. Someone he worked with either misunderstood or disobeyed an order. I prefer to think the latter. I prefer to think *'they'*, whoever *'they'* were, couldn't allow Jay to live. *'They'* thought he was expendable."

"You think Durazo is in league with someone

here?"

"Yes, sir, just like Paul LaRusso, your DEA buddy."

"In that Figueroa building?"

"Sounds too simple, but possibly."

"And you think Durazo will seek retaliation?"

"From his abrupt change of demeanor, I would say that is a definite probability."

"Hmm . . . that's interesting. Good meeting, Alan. Suppose there's any more coffee?"

Chapter 51

After appropriate civilities, Strom departed for Santa Barbara, and with proverbial heartfelt thanks, I bid Walt and his entourage goodbye. I had promised Morris we would go shopping for smart-phones. An hour later the inspector and I were on our way to Cedars-Sinai, smart phones in hand.

Zuzu came to the front entrance, accepted the phone, assured us she would deliver it immediately, and assist Lucy with its use. We sat in the parking lot and waited. Ten minutes went by. Then fifteen. Then Carl's smart phone rang. It was Zuzu.

"Mr. Morris, hi. Your wife is fine, but she's been sedated, she's not able to come to the phone."

"Well, can I see her?"

"Certainly, sir."

Zuzu held the phone on video mode, panning the entire room, zeroing in for close-ups of Lucy lying in the bed. She showed Lucy from many angles; I noticed tears in the inspector's eyes. He whispered, "I love you, Honey, I'm so sorry you were in that car."

Then he turned to me, "It was all my fault, Gumshoe. Lucy is innocent in this entire fiasco from the get-go."

"She'll be out soon, Inspector. A few more days in Cedars, then a couple of weeks in rehab."

We thanked Zuzu and headed back to the office. Morris turned to me. "Rather than staying with you tonight at *Pop's*, would you mind driving me home, Alan? Talking to Lucy, even though she was asleep -- just seeing her, I feel much better. I'll drive myself to Hermosa tomorrow."

"Whatever you say, Carl, but you're no bother."

"I will, however, stop at your shop for a couple of fingers of Martell if your friends didn't drink it all earlier."

"No Martell was offered this morning, Morris," I laughed, "coffee only."

"Then you have some, right?"

"Two bottles, Morris. Why? Want to get drunk?"

"No. I'm just relieved. I saw Lucy today!"

*****

Walt's car was at the curb in front of my office. He and his wife were inside, visiting with Fox. Patting Morris on the back, we walked through the side door to join them.

* * * * *

"Did Gumshoe tell you what happened this morning, Morris?" Walt asked. Fox was busy pulling snifters out of a cabinet and passing them around. She then began pouring Martell into the glasses as I reiterated my morning with Durazo.

The inspector filled the air with expletives, expressing his displeasure. Fox and Walt's wife, Tricia, nodded in agreement.

"But wait, people!" Walt smiled, "Tell them how it ended, Alan."

"Well, we didn't shake hands. I would call it an understanding of opposite sides -- a truce, perhaps."

* * * * *

The party was ready to break up. Walt was slipping a jacket over Tricia's shoulders when an SUV squealed to a stop behind Walt's car; a door was partially opened, something was rolled out onto the sidewalk, the vehicle backed up two feet, then sped off into the waning light.

We rose to our feet as one. Walt and his wife were first through the door; I was one step behind them. Tricia screamed. I looked down at the midnight blue dress. Even before rolling the body over I knew who it was. Pinned to the lady's chest with an ice pick was a note, written in perfect English: *Just housekeeping, Gumshoe -- more to come. T.A.*

* * * * *

Fox covered the body with a plastic sheet we had in the spare office. Morris shook his head and put a call through for a bus. Then the five of us just stood, looking toward the west -- the Pacific, and what was left of the day's light source. The sun's rays splayed up through silver-lined cumulus clouds -- a dramatic, spectacular view.

Sure, I wondered what the others were thinking. I kept thinking of the lady behind us, splayed out beneath the plastic sheet, and the words, *'just housekeeping . . . more to come'*.

Chapter 52

"We talked this morning, Alan!" Morris said excitedly. "I called her first thing. She sounded half-asleep, but she looked really good. Thanks for the phone suggestion."

"You're welcome, Inspector. I'm glad. How was your drive in?"

"Piece of cake. Left home at 6:15, took only twenty minutes."

"So you called Lucy at 6:45? No wonder she looked half-asleep, Carl -- she was."

"Maybe so. Anything new in Manhattan Beach?"

"Naw! a few phone messages -- pawn shop guy, Eugene, in Morningside. Something about a missing heirloom. Then one from Internal Affairs -- don't know what that's all about, but I suppose we'll see. Liz isn't here yet. We're taking my Caddy over to Tony's, then working on some small stuff. Why?"

"I'm pulling the plug on your per diem. Pretty much have everything under control with the assistance of you and ATF. Send me your hours."

"Bull! I'm not sending you a bill, Morris! Had much more fun than being sent to photograph some unfaithful broad. Honest!"

"You won't bill me? Then I'll have to deal with your partner, Gumshoe. You don't work for my house without being paid."

"Aww, c'mon Carl! You're a friend. Fox feels the same way."

"You saved my life, Alan! Mine and Lucy's. Dammit!" There was silence for a moment. "Besides," he breathed though the receiver, "business is business!"

"Okay! Three days at $100 per day. I'll have Fox put the invoice in the mail."

"That's not enough!"

"Okay. Add two bottles of Martell, then we're square."

Fox overheard as she came through the side door. "Who's square?"

* * * * *

"Bossman, what's on the agenda for today? I see we had a phone message from Captain Delaware of Internal Affairs. Wants you to come in for questioning. What's that all about?"

"Beats me, Fox, but first things first. Before anything else, you and I will deliver the Caddy to Tony's to have the body and glass work done; then have breakfast on the way back.

"Then you can call back the pawn shop to get details on the missing heirloom. I'll call Delaware. I doubt it's urgent." In the back of my mind, however, I had the same exact question: *Why does the police 'in-house' watchdog wish to question a private eye?*

* * * * *

Tony was waiting for us. "Nine bullet holes, and two windows, Tony," I told him, handing him my key.

"I'm not going to have a warning shot across my bow, am I, Garrett?" Tony sounded half-serious.

"Not at all, Tony. The threat was eliminated. Ira Sidney is no more." I hopped into the Kia passenger seat and waved goodbye.

"Call you when she's done."

"Where to for breakfast, Fox?"

"We passed a Norm's, they're always good."

"Sounds good to me."

Two blocks later we pulled into Norm's parking lot. I started to open Norm's door, but a voice behind said, "Allow me, Mr. Garrett," and an arm reached around and pulled the door open. Neither Fox nor I recognized the speaker or his female partner, but we frowned and walked in, followed closely by the pair.

"Grab a booth for four," the male instructed, "we'll sit with you if you don't mind."

I didn't feel a weapon poking into my back; I considered minding, but then I thought, *what the hell, they won't start anything in a crowded restaurant, maybe they'll spring for the tab.*

Irritated, Fox asked, "Who are you?"

"Table first; then we talk," the female answered.

* * * * *

The four of us ordered as if we were old friends. I ordered sirloin steak, rare; eggs, sunny-side-up; hash browns, crisp; with hot salsa verde. Fox ordered the same, but chose bacon instead of steak, and kechup for the salsa. Our two new friends ordered coffee -- black.

The fellow sitting across from me was probably ten years my senior, the lady maybe same as me, and I'll be forty in April.

They were dressed like they were strutting down a runway. He: starched white shirt; shimmering gold tie; tailored black suit; polished black shoes. She: flaming red hair; creamy-yellow, knee length, belted shirt dress, a cross between professional and casual. A good look for her.

After thirty seconds of eyeballing each other in dead silence, Fox couldn't handle being quiet. "You obviously know us, so like I asked before, who are you?"

The tall one with the mustache answered, "Gordon Pritkins." He nodded toward his partner, "Mariam Gill. Internal Affairs."

"Huh! Just this morning we had a phone message to come in for questioning." I frowned, "You folks must be in an awful hurry to pick our brains."

"Just you, Garrett. We need you to come in. Delaware sent us."

"How did you find us?" Fox asked.

"We've been a block behind you all the while," Pritkins smiled.

"We'd have picked you up at the auto shop anyway," Ms Gill added.

I looked at Fox with wrinkled brow. She was on the same wave length. "Oh, really?" she asked. "And just how would you have known?"

"Yeah," I agreed, shaking the tines of my fork at one, then the other. "How *would* you have known? Go tell Delaware I'll be there at 3 p.m. -- but first we're going back to the office to sweep it for bugs."

"There are no bugs," Pritkins claimed. "When we saw you take two cars, we put two and two together. That's all."

"We were going to ask you nicely, but now I'm afraid we'll insist."

"So, we're under arrest?" I laughed. "What a load of codswallop! Call your boss. Tell him I'll see him at 3:00. Let's go, Fox. Lost my appetite. Thanks for picking up the tab, Pritkins."

They didn't stop us. In fact I thought I heard a "humph" with giggles. Probably raised eyebrows as well -- we didn't look back.

* * * * *

"What was that word you used in there, Bossman? Sounded like a fish that up-chucked."

"Codswallop?"

"Yeah, is that really a word?"

"Absolutely! Like a load of crap, gobbledygook, bollocks, mumbo jumbo -- pick a word."

"So, we're heading back to the office to sweep for bugs, right?"

"No. There's no bug. The thing about taking two cars was the only clue they needed."

. . . . .

Pop and I had already made arrangements for the use of his car. He said he and Rita were just replanting the garden where it had been trampled by the bad guys.

Chapter 53

"Bossman, those two at Norm's really stressed me out. I could use a Martell right now, but I guess I'll call Eugene at the pawn shop, go over there and get a fix on his heirloom."

"Relax a few moments, Fox. Eugene isn't going anywhere, and he's probably less upset this afternoon than this morning. I'm on my way in twenty minutes so let's leave toget . . ."

My phone rang. "Garrett."

"Haruto here, Gumshoe. Do you have a moment?"

"Certainly. What's up?"

"My forensics team just completed their work at the stash house in Torrance -- you remember, the green hair gal's apartment?"

"Sure do. That was more than two weeks ago, Haruto. You just finishing up with that place?"

"We're like the proverbial tortoise, Gumshoe, slow but thorough. Before you yawn and hang up, I have some interesting news. Hear me out, please."

"I didn't say anything about your information being trivial. Lay it on me, Haruto."

"The apartment unit was on the back burner until yesterday, late morning. Our forensics lab finally started on it, pulled nine prints and some

DNA from the suite. There were the usual suspects, including Belinda, the apartment manager, Michelle, you, Jay, and a couple of others. But two stick out. They should never have been there."

"I'm about to visit IA. Can this wait, Haruto?"

"Give me a listen before you go. We came up with a head-scratcher which may change your mind. DNA from two IA agents were found in the unit: one living, one dead.

"The dead one, name of Ramos, was murdered, you may remember, in LA City Hospital a few weeks ago; the living one, Anita Neubaur, supposedly left Los Angeles, took a position in Phoenix some twelve years ago -- and yet we have her full thumb print partially covering Ramos' finger print in that apartment."

"Are you absolutely sure, Haruto?"

"As sure as triple-checking can be, Gumshoe. We sent our evidence to IA downtown and to Phoenix with an emergency request to confirm our findings . . . haven't heard from Los Angeles, but Phoenix came back positive. Weird huh?

"One caveat: Anita Neubaur never showed up in Phoenix. Their records show that they made several calls and faxes to the Bureau in LA -- answer was always, 'she left for Phoenix on April 4, 2008'."

"That's heavy, Haruto. Thanks. Any ideas why they want to talk with me?"

"Make you disappear?"

"Oh, thanks, Haruto," I laughed. "I was thinking the same thing, but nice to have your stamp on it."

"You want some company?"

"No. Thanks, Haruto."

* * * * *

"Why the frown, Bossman?"

"Just a hunch, Fox; might be getting closer to the center of this case -- you know, the snake's head."

Fox gave me a concerned look as I dialed Pop. "I'll be there in a few minutes."

She drove me up the hill, then she was off for the pawn shop. The time was 2:15 p.m.

* * * * *

The building on North Figueroa was an imposing twin tower affair of twenty-one stories -- joined by a bridge about halfway up. The grounds were sprawling and lovely. I had been in the building a few times before, but never at the request of the chief of the Bureau of Internal Affairs.

* * * * *

The mind is a never-ending warehouse of thought, from normal to bizarre -- pick a drawer. Today, I was approaching extreme.

IA was on the 16th floor -- a long drop over the balcony -- hitting railing after railing like a rag-doll on my way down. Or, I could be offered a position within the ranks, now that Ramos, Sidney, and a few others were no more. That way they could keep an eye on my comings and goings -- *yeah, if I ever had any goings,* I thought.

Somehow, I always knew I would end up here. Fox had asked me weeks ago why I always started at the perimeter and worked my way in. I don't remember our exact words, but we ended up with some convenient humor.

Humor is good, I thought, *but these people police the men and women who wear the badge of authority. They could do about anything they wanted; no one would question it.*

My mind went to Anita Neubaur. "*She pops up in the strangest of places,*" I told myself aloud, "*and over the print of Ramos. Bizarre!"*

Circling the visitors' parking lot of the Figueroa government complex, I found a space and pulled in. *"Get a grip, Alan!"* I whispered to myself.

For the second time I double-checked both my guns. Clips full, extra clips full. Now I'm ready. The time was 3:03 p.m. So, I'm late.

Chapter 54

A young lady smiled down at me as I hopped up the steps to the front entrance. She held out a mask and insisted it be worn. I complied -- slid the mask over my ears, pulled it up over my nose, adjusted my fedora, smiled (although she couldn't see), and entered.

Two security guards met me at a turnstile. Of course I beeped when one scanned me with a metal detector. "Empty your pockets into the tray, please," he said.

Flipped my wallet open, and smiled, "I'm a private eye; license to carry." Still smiling, I tossed change, pocket knife, keys, and extra clips into the tray.

The other guard glanced at my ID and carry card and said, "Guns in tray, Mr. uh, (he glanced again) Garrett."

"But I have authority to carry concealed," I argued.

"Not in this building. Guns in tray." I complied.

"Don't you carry a set of bracelets on you?"

"Oh, yeah, sorry." I reached around and pulled a set of cuffs from my belt. Into the tray it went.

"Now, Mr. Garrett, where to?" I told him.

"Hey, Bob," he laughed, "maybe we should give

him back a gun; he's on his way up to the Bureau."

"You two are certainly comforting," I grinned. "I've been wondering all morning why they want to see me."

"That's why you brought your heavy artillery, right?" the one named Bob asked. The other one just frowned.

"If I'm not down here by 5:30, call my partner, please," I handed him my card.

"We're outta here at 5:00. A new crew comes in. We'll pass your message al . . ." He stopped and looked closer at me. "Gumshoe and Fox? Hey, Bob! This guy is Gumshoe of Gumshoe and Fox. We heard about you, Mister; you're the guy who sat down with that Sinaloa boss on the Manhattan Beach Pier."

Bob walked closer. "That's why they want you up there -- to grill the hell outta you. You'll never get out of the building."

"How do you two know about that meeting?" I asked.

Bob ignored my question. Instead, he dialed a number on a white phone. "A Mr. Alan 'Gumshoe' Garrett here to see Captain Delaware."

After a short conversation he hung up. He gave me back everything but my guns. "Take a seat, Gumshoe. They're sending someone down to escort you up."

I assumed from the phone conversation that my escort would be down in only a couple of minutes, but I waited for fifteen. Finally, a masked, tallish woman rounded a corner and approached.

She held out her hand, "Thank you for waiting. Part of our staff is out with this Covid-19 thing. I'm Sergeant Jill Rainee." I took her hand. The grip seemed a bit clammy.

"You've been a busy boy, Mr. Garrett, or should I

call you Gumshoe?"

"Alan works just fine, Sergeant."

"Actually, I like Gumshoe. Kinda cute."

"Do you know why Captain Delaware wants to talk?"

"Probably something to do with stepping beyond the role of a PI, Gumshoe," Rainee shrugged. She pushed the "up" button for the elevator. "Once you act as a policeman, we can and must get involved."

"I've only been following leads, keeping in close contact with Torrance, Hermosa, even the feds, Sergeant. Never out of my lanes. When Morris in Hermosa was injured, he hired me -- sure, but everything was legit and on the clock. Just yesterday we sent him a bill for our time."

"Tell it to Delaware," she said.

I detected a smirk, but the mask covered her expression. The car opened. "Listen, Gumshoe," she continued, pushing the *ten* button as we shuffled aboard. "You've been involved in at least four deadly force situations that I know of.

"The Redondo pharmacy, the Torrance complex, Lennox, and Beverly Hills homes -- I could continue with another dozen infractionable actions by your agency, but most recently, the murders of Jay Rudolph and Ira Sidney.

"And now," she laughed sarcastically, "colluding with the head of Sinaloa in a public venue. Pretty brazen, *Mr.* Gumshoe!"

As the car rode up I had an epiphany. I couldn't control it. "What happened to Anita Neubaur, Ms Rainee?"

"What?" She was stunned. Her eyes betrayed her, a cross between surprise and fear. A *tell*. I'm a pretty good poker player -- I look for *tells*. This was definitely a *tell*. A major one from the look of it.

"You've been in the Bureau for fourteen years. Surely you remember Anita."

"Yes, I remember Anita. She was here only a short while. Right now we're on our way to see Captain Delaware. No more talk of officer Neubaur."

Her cell rang. "Yes . . . I'm bringing him in now . . . I understand . . . what did I just say?"

I frowned. That authoritative voice sounded rather annoyed, as with an underling, as opposed to an apologetic, "Sorry, Boss," that I would have expected.

She continued, glaring at her phone, "I said one minute! . . . Right -- just be there." She signed off and faced me, her eyes weren't smiling. Everything about this was wrong. She tried to act nonchalant. "He's wondering where I am."

The car opened on level *ten*. We stepped out. "The bridge is just around the corner," she pointed, "then it's up to the Bureau."

"Fine. Lead on," I replied.

The bridge was approximately thirty feet in length, ten feet wide, short wall and windows full length, with domed acrylic roof. A variety of perhaps twelve ornamental trees in large colorful pots lined the walls, staggered six per side -- very attractive look.

We rounded the corner to what was called the East Wing. The two elevators were just to the left, on the outside wall; they were both in use. One was stopped at floor 14, the other was stopped at 9. Lighted digital one inch squares showed us the direction of the cars. Both were going down.

Sergeant Rainee was visibly upset, cursing and mumbling to herself. I was becoming more apprehensive -- *why am I here? where is Delaware?*

My suspicion was confirmed, as moments later a fellow stepped out of the men's room down the hall, and came running toward us, yelling.

"Boss! I couldn't hold the elevator. A group of five or six demanded I give it up, and told me to take the next one."

As he neared, I recognized him. Valmore! The murdering ATF traitor! And I didn't have a gun!

Chapter 55

"We can take the stairs," Valmore suggested as he came close enough for me to slice his neck with my pocket knife -- *but first things first -- what was her play?* I wondered. "Elevator will prob'ly be packed," Valmore continued, "with the goin' home crowd."

"No!" the sergeant spat. "We will go down by the elevator. Next time do your job properly!"

Now I was concerned -- *go DOWN the elevator? I thought, Internal Affairs is on the 16th floor, people!* We stood and eyed each other -- there were no smiling eyes -- I had already put two and two together, but I didn't want to believe it!

Internal Affairs didn't want me to come in for questioning; they wanted to hurt me!

The car started moving down from #14. Next came #12 (there was no floor #13) and it kept coming, stopping at #11 for a full minute before it dropped to #10.

The door opened, crowded with at least eight passengers. I could see some of them had 'Visitor' name tags stuck to their lapels. "Sorry, full up," smiled a labeled, 40ish fellow in a brown suit. His placard read Tom Brenner. "You'll have to wait." Next to him was Joe Kruger. I could tell from the label. My brain shifted into overdrive.

"You might have faster service across the bridge," a lady's voice chirped from the center of the car.

As she spoke I stuck my hand out to Joe Kruger. "Joe! What a surprise! I haven't seen you since the trip to, uh, where was that, Knotts Berry Farm?"

I shouldered my way into the car, patting Kruger (whoever he was) on the arm, and turned to Sergeant Rainee and Valmore. "You won't mind taking the next car, right, Valmore? That way, Joe and I can catch up with each other. I'll see you two tomorrow."

The door closed, leaving the two, mouths agape, in the hallway. I introduced myself to Kruger -- nice guy. He and some others had been visiting the California Property Records Department on the 19th floor.

The car smelled of perfume and cologne, with undertones of a product that the cleaning outfit was partial to -- Pinesol. I added a splash of Old Spice. I figured I was good for ten floors, provided the door opened a couple of times on the way down.

Chapter 56

The security boys handed me back my weapons. I high-tailed it to the office, leaving Pop's car out front to deliver later.

"Hi, Bossman," Liz looked at me quizzically as I walked through the door. "You look a bit frazzled. Delaware called. Wondered why you missed your 3 p.m. Didn't make it to IA, huh?"

"No, but almost. I'll call him back. In the meantime, invite Morris, Haruto, Swazer, and what's her name from Inglewood . . ."

"Captain Wallins?" Fox filled in.

"Yeah, Wallins. Invite them all for a meeting at five o'clock. I'm not sure how to proceed -- it's above my pay-grade, as they say. I'm taking Pop's car back, shouldn't be more than 15 minutes. I'll call Delaware when I return."

I drove up the cul-de-sac, had a short chit-chat with Pop, said goodbye, and walked up to *Pop's Place*. I showered, put on fresh clothes, and walked back to the office. My brush with Sergeant Rainee and serious consequences still on my mind. I guess I was gone a little over a half hour.

"You're late!" Fox chided. Morris, Wallins, and Swazer had dragged chairs from the spare office and were sitting, sipping cognac when I walked in.

"Haruto has a dinner party scheduled," she explained. "It's after five o'clock. You might miss Delaware. I suggest you call now, before you start your meeting."

Right, I should. Yeah, maybe I will, I thought. *In fact, yes! This should be interesting.*

"Hello all," I greeted the three, as I tossed my fedora on the rack. "Sorry I'm a bit late.

"Fox, push the green button," I winked at Morris, "and dial Delaware's number, please. And put it on speaker."

*****

"IAB, Mariam Gill. Who's calling please?"

"Hi, Miss Gill. We met earlier today. Alan Garrett."

"Ah, the Gumshoe! Where are you? You were supposed to be here at three. I assured Gordon you wouldn't let us down. Now I owe him $5.00, and we'll have to come, pick you up."

"Is Captain Delaware available? I'm returning his call."

"It's after 5 p.m. Most days he's gone by now, but I'll check."

As I waited, Fox gave the others a quick rundown on the two IA agents who sneaked up on us at noon, ending with our walking away from the *Norm's* bill. Agent Gill came back on. "Go ahead, please."

"Garrett!" the speaker phone fairly squealed. I yanked the phone from my ear. "Garrett, I called you this morning, left a message to call me. We have questions, Garrett! Then you promised my agents to come to IAB at 3:00 this afternoon, and again you ignored me. This office will not be treated with contempt! *I* will not be treated with contempt!"

As an AFOSI officer, I'd run into this sort of tin

god before; you can't interrupt them, so you wait until they wind down. Then you take your shot. I waited. A minute later my turn came.

"Check your security records, sir. I entered your building at 3:05. Security boys called your office. It took fifteen minutes, but a Sergeant Jill Rainee came down to escort me up. We took the elevator to floor 10, went across the bridge where we met a fellow I recognized immediately as Valmore, a dirty ATF agent."

"Such tripe, Mr. Garrett! You were in the building? That's impossible!

"Rainee, get in here!" he yelled. After a few moments he continued with me, "She's gone home. I . . ."

"Have Miss Gill call Security at the front entry right now. They keep records. In the meantime, what can you tell me about Anita Neubaur?"

"Anita Neubaur? Bureau officer before my time. Moved on. From what I hear, to Phoenix. Why?"

"How many agents in your office, sir?"

"Uh, I think ninety-four, maybe a few more. Jill, uh, that is, Sergeant Rainee would know."

"Who has the most seniority in the bureau, sir."

"I guess Sergeant Rainee."

"How long has Rainee been there?"

"Ten, twelve years. Before me for sure."

"How often do the agents need drug testing?"

"Every six months. We have to be the example."

"How about finger-printing or DNA samples?"

"Upon hiring for sure. Unnecessary after that."

Miriam called Delaware on another line. "Yes!" he bellowed.

"Mr. Garrett did check in at 3:05 as he said, sir."

"Thank you, Miriam. That's all. Drive safely."

"So you were here, you met Rainee and some guy you say was a dirty fed. So you went across the bridge. Then what happened?"

"They were going to take me down, not up to the Bureau. I was able to ditch them in the 'going home' crowd."

"Lie! There is no 'going home' crowd at 3:30!"

"There was a group from California Property Records, so their stickers said. They were visiting floor 19. Fortunate for me that they were on their way down at the time. I think I owe them my life."

Delaware guffawed, "Oooh, so my agent was going to take you for the long one-way ride. Ha! Okay. I saw that group earlier. Fine, Garrett, we've established you were in the building. I still have questions."

"You or Rainee?"

"Uh, I do, and Rainee does as well."

"Shoot! I'm listening."

"Not here, not now. It's late. I'm going home."

"Fine. I have a request. Pull DNA and prints off Rainee's coffee mug without her being savvy to it. Check who her buddies are in the Bureau and do the same. You have a dirty cop or cops inside your organization, and you need to get a handle on it. Cops down here will back you up."

"What cops?"

"Hawthorne, Inglewood, Hermosa, Torrance, Gardena, and more."

"Hermosa. That's the shop we slow-played your sergeant on a shooting?"

"Yes. Now, when and where, Delaware?"

"Uh, first, let me explain. I apologize. Rainee wanted Old Man Morris out, we figured, uh, or at least she and Ira thought it would soon be too much for Morris to handle, so we could install our own man in as chief there. Then along you come and work some cases on a per-diem basis. Rainee became really frustrated. I'm afraid it was my fault. I could have stopped it."

"But you didn't. Who was she hoping to install in place of the old man?"

"Uh, Ira Sidney, I think."

"Figures," I breathed. "Okay, you have questions. When and where?"

"Seven a.m. tomorrow at Security. I'll okay your weapons to go through. Rainee doesn't show up until, uh, 8 -- 8:30."

"I'll be there." We hung up.

*****

"Son-of-a-bitch! They were scheming to push me out of my own precinct!" Morris was livid. "Talk about diabolical pukes! That Delaware has no scruples."

"And no backbone!" Fox added.

"Who knows how far this goes within the county, fellas," Captain Wallins shook her head. "Corruption among the theoretically, 'most pure' among us. Unless something is done to stop it, it could spread throughout the IA ranks. What did Delaware say? 94 agents?"

"That's why I wanted you all here. Who do we go to with this kind of blatant venality?"

"The PSB," Morris was quick to answer, "or Chief of Police, James Sparks."

"Probably the PSB," Wallins nodded her head, "gives them something of value to work on."

"Maybe ATF Strom," Fox suggested. "He's clean."

"I suggest we keep it in-house," I said. "Not in a hurry to get the feds involved. Does PSB have oversight of Internal Affairs?"

"Yeah," Morris said, "but they're all bureaucrats. They'll sit around a table and discuss the correct amount of ice in their water glasses, or the proper weight of a pat of butter."

"So you'd go with Sparks?"

"I'd go with him first. He's a cop, and a damn good one."

I had Fox make copies of the taped conversation. She handed one to Morris, and one to Wallins.

"Who else, Bossman?"

Consensus was reached: a copy each for Haruto, Delaware, and Police Chief Sparks, and of course, one for us. I considered one for Jill Rainee, but we all decided she would hear the conversation from elsewhere -- perhaps in an interrogation room.

*****

"Well, now, that phone conversation covered everything I wanted to discuss. So," I lifted my Martell, "I suppose we can discuss how much a pat of butter should weigh."

"Good cognac!" Wallins said, holding out her snifter. "Could become a habit."

"I'm coming with you tomorrow morning, Garrett," Morris informed me. "I want to look Delaware in the eye as we hand over the tape."

After a Martell top-off, we shook hands all around. The others left; I locked the office; Morris drove me home. *Damn! I forgot to ask Fox about her visit to the pawnshop. I'll catch her tomorrow.*

Chapter 57

The Inspector pulled in at 6 a.m. the following morning. We had a coffee, then headed for the North Figueroa address.

When we arrived, six minutes early, reserved parking spaces were jammed with six or more black and whites, a rescue vehicle, and two ambulances. A cop was directing early morning traffic around the corner, allowing only essential vehicles access.

Morris plopped his magnetic cherry on top and tried to muscle through the chaos, but was forced around the corner with the rest. We did see a couple of blankets in two separate spots on the entry steps -- one midway, one near the bottom, covering two bodies or things of some sort. I went with bodies. Morris agreed. Yellow evidence markers sat atop each blanket.

We found a spot fairly close and walked as far as the cop standing on the other side of the yellow tape. Morris flashed his badge, motioned the fellow closer.

"We have a seven o'clock appointment with Internal Affairs," he told the chunky, brown-haired rookie, handing the kid a card. "Can we get through?"

"I don't think so, sir, but I'll check. Wait here."

He walked to a group of officers huddled around the blanket at the base of the steps. He pointed in our direction; they all looked our way. One of them waved us over. As we approached, Morris whispered, "Captain Sparks."

"Carl! What the hell are you doing so far from home?" He turned to the group. "Fellas, and ladies (there were two) meet Carl Morris, inspector down in Hermosa.

"Carl, you're going to have to introduce me to your friend. Afraid we've not met."

Morris nodded and grabbed my arm. "Best friend and partner a guy could have, for not being a cop, that is," he smiled. "Alan Garrett, private detective from Manhattan Beach. He was an AFOSI investigator for close to 20 years, now in private practice in my neighborhood, so I make use of him when necessary."

The group mumbled a greeting. One of them asked, "AFOSI? Isn't that Air Force?"

"Yes, sir. Office of Special Investigations -- worked out of Quantico, mostly."

Another cop frowned, "Quantico is Marines, Mr. Garrett."

"It was joint. They were happy to have me, sir!"

"So, why are you here, Morris?" Sparks asked.

"A meeting with Captain Delaware of the Bureau, at seven o'clock. He was supposed to meet us here, and escort us up."

Spark's eyes narrowed, "He's here, all right." He pointed to the #2 blanket, halfway up the steps.

"The #1 -- male or female?" I asked.

Sparks yawned and rearranged his cap,"Female."

"Jill Rainee?"

Now a few heads turned my way. Sparks tilted his head and frowned. "Uhhh, yes, we think so, as a matter of fact."

His eyes were daggers, trying to pierce my brain. He chose his next words carefully. "What's going on at Internal Affairs? How did you know that?"

"Same shooter?" I asked, ignoring his question.

"You obviously are in the know. You knew the identities of the victims, you knew there were two shooters, what else do you know, detective?"

I slipped him the tape I had prepared for Delaware.

"Not certain about two shooters, but I suspected. Delaware, long range -- a sniper rifle, perhaps.

"Rainee, up close and personal -- maybe with some facial disfigurement. Payback, probably. Shot elsewhere and dumped here.

"Once you go through the personnel files, I suspect you'll find both Rainee's and Anita Neubaur's files are missing."

"Who is Anita Neubaur, Garrett?"

Without waiting for an answer, Sparks turned to Morris, "Where did you get this guy, Carl?" Morris shrugged and smiled.

"Listen to the tape, Chief," the inspector suggested. "Some things will become clearer."

He turned to me, "Nothing more for us here, Alan. If you don't mind, I'd like to stop by Cedars. Maybe I can visit Lucy."

As we drove out of the lot, Morris noticed a frown on my face. "What's up, Alan?"

"Why Delaware, Inspector?" My thoughts trailed off. *He's a 'yes man' to Rainee -- just a tool! And if Rainee is Lady . . .*

"While you're working on that, we're heading to Cedars," Morris declared.

I decided to worry later, maybe over a Martell. I returned to the present. "Cedars? Absolutely, Carl!

Hopefully, she's ready to come home."

* * * * *

We pulled up in front of Cedar-Sinai visitor's parking spots. Morris put the call through. It rang six times. No response. "We can sit here another ten minutes, Old Man," I patted his shoulder, " I have all day."

We waited another five. The inspector tried again. Still no answer. "No such luck, Alan. Let's go home."

"No, Carl, we're here now. How about some grub? We'll stay in the area a while longer. She's probably having therapy."

Morris put the car in gear and backed out. "Okay, where to?"

"There's a little cafe not far from here. I've been there a couple of times. It's on Wilshire."

* * * * *

Breakfast was enjoyable until I noticed a group of three paying their check at the register. Before walking out, one of them turned, smiled, and 'shot me' with his finger. I acknowledged by glaring and 'nodding' my head up and down.

Morris swiveled in his seat. Turning back, he asked, "Who's that?"

"Delaware's killer, I suspect. Name's Valmore. He's probably part of the crew that rolled you over the cliff as well."

"So why are we sitting here, Alan? Let's go arrest them."

"For what, Carl?"

"For what you just said!"

"Enjoy your breakfast, Morris. There's a time and a place. I have nothing on him that would stick, but it wouldn't surprise me to find them waiting for us in

248

the parking lot."

"Now you're trying to scare me, Garrett." Morris contorted his face to give me his best fearful look -- really quite awkward, but funny. He continued, "Not sure I want to step outside."

"So let's finish eating, have another coffee, call Lucy one last time, then either head home, or go pick her up."

My cell rang. It was Fox. "Gumshoe, Durazo just called. He said he's done with housecleaning, but wants to speak with you."

"Did you give him my number?"

"No. He left his."

"Good." We ended the call.

The inspector placed his call. It rang at least six times, and as before, there was no answer. Disgusted, Morris disconnected. "Let's go home, Alan."

"Maybe you should call the front de . . ."

The inspector's phone rang. He looked at me, with a look of jubilation, and whispered, "It's Lucy!" then, "Hello?" Lucy's face showed up.

"Carl? You've been trying to call me I know, but they've kept me busy." Her voice was weak but positive.

"Lucy!" Morris sounded relieved. "Oh, Lucy, I was worried about you. How are you feeling?"

"Ready to come home. That's what I meant by saying they kept me busy. The doc says he . . ."

"We'll be right there. We're actually in . . ."

"Shush, Carl, and let me talk. The doc says they are happy with my progress. He wants to do a final check of some kind tomorrow morning, and if it meets his standards, I'll be released by 10 a.m."

"I'll be waiting. They're still not letting me come inside -- the bastards."

Lucy went on for a few minutes, Carl managed a few words, the two kissed their screens and waved goodbye. She was gone. Carl stared at the screen for a moment more, then finally pressed 'end'. I began to form a real hatred for covid 19.

* * * * *

No one was outside the cafe to ambush us. We drove home with Lucy's good report on our minds. Carl asked me to join him in prayerful thanks to Our Creator. I did so happily -- just as I had for Pop and Rita.

"I'm afraid I'll have to drop you off, Alan. I have a precinct to run."

* * * * *

Sighing long and deep, I walked through the door and tossed my fedora on the rack. At my request, Liz called the other local precincts for any updates they may have. I took the phone from her -- spoke with Haruto while she motioned for me to sit at her desk. I declined, and paced back and forth instead.

"We were in a short gun battle with Michelle and Camacho her boss," Haruto began. "Camacho was a procurement agent, a lieutenant for the Sinaloa."

"You say that like he's dead. Is he dead, Haruto?"

"No, he's in custody in San Diego. Michelle and two others are dead. We turned three illegals over to Border Patrol. Not sure what happened to them."

* * * * *

"So, Bossman, tell me about your meeting with Delaware."

"Didn't happen. He was wrapped in a blanket, and surrounded by cops when we arrived on scene."

"Wow! That's gotta shake up Internal Affairs! When did that happen?"

"Sometime between 6:15-6:30. When we arrived at 6:50, he was still warm, but already cordoned off with yellow tape and six or seven cops. I met Chief Sparks and some of his boys."

"Wonder who did that; you think maybe that gal, Rainee?"

"Good guess, Fox. That would have been my first guess, too, except for the obvious. Her body was at the bottom of the steps, also wrapped in a blanket."

"Double wow! Then who, Gumshoe? Who would do this?"

"I think Rainee was taken out by one of T.A. Durazo's crew; didn't you say he called to tell us he's taken care of retaliation for Jay's death? She was killed close up by a handgun, and her body moved to the steps of the building. But Delaware -- now that Jill is, shall we say 'cleared' -- well, he remains a mystery."

"T.A. wants you to call him, remember?"

"I know, but before I do, what happened with that pawn broker, Eugene? Did we take on that case?"

Fox laughed. "I go there. We talk. He describes a 18k gold necklace -- 24" with a three carat diamond drop. He says the last time he sees it was last night as he closes up. He says he's worried sick. As he's talking, I'm looking at it -- around his neck!

"I say, 'Does it look like this?' I hold it out so he can look down and see it. Talk about embarrassed! We end up laughing. He insists on giving us a 30% discount on any purchase we make in his shop."

"Solved another case, Fox. Okay, let's see what T.A. has to say. Give me his number. Push the green light, too, please."

* * * * *

As I dialed, I reached into the fridge for a Bohemia. Durazo answered on the first ring. I didn't have time to crack the tab.

"Mr. Gumshoe, I understand you were there when my package was delivered to the steps of the building."

"Just after, Durazo. Why was she necessary?"

"We had a partnership. Passing out guns and ammunition to teens, homeless, depressed, down-and-outers, creating chaos in the inner cities was just the beginning. We had big plans. But she double-crossed me, Mr. Gumshoe."

"How?"

"She was in my employ for 11-12 years."

"Was she the Lady I've been hearing about?"

Durazo laughed. "Lady? No! Lady is smarter than both of us, amigo. Now just listen. For years Rainee fed information to Sinaloa, all the while hiring dirty agents to feed her own bank account. We knew all that, but we were good with it.

"Then, about a year ago someone started feeding Timeo information. For a while I wondered how he was able to outsmart me, providing product to my regular customers! Me! Then I learned it was Ms Rainee who was double-dipping me, Mr. Gumshoe! I thought she was my friend! Feeding Los Zetos my customers? I had to take them out, and Lady agreed!"

"Them? You took out Timeo Banderas up in Montecito?"

"Sure, and that fed bigmouth, LaRusso, too. Just sorry we couldn't work them over some. Too many cops swarmed in."

"Tell me this, Durazo. Did you off Delaware as well?"

"Delaware -- the IA captain? No! Why would I?

Useless as most of your government agents. Harmless blowhard, pencil pusher, I think you Americans might call him. But kill him? No!"

"Yeah, you're right. That doesn't fit. My guess is Valmore."

"Who? Aah, Gumshoe, so *that* was her new partner. Like I said, she sold me out. Ha! Valmore. I know him! You want, I'll give him to you, too." Durazo laughed again. "You can count on me, mi amigo."

"We're not friends, Durazo!"

"Aah, but, amigo, we broke bread together. Maybe when I finish with this Valmore, I'll swing by with Lady for a chat and a Martell cognac." He laughed and hung up.

I stared at the phone for only a couple of seconds, then called him back. When he answered, I chuckled, "We have a misunderstanding. We were not breaking bread, Durazo, we were laying out ground rules. You come into my backyard and destroy lives, perhaps thousands -- as you say, from Tijuana to Laredo.

"My goal has been to destroy the snake, from tail to head -- be it in Montecito or Ensenada. You have been a willing tool in my hands, and for that, I thank you. But you are not a friend. Not a partner.

After a slight hesitation, "Aah, as you wish, Mr. Gumshoe. I thought we could become friends, but, alas, we are enemies. So be it." He laughed a cruel laugh. We hung up. I felt better.

"By the way, Bossman, Tony called. Your Caddy's ready."

"Great! Tomorrow morning, first thing!"

"Not this afternoon?"

"No, I'm tired." I cracked the tab on my Bohemia, and dropped into a chair in the main office, sighing, and mulling over the events of the past month.

"What do you think, Fox? Is Durazo trying to buy our affection? Trying to recruit me? First, he removed the dirty lawyer, then Rainee, and now the promise of Valmore. It's a head-scratcher.

"Durazo is not stupid. What's he looking for? Protection? A new partner?"

The snake was still out there, but we wounded him for sure. Still, he found a way to taunt me with the idea of *swinging by with his lady for a chat and a cognac.*

I must have fallen asleep, because the next thing I felt was Fox carefully pulling the beer from my hand.

Back to dreamland; a mixed bag of vignettes:

In one, I was questioning five women as to which of them was *Lady.* Rainee sat up, rolled a blanket off her body and said, "I am." Another, sitting to her left, pulled Rainee's hair and declared that she, Anita Neubaur, was the real *Lady.* All five "ladies" then engaged in a scratching, gouging slug-fest, claiming ownership to the title. I stepped out of that scene into a big, yellow Ford van full of snakes and blood. Captain Sparks was hosing out the blood. He looked up and growled, "About time! You're late!"

I scrambled out, set up a ladder, and commenced painting the words, *Be Very Afraid* on the exterior of a multi-story apartment complex, staring into the windows where more interesting clips flashed by.

An old woman with white hair looked up at me from her rocking chair, holding out a western novel in one hand, beckoning me with the other. "You remember me, don't you, Mr. Gumshoe? I'm Katie. My husband was found guilty for killing that boy, and he wasn't even dead. I don't understand."

Morris was being lifted up from a canyon by tow truck cables, Valmore was at the truck's controls, Lucy was waving for Valmore to lower Morris who was dangling from the truck's boom.

T. A. Durazo clapped me on the shoulder (not sure how I descended the ladder) and said, "He'll be fine, Mr. Gumshoe. You and me, Amigo, we'll break bread together." I joined him on the pier, but a gent serving our table brought us two Bud Lites.

"*That's not beer!*" I shouted at him.

*****

I woke with a start. "Did I just yell?"

"Bossman, you were so cute; you were chewing someone out, I think, for drinking."

"Sorry! Just glad I didn't fall off the ladder."

"Huh?"

"Never mind, Fox. Just a dream. Vivid, though," I laughed. "What happened to my beer?"

"I took it away from you so you wouldn't spill it. Then I drank it."

"Aah, waste not, want not."

"That's what I thought."

Chapter 58

The afternoon went smoothly. Pop came by for a short visit, asked about the Inspector and Lucy, which reminded me to call Morris for an update. I placed the call while Pop was with us. It went something like this:

"Hi Carl, how are . . ."

"Oh, hello, Alan, I've been meaning to call to thank you for your company this morning. Lucy is in awful pain. I gave her some soup and a pain pill. She's sleeping now. I don't know when I'll feel it's safe enough to leave her.

"She's so frail, Alan. Can you call Brad and ask him to give me a couple more days?"

"I can do that, sir. Anything else I can do?"

"I don't know, Alan. I almost feel like a failure, I mean, here I sit, frustrated -- can't go to work because of the situation, which makes me feel disgusted with myself for feeling frustrated. Little voice says, 'it's one or the other -- love your job or love Lucy'."

"You and I know that's irrational, Morris. We all run into the unexpected at times. Every one of us love both you and Lucy, and . . ."

Pop interrupted me. "Alan! Give me the phone! . . . Carl! It's Roland, Alan's dad. I have a whole raft of people who will help you take care of Lucy, starting with Rita and me. Take a day or two more, and then call us. We'll have a team ready to step in. And believe me, Carl, they are all qualified."

"Thanks, Roland. I feel better." They hung up.

"Thanks for being here, Pop."

"I'm going home now; can you two get along without me? Want a ride up the hill, son?"

"Naw. I'll stick around here for a while. You can run off, too, Liz."

*****

They left together, leaving me nursing a Martell and a giant dill pickle I found in the office fridge. I thought about Lucy -- and thought, *good thing you're not going to be looking after her, Garrett.*

Just preparing to leave, the office phone rang. I answered, "Garrett here."

"Gumshoe? Hi. This is Katie, remember me?"

"Of course, Katie, how are you? How's Randolph?"

"Thank you for getting Randy off with just a warning."

"You're very welcome, Katie. How is he?"

"Better. He's out of the hospital, and stable now; they took the shackles off him the day following your visit. That's all I wanted to say. Goodnight, Mr. Gumshoe. Oh! and the book is a delight!"

*****

Not often do I spend any length of time alone in my office, but this afternoon felt different, reflecting on all that had happened up to today: Delaware and Rainee are dead; Lucy is back home; we foil the plan of Durazo and Rainee to put more than 150 small arms into the hands of tent city occupants; Durazo admits to the killing of Rainee, knows nothing of the killing of Delaware, and is trying to recruit me. Tells me Rainee isn't Lady.

Next, some strange, disjointed nightmares; then Katie calls, thanking me for being instrumental in getting her husband off with only a warning. Are we missing something?

*****

Was there anything more to this case we should pursue? My brain was saying, *Think, Alan!* We had had some successes, but did we turn over every rock to find Lady, the *"You are a problem, Mr. Gumshoe Garrett. I'll need to deal with you, and soon"* woman?

No! I decided to stick around and think in the quietness of my office. First, I hit the shower, threw clean shorts and a clean shirt on. Then I grabbed a new bottle of Martell and the "Swazer Case" folder from the filing cabinet. Thus armed, I headed for my personal office.

Dummy! You forgot a glass! I thought. Back in the main office I pulled a brandy snifter from the liquor cabinet. The sky was changing color; less than half of the sun was now floating atop the Pacific.

I poured myself a Martell, took a sip, and began writing notes:

> *1. Swazer's shooting in the pharmacy that Sunday, November 24, 2019, and the subsequent benching of Swazer while Internal Affairs investigated the shoot. Only Agent Ramos ever entered Hermosa Precinct. His partner, Sidney, never came in.*
>
> *2. Early December -- Delivery of an empty box by Smith and Friday from Inglewood (T V Dragnet cops). No guns! How could that be?*
>
> I took a sip of cognac, and continued . . .
>
> *3. Inglewood says they don't have a Smith or Friday. (No kidding!) So, who are they? Where did they come from, and where did they go?*

4. Per fax from IAB, officers Ramos and Sidney were phonies -- no longer IAB members.
5. IAB officer Ramos murdered --why?

Wait a minute! Back to point 3. An inspired thought struck the left side of my brain. I flipped back through my notes as I took another sip of Martell. *What was it Captain Wallins said when we first met?* I found the exact quote.

". . . unfortunately, we just discovered, thanks to you by the way, that all of our paperwork is missing as well."

Huh! She acknowledged that she was aware the guns were sent. She, or someone in the precinct, must have the names of the two delivery officers.

Speaking aloud to the lamp on my desk, "I'm going back to Inglewood tomorrow, as soon as I have my wheels." I finished my Martell and leaned back in my chair. Woke up at 9:22 p.m., turned off my desk lamp, and settled in for the duration. Comfy chair.

At 4:45 a.m. I was jolted awake by pounding, and a man's voice calling my name at the front door. *That's Bradley Swazer!* I thought. *Now what?*

*****

"Mr. Garrett!" Brad was all worked up as he stood at the door. "You need to get home now!"

"Calm down, Bradley!" I tried to settle the young sergeant. "Is my house on fire?"

"You'll see. Put your shoes on, sir. I'll drive."

*****

The first thing I noticed was a light burning at Rita's as we passed, then I saw a cop car parked on the street, and a coroner's wagon backed into my driveway. *That's not good*, I thought.

"Notice anything strange on your porch, Mr. Garrett?" Swazer asked.

Pop was talking to the cops and the forensics examiner, blocking my view of the porch. I have two chairs up there and I . . . "Oh, wait! Yes, Brad, there's someone slouched over in one of my chairs!"

"We wanted you to see him before we zipped him up for the morgue, sir. Face and hands have been . . . uh, altered. He's been here for only about two hours. Strange thing is, we still have an unmarked car here 24/7 watching over Rita's place.

"It's scheduled to remain 'til March 10. Not sure how he slipped through. There's a note on the body."

"Valmore," I shrugged and shook my head. "Gotta be Valmore. But let's go up and take a look."

*****

The body was too disfigured to identify, but the terse note was sufficient for me: *"As promised, amigo."*

"Send a DNA sample to ATF Strom up in Santa Barbara for confirmation," I directed. "You'll find I'm correct."

Chapter 59

Pop stayed behind as the official vehicles left the cul-de-sac. He volunteered to hose down the porch in exchange for a cup of coffee. Good trade-off.

While I poured, Pop walked around my kitchen, offering praises for the new appointments and workmanship.

"What was all that about, Alan? That poor fellow was a total mess."

"That poor fellow tried to kill me just two or three days ago, Pop. Dirty ATF agent. T.A. Durazo promised me he would take him out as a favor between *amigos*."

"What did you promise him in return, son?"

"Not a thing, Pop! I promised him nothing."

"Well, he certainly made a show of it."

"Maybe he was trying to prove he could be as stealthy as I. On the pier, I threatened I could sneak up on him and put a knife to his neck before he even realized I was there."

"Could you?"

"Ha! Who knows? We were exchanging vials of testosterone, Pop. He threatened me with what he just did to Valmore, so I suppose I should take him seriously."

"You suppose?" Pop was incredulous. "Don't be

flippant with that monster, Alan! That wasn't an empty threat. Now, what are your plans for today?"

At that instant something else struck my brain with a *"whump!"* I frowned, ignored Pop for a moment. *What was it that Durazo had said in that phone call?* "Sorry Pop, my mind was somewhere else." I pushed the thought to the back of my brain.

"Today? I'm heading to the Inglewood cop shop with a few questions for the captain, Pop. In January, Fox and I asked her which two of her officers delivered a gun package to Hermosa. She denied knowing, yet in the same conversation she acknowledged the delivery."

"So someone in Inglewood must know."

"Exactly, Pop! So I'm on my way there as soon as Fox comes on board. She'll take me to Tony's to pick up my Caddy."

"You watch your six, Alan!"

"I intend to, Pop."

Chapter 60

The Caddy was back to being a showroom beauty. I thanked Tony, paid him, kissed Fox on the cheek, and headed for the Inglewood precinct. It was 8:15. Captain Wallins should be in by now.

* * * * *

Desk Sergeant Gibson came around his desk to greet me. "Mr. Uh . . . Garrett, I believe. So where is your lady friend?"

"She's tied to her desk with a four inch stack of paperwork to catch up on. How are you, Sergeant?"

"Too early to tell. The captain isn't in, yet. Has appointments until this afternoon."

"Too bad. Well, maybe you can help me out. We still have the issue of six weapons that were supposed to reach Hermosa back in December. Your records and their records are missing. That's too coincidental, don't you think?"

"Seems so. But what can I do for you?"

"Ask around. Find out who took the box to Hermosa. Must have been someone from here."

"Wallins would have my head. She was fuming about you two coming in here asking your questions the first time! Very protective of her precinct."

"Interesting, Sergeant. How long have you been here?"

"Me? Nine years."

"How about Wallins?"

"Ten-twelve years anyway. Before me, but not by much. Why? She's good police."

"I'm just trying to get a feel for your two precincts. Hermosa keeps their open files up front for a minimum of thirty days, then, if required, they are assigned to an investigator or team and the folder goes into a *Records Crib.* Is that how you treat yours?"

"Essentially, yes."

"Do actions go on a memory stick?"

"A flash drive? Yes, a daily record -- also under lock-up."

"Okay, sergeant. I'm sorry the captain isn't here this morning. Thanks for your time. What kind of car does she drive? I might swing by again for a chat if I see it in the lot."

"Black Honda, brand new." Can't miss it. Parks right in front."

"Thanks. I might wander back. Oh! one last thing. Where did Wallins transfer in from?"

"You'll have to ask her that question," he smiled.

We said our goodbyes. I drove back to Manhattan Beach with many thoughts rolling around in my brain, not the least of which was the head of the snake! Now I was sure of it -- we were staring into its mouth, fooling around with its fangs.

Chapter 61

"What's our next move, Bossman?"

"Get ATF involved. Strom should have the clout to pull a court order for a federal warrant. After all, six handguns are missing."

"Makes sense."

I placed the call.

* * * * *

"I'm with you, Gumshoe. I think there's enough for a warrant."

"Thank you, Strom. As broad as possible. Someone there is hiding something. I'd also like background checks, DNA samples, whatever I'm forgetting."

"I'll see if I can't expedite it. Call you tomorrow morning." Strom signed off.

* * * * *

Fox and I walked to the *Shellback* for a quick lunch. While waiting for our burgers, Morris called.

"Just wanted to thank you folks, Alan. Your dad and Rita are here, bless them. They just took over the chores with Lucy. You have a good dad, Alan. I'm all thumbs; afraid to touch her. Rita has an angel's touch, and I'm breathing easier. That's all I wanted to say." The inspector hung up. I smiled.

Fox, who had overheard, said, "Poor man would

have been lost but for friends like your pop."

"Truth be spoke, Fox. Pride gets in the way sometimes, doesn't it?"

Our order came. Fox grabbed the ketchup and squirted some on her plate. As she picked up a french fry, she paused before dipping it into the red stuff, "And on the other end of the spectrum is vocalizing thankfulness for the kindness." I nodded in agreement. "Which reminds me, Bossman, I am truly thankful for my job . . . and I couldn't ask for a better boss."

"And I'm happy to have you on board, Fox." I dipped a fry into her ketchup, and grinned. "We do work well together, don't we?"

Fox stared at me and raised an eyebrow, "Now you're just plain taking advantage of me, Mr. Gumshoe!"

* * * * *

All was quiet until 3:30. I was jotting a few pertinent thoughts on the chalk board side of my flip board. Fox was just walking through the door with her arms full of needed supplies when the first of two calls came in.

"Who do you think you are, Mr. Gumshoe, asking questions, snooping around my precinct while I'm out?" The call was loud, angry, and over before I could say more than hello.

Less than a minute later, ATF Chief Strom called. "Garrett! I got it! I got the warrant! We're in!"

"That's great, Strom, but you say 'we'. I'm not a federal officer. Are you including me?"

"Absolutely! I'll swear you in, put you on the official payroll for forty-eight hours, subject to renewal at your discretion."

"You can swear me in for the warrant, sir, but no

payroll."

"Fair enough. See you tomorrow morning, 9:30 sharp, Inglewood Precinct. I'll have six with me. Two will be forensics techs. Sure hope your hunch is right."

"More than a hunch, Strom. I'm looking forward to it, sir; should be fun."

Chapter 62

Three black Suburbans were already in the visitor's parking lot when I pulled in alongside them. I nodded to the occupants in the one closest.

As if on cue, doors opened and I found myself surrounded by seven dark blue windbreakers -- bold, yellow initials, ATF, sewn on the backs. Strom tossed a jacket and a vest to me. "Put these on; we'll wait." I protested, but at his insistence I strapped on the Kevlar vest and put on the jacket.

"Her black Honda," I pointed to the car in a front parking spot.

A couple of young police officers looked at us curiously. One approached, "Why is ATF here, fellas?"

Strom answered with a grin, "A gun matter, son, you might want to hold off going in."

We continued inside. Sergeant Gibson looked up from his desk, frowned and cocked his head at me.

"Looks official, Gumshoe. Who are your friends?"

Strom took over. "We're here to carry out a search warrant. Please step away from your desk, sir. If Captain Wallins is available, please go, instruct her to come here." He turned to one of his men, "Jerry, accompany officer Gibson."

"I can just call her, sir," the desk sergeant offered.

"No! I want her in here, now."

* * * * *

Captain Wallins, a determined look on her face, came rushing to the front desk, seething with rage at the insolence perpetrated upon her domain.

"Let me see that paperwork!" she demanded! Spying me, she spat out venomously, "You! You did this!"

Strom calmly handed it to her. "No, Ma'am. This warrant emanated from federal headquarters in Santa Barbara."

"We'll see about that!" she screamed. "I'll have you stripped of your badges! And you!" she turned to me, "you'll end up in . . ."

"Your phone, please, and step aside, Ma'am." Strom instructed, holding out his hand.

Defiantly, she ripped up the warrant and tossed it on the floor. Then exploded, "You're getting nothing from me!" she shrieked. "This is *my* precinct!"

"Cuff her!" Strom instructed the nearest agent calmly. "Relieve her of purse and weapons, then put her in a wagon."

Turning to Gibson, he said, "Sargeant, you will accomp . . ." A skirmish caused everyone in the room to react audibly.

Wallins had jerked away from the agent, drew her weapon, and pointing it at Strom, screamed, "Take your men and leave my precinct! Leave Mr. Garrett here with me."

"I can't do that Ma'am. If you shoot one of us, you will be brought down within seconds."

"Move aside! Now!" She waved her gun at Strom, then shouted, "Gumshoe! Front and center!"

Like the others, I had pulled my weapon and pointed it at Wallins. I stepped in front of the ATF leader.

"Anita Neubaur," I started. "Why didn't you transfer to Phoenix?"

Her eyes flared, and a shocked look crossed her face, then it turned into an evil smile. "I got a better offer. Why didn't you keep your nose out of our business? We had people in place; we were ticking like a well-oiled machine. You had to spoil it."

"Rainee, Durazo, and you. Who else, Anita? Mixed metaphors by the way."

"You think you're so cool, Asshole!" she sneered. "You'll never discover who else, Mr. Big Shot Gumshoe!

"Durazo?" She scoffed, "He promised to bring you on board. Another asshole! Instead, he *leads* you to me!" She shrugged, "Only one thing now for me to do."

Before anyone in the room understood what was happening, Wallins pulled the trigger. I staggered backwards as two rounds struck my chest at close range. Next, she put the gun to her temple and pulled the trigger.

* * * * *

For the next several minutes I sat on the floor, recovering from the two shots to my chest. Strom knelt beside me, asked if I was okay, asked if I needed a bus to the hospital. I shook my head.

"Give me five minutes." I winced. Tried to get up. Sat back down. He mentioned something about the bulletproof vest, made some sarcastic remark about macho, then began barking orders to his crew.

"Someone call for the coroner! Bring a bus for Mr. Alan *Macho* Gumshoe as well. Gibson, show me the personnel files."

The sergeant led him to an ante-room. "Alright, two of you take Gibson to the Captain's personal office to search it thoroughly. Gibson, hustle back here and show the others the locker rooms; stay with them, then proceed to the contraband crib.

"I'll be going through the personnel files for any clues as to whom she may have been working with. Oh, Ronaldo," Strom continued, "before you go, take prints and photos of the body. Take a couple shots of Garrett, here, as well.

"Last thing before we leave, I'll want you two techs to go through, with a fine tooth comb, the black Honda parked out front. You know the drill, folks. Let's not dawdle."

Chapter 63

The bus ride to Kaiser made a quick detour to my office (I insisted, vehemently) before continuing to the hospital.

Fox became almost hysterical with news of my close call, then she bucked up. "Why is he going to Kaiser?"

"Just cautionary, Ma'am," one paramedic spoke up. "Bullet may have split a rib, pierced a lung or the heart. Could be bleeding inside. He was shot with a .44magnum at close range. He'll have x-rays taken, then, if all is well, he'll probably be released."

"Will you bring him back?"

"No, Ma'am. We have other calls to make. Swinging by here is highly unusual. Don't you tell anyone," he laughed.

* * * * *

I'd never been shot before. Talk about a surprise! Talk about shock! Talk about pain! I even tried to shake it off and rise from my butt on the Inglewood PD floor, but I collapsed a second time. Strom then called for a bus for me. *Why?* I thought; *I have my Caddy. I can drive home, no problem.* I tried to rise once again, but a flush of pain drained the blood from my face and brought me back down to my knees.

One of the techs told me to stay put, that I could have internal organ damage. I decided to obey. So now, 10:25 a.m., here I am on a gurney in the Emergency hallway at Kaiser. And I'm waiting, and waiting, and . . .

* * * * *

Fox and Pop arrived just before noon. Security wouldn't allow them in.

Pop called on the cell. "All done, Alan?" he asked. "Ready to go home?"

"They haven't seen me yet."

At that moment a nurse, Maria, came around the counter, smiling at me.

She set a folder on my gurney. "Good timing," I said to Pop, "looks like I'm finally going to be checked over." Two staff members appeared, glanced at the instructions stapled to the jacket, and pushed the gurney to an elevator. I was aboard.

* * * * *

Forty-three minutes later I came back into the hallway. I called Pop and Fox. They were still outside.

"So? What's the news, Bossman? You good to go? We picked up your Caddy, by the way. It's parked in our lockup."

"Thanks. I don't know about being released. They took some x-rays, probed around my innards for a few minutes, but didn't utter a word. When everything was done they said 'go back downstairs and wait'. So I'm waiting. My chest looks like a topographical map with two black volcanoes, one just above my heart, one an inch lower on the right side. I need to send Strom a bouquet. He insisted I wear that damn thing."

Maria came my way from behind the counter. "Okay, Mr. Garrett. How are you feeling?"

"Like I've been run over by a herd of elephants. Can I go now?"

"Here's the deal," she said, looking at her notes, "you have two broken ribs, and a bit of internal bleeding. You may leave, but Dr. Martinez wants to see you tomorrow at 4 p.m. for a follow-up to make sure the bleeding is nothing to be concerned about.

"Here's a prescription for pain pills. You'll want to fill that prescription tonight. The pain will increase to eleven on a scale of one to ten. Are your friends still around?"

"Waiting right outside. I've decided to leave, Maria. When is this covid thing going to end?"

"Who knows? Okay then, climb aboard, Mr. Garrett, I'll wheel you outside."

Maneuvering myself into the wheelchair was much easier than I thought -- being, of course, wrapped like a mummy from armpit to just above my belly button. Pop and Liz were chatting with the security officer outside when the automatic doors opened.

"They're saying I shouldn't go back to work for a few days. That I should take it easy."

Maria leaned into Pop's open window, "He has a prescription; I recommend filling it before he gets home." We took her advice.

* * * * *

The second day was painful. Liz drove me to Kaiser for my 4 p.m. check-up. The doc was satisfied; he cut the mummy-wrap off me and took x-rays.

"You won't need binding anymore, the bleeding has stopped, and the ribs should mend nicely over the next five to six weeks.

"I'm giving you some breathing exercises. The

first is to breathe deeply, hold it a bit, then release slowly. The second is to cough a couple of times an hour for the next two or three days."

I'm glad he was satisfied; I could hardly handle the pain. The third day was the worst, but I was still coughing and breathing; and most importantly, I was still above ground. Thank You, God! And thank you, Strom!

Day four, I walked down the hill to the office, thinking about the short exchange I'd had with Captain Wallins, aka Anita Neubaur before she offed herself:

"Rainee, Durazo, you, and who else, Anita?"

"You'll never discover who else, Mr. Big Shot Gumshoe!"

With every jolting step down the hill, that short conversation became a sort of 4/4 cadence for my march:

Rainee, Durazo, and you. Who else?

Rainee, Durazo, and you. Who else?

You'll never discover who else, Gumshoe.

You'll never discover who else, Gumshoe.

"The hell I won't, Anita." I thought, as I opened the office door.

Fini

Epilogue

In the first few days that followed, I neither saw nor heard from Durazo or the feds, or, for that matter, the *"big cheeses"* downtown. But, at the end of the day, Thursday, March 13 -- fourteen days after I was shot -- I poured two fingers of cognac and was just sitting down when the desk phone rang.

"Amigo! My lady shot you in the chest two times, and you still live! I hear you were standing only eight feet from her and her powerful gun! I am impressed! You are like a cat, amigo. How many more lives do you have?"

I started to say something flippant, but he cut me off.

"Oh! Did I tell you, amigo? No? Jalisco Nuevo Generacion has joined the Sinaloa with a common target -- your recintos policiales -- how do you say, police precincts?" He let out one of his patented, cruel laughs. "And you, of course, amigo! We're coming for you!" He hung up.

Passersby as far away as the pier may have heard as I shouted, "Son-of-a-bitch, Duranzo!" I quaffed down the Martell; splashed another two hefty fingers into the snifter; leaned back; set my feet on the desk; unholstered my Glock, and set it beside the bottle. Then I picked up the phone and called Morris.

APPENDIX 1

APPENDIX 2

Also From the Author

All are available at ferdigwerks.com

•**A LAD FROM SARDINIA** -- The Adventures of Morgan Harmony

A High Seas Adventure in the Mediterranean Sea in the 1600's. A page-turning Christian YA favorite the entire family will enjoy! Pirates, ghost-ships, romance and more! Story set in prose poetry.   ISBN #978-0-9966042-0-8

• **POETPOURRI** -- A Labyrinth of Wandering Thought

A Collection of Short Stories, Poetry, and Prose Poetry from the Ridiculous to the Sublime.   ISBN#978-0-9966042-1-5

•**A RANGER'S TALE** -- Jacks' Vendetta

An Old West adventure revolving around the fledgling band of Texas Rangers in pursuit of the Jacks' gang.   ISBN #978-0-9966042-3-9

Cowboy Justice series

•**COWBOY JUSTICE** -- On The Border

A fictional account of an Arizona lawman who joins a vigilante group to rid the influx of illicit drugs and entry by undocumented migrants along the southern U.S. border.   ISBN #978- 0-9966042-4-6

• **A CRY FOR JUSTICE**

Continuing the fight against corruption, trafficking, and drug-running . . . ugly, ongoing problems, not just in Arizona, but in every state . . . and now, as a couple, Frank and his bride feel a shared obligation to follow the desperate cry for help whenever and wherever it presents.   ISBN 978-0-9966042-5-3

Gumshoe & Fox Mystery series

•**THE REUNION** -- a Case of Revocable Trust

a Gumshoe & Fox Mystery A story that begins with a high school reunion . . . should be filled with fond memories, a few drinks, some dancing, and some back-slapping, right? But it ends with murder . . . and not just one murder, but four!   ISBN # 978-0-9966042-6-0

•**THE DERELICT** -- the Key West Caper

When Brigadier-General Maggorie sent him $20,000.00 as a retainer to find and return his missing teen age son, Alan Garrett, a.k.a. Gumshoe, took on the assignment. The general's teen-age son was last seen on the Atlantic coast heading south. Garrett gave the assignment to his subordinate, Fox. Good plan -- or was it?   ISBN # 978-0-966042-7-7

A YA Western

•**THE BLACKSMITH** and the Sheepherder's Daughter

1845 - New Mexico Territory - A savage attack on a family of sheep-herding immigrants leaves ten year old Molly Broderick, the only survivor. She is mentored by several residents of this wilderness community -- among them Jake, the saloon owner; Doc Ford; Mr. Royston, the banker; Margaret, the general store owner; and especially Uncle Buzz, the Blacksmith. Our adventure wends its way through the lives of these folks and others as Molly grows into a mature young lady.

An exciting, action-filled "Y A" story for all ages.   ISBN # 978-0-9966042-8-4

APPENDIX 3

Books have always been highly prized by Myron, from school books to novels. It seemed almost criminal to deface a book, whether it be dog-earring a corner, doodling, or writing notes in the margins.

As a boy, he read everything he could get his hands on -- from *Men of Iron, The Yearling, Tarzan, The Cardinal, Old Red,* to *The Old Man and The Sea.*

Favorite authors included Zane Grey, James Kjelgaard, Joseph Altsheler, and Edgar Rice Burroughs

His first writings included short stories, poems, and songs. His first book, *A Lad from Sardinia,* was self-published in 2015 at age 73.

His eighth book, *The Blacksmith and The Sheepherder's Daughter,* was published in 2022.

When not writing, he might be found playing guitar and singing, or out for a morning walk with his dogs.

He lives in Southern California with his wife, Darlene, and their two rescue dogs, Thatcher and Shylow.

We named Thatcher the day Margaret died -- some 11 years ago. When she first came to us she was a 60lb pup. At 77 lbs, she still thinks she's the Iron Lady.

Shylow is probably 13 years old. We drove 60 miles to a rescue organization 2 1/2 years ago to pick her up. The folks there said she was one of 27 dogs that had been dumped in the Mohave desert.

Blind in one eye and selectively deaf, it took more than a year to convince her she's safe in this household ... thus the name Shylow.

I asked the vet what mix of breed she might be. He asked, "What street do you live on?"

I said, "Helendale."

He assured me she's a Helendale Retriever. No need for a DNA test.

www.ingramcontent.com/pod-product-compliance
Lightning Source LLC
Chambersburg PA
CBHW071246300726
48975CB00002B/567